HOW TO DATE A FLYING MEXICAN

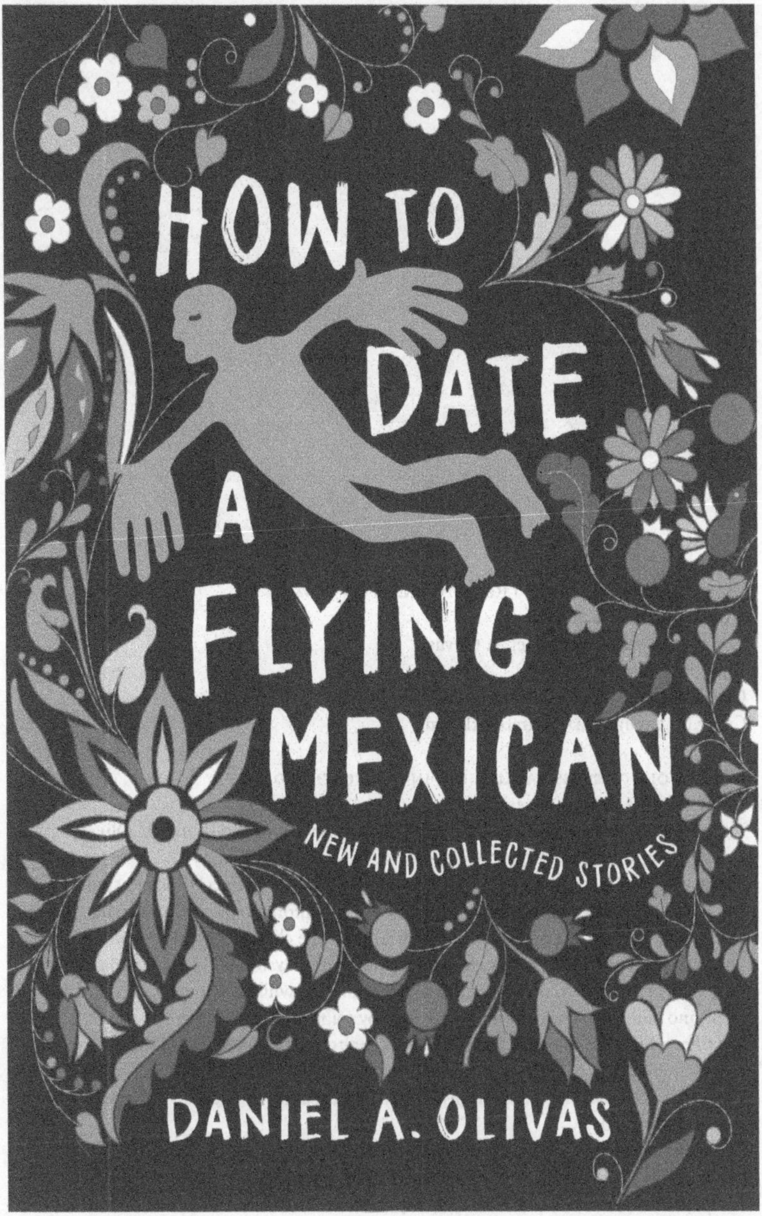

UNIVERSITY OF NEVADA PRESS | *Reno & Las Vegas*

University of Nevada Press | Reno, Nevada 89557 USA
www.unpress.nevada.edu

Cover design by Trudi Gershinov / TG Design
Cover art © OlgaSka / Shutterstock.com

LIBRARY OF CONGRESS CATALOGING-IN-PUBLICATION DATA
Names: Olivas, Daniel A., author.
Title: How to date a flying Mexican: new and collected stories / Daniel A. Olivas.
Description: Reno ; Las Vegas : University of Nevada Press, [2022] |
Summary: "The book is a collection of Daniel A. Olivas's distinct, Chicano short stories-sharing once again some of his best-loved, unforgettable and somewhat strange tales, and also introduces readers to new stories. The characters and episodes in the book explore worlds of magic, fairy tales, fables and dystopian futures, and confront questions of morality, justice, and self-determination while being deeply steeped in Chicano and Mexican culture" —Provided by publisher.
Identifiers: LCCN 2021041559 | ISBN 9781647790363 (paperback) | ISBN 9781647790370 (ebook)
Subjects: LCSH: Mexican Americans—Fiction. | Hispanic Americans—Fiction. | Short stories, Mexican.
Classification: LCC PS3615.L58 H69 2022 | DDC 813/.6—dc23
LC record available at https://lccn.loc.gov/2021041559
The paper used in this book meets the requirements of American National Standard for Information Sciences—Permanence of Paper for Printed Library Materials, ANSI/NISO Z39.48-1992 (R2002).

FIRST PRINTING

Manufactured in the United States of America

For my father,

Michael Augustine Olivas (1932–2020)

The simplest answer is
you can't footnote a dream.

—Luis Alberto Urrea
(from an interview with Daniel A. Olivas)

CONTENTS

Acknowledgments

GIVING THANKS is fraught with peril because it is impossible to list every person who played a role in the birthing of a book. But I will try and, if your name does not appear here, you know who you are and I am deeply indebted to you.

Many thanks to those passionate, brilliant editors of the presses, literary journals, and anthologies that published these stories for the first time. I specifically and proudly acknowledge your publications, by name, at the end of this book.

I deeply appreciate the enthusiastic response I received from the fine folks at the University of Nevada Press when I submitted this manuscript for consideration. I know many proposals come in each day, so it meant that much more to me that you moved with such alacrity in completing the peer review process and then making the offer to publish. I have enjoyed reading your titles throughout the years. It's a delight to be part of the family. And a million thanks to my copyeditor, Robin DuBlanc! I could not have asked for a sharper eye or a more thoughtful collaborator.

A big Chicano abrazo to the many gifted and committed writers who have encouraged and inspired my literary life. And as I have done so often before, I offer additional thanks to my fellow bloggers at the online literary site *La Bloga*: You never fail to offer communal support for our curious vocation.

As for my day job, I offer thanks to my friends at the California Department of Justice who have read my books and attended my various book readings. You continue to help me integrate my life as a lawyer with that of an author. You have also inspired some of the fiction in this collection, especially "Good Things Happen at Tina's Café." Together we have worked hard for the people of California, and we have watched our former boss take her seat in history as the first woman of color to become vice president of the United States. Sometimes dreams do become reality.

I thank my parents, who always made certain that we were a family of books and that we freely used our library cards. You taught your children to love and appreciate reading, the arts, and our culture. I know that my father is looking down and smiling at his son who became a writer. I love and miss you, Pop.

Finally, I thank my wife, Susan Formaker, and our son, Benjamin Formaker-Olivas. As I have said before, I am nothing without you. I hope that you enjoy my new book.

INTRODUCTION

As I write this, we are in the tenth month of sheltering in place while the pandemic wreaks havoc on our country. We also nervously await the inauguration of a new president as our nation's Capitol is militarized in anticipation of further acts of insurrection.

And I am still mourning the passing of my father, Michael Augustine Olivas, who was called back on September 23, 2020, after a long illness. The son of Mexican immigrants, my father had dreamed of publishing his fiction and poetry, but to no avail. He destroyed all of his writings and got on with his life of being a loving husband and father of five children. Though he never explained to me why he took such permanent drastic action, I suspect the rejection was just too much for my father, and he decided to snuff out all physical evidence of his literary dreams. But he took great pleasure in the fact that I became a published author, and my last visits with him were filled with joyous discussions about books and my latest literary projects.

I am also a person with two lives. On the one hand, in my "day job" as a senior attorney with the California Department of Justice, I supervise a team of just under fifty attorneys and paralegals in the areas of land use, environmental enforcement, and affordable housing. My days are filled with video meetings, phone calls, memoranda, legal briefs, and assorted correspondence—all while I sit at our kitchen island as my wife also teleworks and supervises a team of administrative law judges from our home study. I work with committed, brilliant professionals who have "kept it together" despite being forced to work from home, sometimes with young children to care for and educate while juggling a demanding legal practice. And some of this legal work involves fighting the Trump administration's policies targeting our immigrant communities with regard to basic needs such as housing. So in terms of my day job, my plate is full, as they say.

In my other life, I write fiction, poetry, essays, author interviews, and plays. And after almost twenty-five years of writing short stories of various genres, I realized that many—though not all—of my narratives fell within the world of magic, fairy tales, fables, and dystopian futures. A few months ago, I decided to read through my published stories and select some of my favorite, more curious tales. Our strange times seemed to call for it. In compiling the stories that make up this volume, I noticed that many of them confronted—either directly or obliquely—questions of morality, justice, and self-determination while being deeply steeped in Chicano and Mexican culture. A few of my tales simply focused on the way that we, as people, often hurt those we love for reasons that are as cruel as they are confounding. And the final two stories in this collection represent my newest pieces, written in 2019, both of which confront Trump's anti-immigrant rhetoric and policies; in one, I utilize a dystopian narrative that now seems a bit too close to reality, while the other is imbued with magical realism.

As I reread my stories and assembled this collection, I found myself falling back into memories of writing these tales throughout the last quarter century. Our son was quite young when I wrote many of these stories, and as he matured and became more sophisticated, I would like to think my storytelling abilities did so as well.

I also pondered a question that I have explored in my dozens of published interviews with other authors: Why do I write? While many of the authors I have interviewed throughout the years eloquently explained what inspired them to become writers, I truly do not know why I must write. I *do* know that I attempt to express the beauty and complexities of my culture rooted in Mexico, the home of my grandparents. Moreover, inaccurate depictions of my culture are too common, and I believe I have a moral duty to correct those depictions through my own storytelling.

You could say that when I write, I am making a political statement because I am adding my voice—my very Chicano voice—to the artistic conversation of our country. I think this inherently political element is inevitable for all writers who come from marginalized communities. And I know that my parents encouraged my siblings and me to express pride in our culture in whatever form we felt appropriate.

Why did I choose "How to Date a Flying Mexican" as the title story? Two reasons. First, of all the stories I have read to audiences throughout the years, that is the one that has received the strongest response: in the form of laughter but also recognition of the cultural touchstones that it describes. Second, it was one of my late father's favorite stories of mine. The title alone made him laugh—a laugh I miss more and more each day.

My father was a proud Chicano who—along with my mother—made certain his children were exposed to Mexican art, literature, and culture. And this collection is imbued with that cultural pride. In one of my last conversations with my father, I told him I was working on this manuscript and that I had chosen his favorite piece as the title story. He smiled. He approved. A son could not ask for more.

If you have read most of these stories before, I hope you enjoy them again. And if my stories are new to you, let me say: Welcome to my strange little world.

HOW TO DATE A FLYING MEXICAN

HOW TO DATE A FLYING MEXICAN

Rule 1 ~ Don't Tell Anyone About the Flying Part

AFTER THE SECOND NIGHT Conchita witnessed Moisés flying in his backyard under the moonlight, and after the first night they shared her bed (which happened to be the second night she witnessed him flying in his backyard under the moonlight), she realized that no one, not even her sister Julieta, could learn of her new novio's extraordinary talent. What would people think? Certainly gossip would spread throughout the neighborhood, eventually migrating south out of Los Angeles and down below the border to Conchita's hometown of Ocotlán via whispered phone calls, wisecracking emails, and even terse though revealing postcards. Yes, the chisme would most certainly creep out of the city limits, inexorably spreading like a noxious fog, finally reaching all of her friends and family, who would shake their collective head about poor Conchita Lozano de la Peña finally going loca. And, of course they would proclaim, such madness involved lust. See what happens when you don't settle down like all good Catholic Mexican women and marry a man who can give you children and something to look forward to in old age! No God-fearing woman should enter her sixth decade of life—as Conchita had two years earlier—without having walked down the aisle to accept the sacrament of marriage. And it makes no matter that Conchita certainly doesn't look her age—with skin as smooth as Indian pottery combined with a voluptuous figure that would knock the false teeth out of any mature (and eligible) man. But that's the problem, you see. Too much fun, not enough pain. And now Conchita thinks she has fallen in love with a Mexican who can fly. ¡Ay Chihuahua!

So, you see, no one can find out about her novio's penchant for flying. Period. Conchita's good fortune cannot be tarnished by this slightly odd behavior. While keeping this secret, she will proudly introduce him to her comadres at tardeadas, quinceañeras, and funerals even if they have already recognized Moisés Rojo as Conchita's recently widowed but still vigorous next-door neighbor. And people will, indeed, nod with approval because this woman (¡finalmente!) has found a solid, handsome, and age-appropriate gentleman who maybe—just maybe—will ask her to marry him. And perhaps—they will say—Conchita will come to her senses after all these years of "dating" charming but useless men and allow the Holy Catholic and Apostolic Church to bless their union in a proper Mexican wedding. Because in God's eyes, it is never too late for sinners as long as they are still living and breathing and taking up space on this miraculous place we call Earth.

When Conchita finally broached the subject with Moisés—about his flying, not marriage—he held up his right hand, palm out to his new love, and corrected her: "I do not fly, mi amor," he said softly. "I levitate."

"And what exactly is the difference?" she asked.

"Planes fly," he explained. "Birds and mosquitoes and kites fly. People levitate."

"Oh," said Conchita. "That's clear. But what should I tell people?"

Moisés only shrugged. A few minutes later, when Conchita attempted to return to the topic, Moisés grabbed her shoulders and kissed her full on the mouth. Conchita surrendered to his taste, smell, and touch as if this were their first kiss. Moisés pulled back and looked into his novia's eyes. "Tell people whatever you wish," he said. "To me it makes no difference."

And so it was: Conchita decided never to share her secret with anyone.

Rule 2 ~ Don't Try to Understand How He Does It

OTHER THAN THE FLYING PART, Conchita found Moisés to be quite normal. He ate, slept, read the paper, and loved her as any ordinary man would. When Conchita asked him one day why she couldn't fly unless she held his hand (in which case she would rise effortlessly from the Earth as if she were filled with helium), Moisés, of course, corrected her terminology ("I levitate, I don't fly") and then explained that after his wife died, he had fallen out of balance. So he took up yoga and transcendental meditation.

"How did you learn of these things?" asked Conchita.

"I went online and typed in: OUT OF BALANCE," he said. "I found many excellent websites and articles."

"And?" Conchita pressed.

"And after much study, I became a disciple."

"A disciple of what?"

"Of balance, mi amor," Moisés answered. "Balance."

"And if I studied yoga and transcendental meditation," ventured Conchita, "I, too, could learn to fly?"

"Of course not," he said. "I read nothing of levitation. It just happened one night as I sat in the lotus position while chanting my mantra."

Conchita skipped asking what a mantra was but nonetheless continued her cross-examination on the crucial issue at hand: "Must you have moonlight to fly?"

"No, no," said Moisés, betraying a bit of impatience. "This is not magic. It is pure physics."

"I knew it!" exclaimed Conchita. "No magic, just magnetic fields, right?"

At this, Moisés simply sniffed and reached for his cup of coffee. Conchita stood at her kitchen sink waiting for an answer to her question.

"You make the richest coffee I've ever tasted," Moisés finally offered. "What do you do to make it so delicious?"

"It's my mother's little secret," she said, pleased by the compliment but annoyed at the evasion.

Sensing Conchita's conflicting emotions, Moisés said: "Magnetic fields could certainly be at work."

Conchita smiled and refilled her lover's cup with fresh coffee.

Rule 3 ~ Don't Lie About It to Your Dead Mother

ON THE THIRD NIGHT they shared her bed, Conchita's late mother, Belén, appeared to her daughter. Moisés snored softly, curled up like a milk-drowsed baby, while Conchita sat by his side, propped up on two pillows, surveying her new and quite delightful situation. And then, in a blink, there stood Belén at the foot of her bed dressed in the pretty floral print she'd been buried in, holding a cup of coffee and puffing on a fat hand-rolled cigarette.

"Ay, mija," said Belén after she exhaled a large billow of white smoke. "Another man?"

"Mamá," whispered Conchita. "How long have you been watching?"

"Oh, mija, I saw the whole thing."

"¡Ay Dios mío!" exclaimed Conchita through tight lips. "This is so embarrassing!"

"Don't worry, mija," said Belén. "I'm dead. Nothing embarrasses me. You ought to see what your sisters do."

Conchita was partially placated by this thought but she wondered if, in fact, her younger sisters really enjoyed themselves with their men and whether they were having more fun than she. But her mother interrupted such musings.

"So, mija, your new man flies, eh?"

"I don't know what you mean, Mamá," said Conchita as she crossed her arms and turned to gaze upon a slumbering Moisés.

"Don't lie to your mother," said Belén. "The Fourth Commandment forbids it, as it is numbered by the Roman Catholic Church."

Silence.

"It is useless anyway," reasoned Belén. "I know all. Mothers always do."

Conchita knew that her mother spoke the truth.

"So, otra vez, mija, I ask you: Does your new man fly?"

"If mothers know all," said Conchita with a sly smile, "why do you ask?"

"Because mothers want their children to admit things," she scolded. "Does your novio fly?"

"No, Mamá, he levitates," said Conchita as she turned to face her mother. "Planes fly. And so do mosquitoes and birds and other things. But people levitate."

"Ni modo," said Belén with a wave of her cigarette. "It's all the same. He's up in the air like a plane or a bird or a mosquito or whatever." With that, Belén sipped her coffee and let out a little burp.

"But his special talent doesn't make him a bad person, Mamá," said Conchita, feeling a bit defensive.

"You're right," said Belén. "Sabes qué, mija, before I met your papá, I dated a man who could do things with his mouth that were simply miraculous."

"No, Mamá, I don't need to hear this."

"Oh, mija, that man," continued Belén, "that man could make me fly!"

Belén let out a little laugh as her mind wandered to ancient memories.

And Conchita let out a sigh.

"His name was Francisco," said Belén after a few moments.

Conchita blinked. "You mean the butcher?"

Belén nodded, took another sip of coffee, and then puffed heartily on her fat cigarette.

At that moment, Moisés woke with a start. "Did you say something?" he asked without opening his eyes.

Belén blew a kiss to her daughter and disappeared.

"No, mi cielo," said Conchita. "Back to sleep; it was nothing."

"Have you been smoking?" asked Moisés as he sniffed the air and opened his eyes to a mere slit.

"No, mi cielo, no," said Conchita as she pushed down her pillows and snuggled near her man. "You know I don't smoke."

Moisés closed his eyes and started to snore softly.

Rule 4 ~ Don't Grow Weak in Your Resolve to Keep the Secret

Each morning before 7:30 a.m., except on Sundays, Conchita asks Moisés to go back home. It's not because she doesn't appreciate the intimacy that only long, lazy hours in bed can bring. No. It's because her sister Julieta drops by each morning at 7:30 a.m. sharp, Monday through Saturday, to end her power walk and have a little chat with her hermana. After sharing a little family time, Julieta walks home, showers, and meets her husband at their camera shop for another full day of keeping their fussy customers happy. Having Moisés leave before Julieta arrives is not for Julieta's benefit. Not at all. Julieta knows that, throughout the years, her older sister has enjoyed almost countless men. And, being sisters, they have shared many naughty stories, though most of them came from Conchita, not Julieta. In reality, Conchita wanted to spare Moisés the embarrassment of having to socialize with Julieta after spending the night in Conchita's warm, entertaining bed. He was a sensitive man who read books, enjoyed art and, most important, was still healing from his wife's death, though he tried mightily to hide his grief from Conchita.

So Conchita would wake to her buzzing alarm clock at 6:00 a.m., slide herself on top of Moisés for a delicious bit of lovemaking, serve a wonderful breakfast of tamales de puerco and hot coffee along with the newspaper, and then direct her man out the front door. Moisés obliged without argument, subdued by love, food, and the morning news. He'd walk next door to his home, shower, and then meditate in his living room while Conchita and Julieta visited.

During the first two weeks Conchita had enjoyed her new relationship, Julieta used her morning visits to pepper her older sister with questions. Julieta's preliminary queries were somewhat benign and quite general, such as "Does he snore?" and "What's his favorite food?" But then, after a couple of days, Julieta dug deep: "How often do you make love?" and "How big a wedding do you want?" Such questions didn't bother Conchita. Indeed, she'd be insulted if Julieta failed to probe into her love life. But one morning, her sister surprised Conchita with a particularly insightful query.

"What makes Moisés different from all the other men you've been with?" she asked as Conchita served coffee.

This was precisely the kind of question that Conchita had feared. She'd always shared with Julieta the deepest, most personal elements of her dating life even though Julieta, after drinking up every delicious detail, would eventually scold her older sister for not settling down. Would it hurt if Conchita revealed this little secret to her best audience? What's the worst that could happen? Julieta would think she's crazy? No big deal. But perhaps Conchita shouldn't move too fast on this. Maybe she could drop little crumbs of information to see how Julieta reacts.

"He's very spiritual," answered Conchita, relying on every ounce of self-control that she could muster.

Julieta perked up. "Spiritual?" she asked. "You mean he prays to todos los santos and goes to Mass a lot?"

"Not quite," answered Conchita, looking over to the kitchen window.

"Well, what do you mean, hermana?"

Conchita turned back to her sister, brought the coffee cup to her lips, and said: "He meditates."

"Meditates?"

Conchita drank and then slowly lowered her cup until it met the wooden tabletop with a muffled *clink*. She nodded and waited.

"Meditates?" Julieta spat out again. "What is he, some kind of. . .of. . .of. . .agnostic?"

"Well, I wouldn't say that."

"But meditation?" continued Julieta. "What kind of man meditates? What's wrong with saying a rosary? That works for me. It works for all good Catholics, right? A good rosary and I'm ready for bed and a good night's sleep."

At that moment Conchita realized that it would be a mistake to tell her sister that in addition to meditation, Moisés also levitated. So much for sharing.

Rule 5 ~ Don't Google the Word Levitation

THE SAME MORNING Conchita decided, once and for all, that it would be best not to share with Julieta her little secret, she decided to do some research on her novio's special talent. She typed in "levitation" on Google and got over 2 million hits. Too many to go through. How could she limit her search? Ah! One of the books Moisés loved to read was entitled *The Gateway to Eastern Mysticism*. Conchita added the words "eastern mysticism" to "levitation" and got 15,263 hits. Much more manageable. After going through several websites, she found one that seemed promising. The first paragraph explained this phenomenon:

> The reported instances of levitations have been observed in connection with hauntings, shamanistic trances, mystical rapture, mediumship, magic, bewitchments, and (of course) possessions of various types (e.g., satanic or demonic). Based on documented events, many if not most levitations last a short time, perhaps only a few seconds or minutes. In the field of parapsychology, levitation is considered by many as a phenomenon of telekinesis, also known as "mind over matter."

The first part sent an electrical current of panic through Conchita's entire body. Hauntings? Satanic possessions? ¡Dios mío! What had she gotten herself into? She pushed on:

> Not a small number of saints and mystics reportedly levitated as proof of God's great power over the incarnate form, in holy rapture, or because of their saintly nature. Reputable reports documented the abilities of the seventeenth-century saint Joseph of Cupertino, who could levitate. Indeed, the reports indicated that he could fly in the air for longer periods of time than ever documented with other similar instances of levitation. Conversely, in Eastern mysticism, levitation is an act made possible by mastering concentration as well as breathing techniques that are at the core of the universal life energy.

Ah! Saints! Perhaps Moisés was a modern santo! Conchita wiped her upper lip with the back of her hand and began to calm down. Maybe levitation wasn't so odd after all. She went to Wikipedia, typed in "St. Joseph of Cupertino" and read:

> Saint Joseph of Cupertino (Italian: San Giuseppe da Copertino) (June 17, 1603–September 18, 1663) was an Italian saint. He was said to have been remarkably unclever, but prone to miraculous levitation and intense ecstatic visions that left him gaping. In turn, he is recognized as the patron saint of air travelers, aviators, astronauts, people with a mental handicap, test takers, and weak students. He was canonized in the year 1767.

Conchita read about Joseph's father, who was a carpenter and a charitable man. But he died before poor Joseph was even born, leaving his wife, Francesca Panara, "destitute and pregnant with the future saint." Conchita eventually came to this:

> As a child, Joseph was remarkably slow witted. He loved God a lot and built an altar. This was where he prayed the rosary. He suffered from painful ulcers during his childhood. After a hermit applied oil from the lamp burning before a picture of Our Lady of Grace, Joseph was completely cured from his painful ulcers. He was given the pejorative nickname "the Gaper" due to his habit of staring blankly into space. He was also said to have had a violent temper.

Such miserable lives these saints lived, thought Conchita. Clearly, that's why they became santos. ¿No? But what of levitation? Conchita wanted to know the details. She scanned the article further, her heart beating fast. This Joseph of Cupertino was a real misfit who had been teased endlessly by his classmates when he had holy visions at the age of eight. Eight! So young to be seeing things. Because of his bad temper and limited education, he had been turned away, at seventeen, by the Friars Minor Conventuals. Eventually, Joseph was admitted to a Capuchin friary, but was soon removed when his constant fits of ecstasy proved him unsuitable. In his early twenties, he was accepted by a Franciscan friary near Cupertino. The article continued:

> On October 4, 1630, the town of Cupertino held a procession on the feast day of St. Francis of Assisi. Joseph was assisting in the procession when he suddenly soared into the sky, where he remained hovering over the crowd. When he descended and realized what had happened, he became so embarrassed that he fled to his mother's house and hid. This was the first of many flights, which soon earned him the nickname "The Flying Saint."

And finally, she read that when this saint heard the names of Jesus or Mary, participated in the singing of hymns during the feast of St. Francis, or prayed at Mass, he would go into a trance and soar into the air, "remaining there until a superior commanded him under obedience to revive." His superiors eventually hid him away because his levitations caused great public disturbances. But he also gave off a sweet smell because he was pure.

Poor St. Joseph of Cupertino! A prisoner of his own holiness. Would that be her new man's fate if anyone discovered his secret? Would the government or even the Catholic Church want to hide Moisés away so as not to cause public disturbances? No, it was clear to Conchita. Moisés must keep his levitation a secret from all. Period. End of story.

Rule 6 ~ Don't Forget to Breathe

CONCHITA AND MOISÉS made a compact. If she taught him the secret of her delicious coffee, he'd teach her how to meditate.

Moisés quickly mastered Conchita's brewing techniques. However, introducing Conchita to the art of meditation was an entirely different affair. Oh, she easily became skilled at sitting in the lotus position—due in large part to her great flexibility, which also made her a delight in bed. But Conchita wrestled mightily with the meditation part of it.

"I'm distracted," she complained as she sat on his living room carpet. "I can't keep my mind from bouncing from thing to thing."

Moisés counseled her: "Mi amor, the most important moment in meditation is when you realize that you are, in fact, distracted."

"¡No es cierto!"

"Yes, it is true," he cooed. "Say to yourself: I am now distracted."

"But I can't empty my mind," she protested.

Moisés said, "Meditation is *not* the absence of thought."

Conchita opened her eyes and turned to her man, who kneeled next to her. "What the hell is it, then?" she asked.

Moisés gently turned Conchita's head, closed her eyes with his fingertips, and pressed his right palm onto her lower back, his left onto her abdomen. "Don't forget to breathe," he said.

Conchita obeyed her teacher and inhaled deeply.

"Now exhale," he instructed. "Let your thoughts come and go without clinging to them so that you can focus on the meditation."

Conchita inhaled deeply again. And after a few moments, she exhaled with a soft *whoosh*.

This is really stupid, she thought. I'm such a pendeja.

"Tomorrow," said Moisés, "we'll discover your mantra."

"Perfecto," said Conchita. "Perfecto."

"Do you mean it?"

"Yes," said Conchita. "I've always wondered what kind of mantra I would have when I grew old and senile."

Summing Up ~ Let Us Review

FIRST, never, under any circumstances, let anyone know that your new lover can fly. This will cause your family and friends great consternation and might lead to the government or Catholic Church locking him up to prevent public disturbances.

Second, don't lie to your dead mother about it. She is dead, after all, so she won't be disturbed by the news. Besides, nothing escapes her so you might as well fess up. The Fourth Commandment (as it is numbered by the Roman Catholic Church) is, indeed, the most important one of all. At least for dead mothers.

Third, do not conduct internet research on your lover's levitation skills. What you find will only cause great agitation and make you perspire profusely. Sometimes controlled ignorance is the only way to get through life.

Fourth, enjoy your flying Mexican. Life is short and we all need to take delight where we can find it. A corollary to this is that you should learn to accept your lover's special talents even if they're annoying.

And finally, we hope that you remember the most important lesson of all: Do not forget to breathe.

AFTER THE REVOLUTION

AFTER THE REVOLUTION, after the last ringing "¡Basta ya!" echoed through the plazas, calles, and ranchos of Mexico, after the murders of Emiliano Zapata and Pancho Villa, and after the drafting of the new Mexican constitution, Lázaro Mayo Cisneros worked with all his soul, all his essence, all his sweat to rebuild his wealth and power.

The agrarian reforms inexorably led to the confiscation, division, and distribution of Lázaro's once vast, lush rancho. Out of pity, the Revolutionaries left him with a few acres of rocky terrain at the outer edges of the pueblo. But he was a realist. Lázaro asked himself: What could I do with all that wonderful grazing land when my fine cattle has been taken away as well? And he answered: Después de la lluvia sale el sol. Things must get better after such a calamity. ¿No? Lázaro looked in the mirror and saw a healthy man of thirty-two years. The Revolutionaries could not take this from him. So he accepted the unusable acres with a smile and an elegant bow, and pledged on the memory of his late parents to begin anew in this measureless land of Mexico.

Aside from his youthful vigor, Lázaro enjoyed several other advantages. First, he benefited from a keen mind, one that not only gathered and retained limitless quantities of facts, but one that never ceased to assimilate these facts—whether during working hours or in the dark depths of his hard-earned slumber—so that they could be used in the most efficient and lucrative manner.

Second, Lázaro possessed a diplomatic nature and a graceful bearing so that even the Revolutionaries took great delectation in his company. Indeed, the Revolutionaries grew to trust Lázaro's opinions on politics, ranching, and science.

Finally, Lázaro enjoyed immense luck. One crisp morning he discovered that his rocky plot of land was nothing less than a boundless source of fine granite that could be quarried to build the many new edifices the pueblo desperately needed to take advantage of the blooming economy. Realizing that much more money could be made from his land, he hired an architect and an engineer so that he could not only sell the granite, but also offer the services of his newly formed company to design and construct the new courthouse, mayor's home, and plaza. It wasn't long before the surrounding pueblos learned to appreciate his structures. A Mayo edifice was solid, dependable, yet handsome and graceful, not unlike Lázaro himself.

Lázaro's popularity grew almost as rapidly as his wealth. He employed scores of men from the pueblo, which made him that much more appreciated. Indeed, at the end of three years, several of the more ardent Revolutionaries cajoled him into running for mayor, which he did, reluctantly. Lázaro won the election—no opposition candidate having entered the contest. Yes, three years after the Revolution, Lázaro had risen like his namesake Lazarus. But where he had been merely a wealthy landowner, he now possessed not only money but the respect and support of the entire pueblo.

Yet at the age of thirty-five, Lázaro still lacked a wife and a male heir. So he set about the task of filling this one void in his otherwise full life. If he suffered from a personal failing, it was this: Lázaro knew nothing of the fine art of romance. True, he was sturdy and handsome, and when dressed in his Sunday finery, Lázaro attracted many appreciative feminine eyes. But he approached the idea of starting a family the same way he constructed a building: he carefully drew up plans, thought about what kind of foundation to use, and considered how long the entire process would take.

One night Lázaro closed himself up in his study with strict instructions to his ancient but competent housekeeper, Marta, that he should not be disturbed until he opened the door. He asked Marta to brew a large, strong pot of coffee because Lázaro appreciated the importance of the task before him, and he needed to be alert—but he did not let her know what he was doing because he was a bit embarrassed by it all.

Once he settled at his desk, and after a few sips of Marta's wonderful brew, Lázaro pulled out a large piece of parchment, dipped his pen into the inkwell, and with great deliberation wrote three names separated by vertical lines running from the top of the page to the bottom. He sat back and pondered the first name: Celia. Oh, beautiful Celia! Her father, Miguel, who owned the pueblo's largest restaurant, had previously hinted that he would not mind such a match. But Lázaro, at that time, was not interested because he had too much to accomplish to rebuild his fortune. Now his mind's eye washed over the few furtive glances he had thrown Celia's way when she walked through the pueblo. She reminded Lázaro of a brilliantly plumed parrot: exquisite and proud. But then Lázaro's mind stumbled into a memory of his one conversation with Celia. In a particularly mellifluous voice, she expressed no opinion about anything, not even the weather—indeed, she said nothing of any importance, though she said it quite beautifully. Surely he would grow bored living his life with this woman.

Lázaro took a sip of coffee and then turned to the second name: Hortencia. Though not as beautiful as Celia, Hortencia, the daughter of one of the more affable Revolutionaries, was a robust young woman who wore glasses and loved to read Russian novelists and German poets. Perhaps she could keep Lázaro content and produce an intelligent son who would eventually take over the family business. The downsides to Hortencia? Lázaro could not think of any, other than that Hortencia enjoyed polemics, intense debates, controversy. But was this an unwanted trait? Would it not benefit Lázaro to live his life with a woman who had the intelligence to point out the pitfalls of this business venture or that? Interesting question. He underlined Hortencia's name twice.

Finally, Lázaro looked at the name Socorro on the parchment. Why he had written it he did not know. Socorro was the last woman in the pueblo to be made a widow by the Revolution. She had been married to Lázaro's friend Manuel Osorio Martín. Oh, poor Manuel: he was a fine man but stubborn beyond belief. When the Revolutionaries took his land, he spat in their faces and told them to burn in hell. And one bullet ended this great man's life, leaving behind the handsome, seventeen-year-old

Socorro and no children. Before her husband's death she had been gay but not frivolous; practical yet not boring. But when she held Manuel's lifeless body on that horrible day in October, her soul crumbled, caved in, became a cheerless abyss. And for a full year Socorro wore nothing but black and shielded her ethereal visage with a veil. When she finally discarded her mourner's apparel, she went about her business avoiding eye contact and trying not to make a ripple in the pueblo's activity. But once, and only once, on one of Socorro's rare visits to the mercado, Lázaro caught her eye. And she gave him a smile—not much of one, a mere shadow of an upturned lip—but it was enough for Lázaro to catch his breath, trapped for a moment in the beauty and sorrow of his late friend's widow. Was there a downside to choosing Socorro? Perhaps only her poverty could be considered a disadvantage, but money was not at issue here. Finding a true helpmate, a mother for his future male heir: that was the only important thing.

Lázaro's task had kept him so enthralled he had not noticed the passing of the hours. A sharp rap on the study's door snapped him from his musings. The heavy wooden barrier creaked open and there stood Marta, holding a large silver tray of breakfast, shaking her large head back and forth, clucking her tongue, as if she had come upon an unruly child torturing the household cat. "No sleep," she said, a statement of fact rather than a query.

"None," offered Lázaro, feeling just like that unruly child.

Marta shuffled to her master's desk, set the tray down, and crossed her arms. "Eat before it gets cold," she said, with more concern for the fine meal she had prepared than for Lázaro's health. She handed a napkin to Lázaro.

He took it, spread it upon his lap, and gazed upon his breakfast of huevos, frijoles, tortillas, and coffee. Despite her personal failings, which included an extreme lack of warmth, Marta was an accomplished cook who ran an efficient household.

Suddenly, as she started to walk away, confident that Lázaro would eat his food, Lázaro had an idea. "Marta," he began. "Look here. Look at what I have been writing."

Marta let out a sigh, not even attempting to conceal her annoyance. "I have much cleaning to do," she said as she turned back to the desk.

"This will not take long," said Lázaro. Then he corrected himself: "This will not take *you* long at all."

She scanned the parchment and made a small whistling sound through her narrow nostrils. "And what am I looking at?" she said.

"I am deciding who should be my wife," said Lázaro, pushing aside his embarrassment, for he was at a terrible impasse.

Marta fell back upon her heels as many thoughts invaded her mind. *Wife?* she thought. *What of me? Will she replace me?*

Lázaro, sensing her panic, added: "It is important for you two to get along because you will be with me for as long as God allows."

Marta recovered her bearings, for her master was nothing if not an honest man. She squinted at the parchment. For a full five minutes, she offered nothing more than a cough as she absorbed Lázaro's elegant notations. Lázaro's heart beat harder with each minute Marta mused in silence. He respected this tough old woman's opinion.

Celia, Hortencia, and Socorro. Marta recognized each name. And this is what she thought: *¡Ay! Why must Lázaro make such a change in my life? Things are so good, under control, and predictable for me! Oh, what a hard life God has given me! So who would cause the least damage to me? Who? Celia? She is pretty. Too pretty! She will have me doing much more laundry just to keep her looking lovely in her frocks. She would be the end of me! I would surely die of exhaustion! And Hortencia? She is no fool and she does not worry much about how she dresses, either. She might not bring too much misery to my life. But she does love argument, does she not? In fact, she seems to love debate for the sake of debate. I heard her engage the wonderful, patient butcher Alonzo in an argument about the name of a certain cut of beef! Poor Alonzo! He had customers piling up behind Hortencia, but did she care? No, she had to argue! She will ruin my life! She will turn everything I do into fodder for a diatribe! Let me see: Socorro. Poor woman. So young to lose a husband. And she very properly wore black for a year. She knows her place. Socorro. ¡Sí! It will be Socorro who will bring me the least trouble!*

Marta pulled herself up straight and cleared her throat as

Lázaro waited anxiously for her opinion. "Well," she began, "you have listed three of the finest women in the pueblo."

Lázaro smiled and nodded.

"And your notations are not only beautifully written, they are accurate as well."

"Yes?" said Lázaro. "Go on."

"So the question is which of these fine women will make you a solid wife, a good mother for your future children." She added: "The most important thing is which woman would be best suited for you and only you."

"And your thoughts?"

Marta paused for emphasis. "These are my thoughts: there is one woman on the list who will make my life more difficult but who will be the best match for you."

"But it is not my intention to make your life more difficult," said Lázaro.

Marta waved her callused, veined hand. "I am not important. You are. So let me speak."

"Yes, I am sorry. Who would be best? For me?"

Marta paused again. She finally said in soft voice: "Socorro."

Lázaro looked down at the parchment. "Socorro," he whispered. "Socorro," he said again.

"Socorro," echoed Marta.

Lázaro dipped his pen in the inkwell and crossed out the other two women's names. "Socorro it is, then!" he said triumphantly.

Marta smiled and poured coffee into Lázaro's large cup. "Please, now, you must eat breakfast. You have much to do today." With that, Marta left the study triumphantly.

Lázaro grinned a wild grin and ate his breakfast with great vigor while the image of Socorro swirled about his mind. He saw the faces of his future children: a firstborn son who would be named after him, and maybe a daughter or two to keep Socorro contented. And he saw a wonderful retirement with grandchildren running about the house. Most important, there would be a competent, successful son taking over all of his business ventures someday. Yes! But first he must woo his choice. Oh! If he failed, what would he do? Though Lázaro believed he could bend the will of any businessman, a woman's heart was of a nature quite different and made more complicated by the great suffering

Socorro had endured with the loss of her beloved husband. A momentous task lay before him.

After a joyous breakfast filled with reverie interrupted by momentary lapses into trepidation, Lázaro bathed vigorously and then shaved his smiling face while Marta set out his finest outfit. As he dressed, he wondered how he should broach the subject of matrimony with Socorro. Lázaro had not spoken many words to her since Manuel's death, but he felt a connection with her. So did it much matter? He would have a message delivered to Socorro inviting her to dine with him at the pueblo's finest restaurant. It is so easy to discuss business over a delicious meal and delightful wine, he reasoned.

As Lázaro directed two boys in the washing of his Model T, Marta hired another boy, Tito, to deliver the invitation to Socorro. A half hour later Lázaro proudly gazed upon his gleaming automobile. As he wiped away a stray fleck of soap, he observed in the reflection Tito wandering up the road. *Ah!* he thought. *He must have the response from beautiful Socorro!* The front door opened and Marta went to meet the boy. As Lázaro happily fussed with the Model T, he heard Marta's voice become shrill and scolding. Alarmed, he turned in time to witness Marta slapping Tito across his bony face.Lázaro ran to his housekeeper and the boy. "What is this?" he yelled.

Marta pulled her hand back and slapped the boy again. "This boy," she said with a sputter, "did not deliver the invitation as instructed!" Lázaro motioned for Marta to leave. After a moment of hesitation, she let out a huff and walked back to the house.

"Well," he said to the frightened boy. "Is this true?"

Tito kept his eyes on the ground and slowly nodded. Tears rolled silently off his high cheekbones and hit the dusty cobblestones with surprising force. Lázaro leaned closer to Tito. "What happened?" he gently asked the boy.

After a few sniffles and a wipe of his nose on his soiled cotton sleeve, Tito said: "I gave it to her but after she read it, she handed the invitation back to me."

"Really?"

"Yes. This is the truth."

"Did she say anything?"

Tito thought for a moment. He was now calm, secure in the

belief that Lázaro was not the type of adult to hit a child indiscriminately. "Not really," he said slowly.

"Not really?"

"Well, she did laugh," the boy said.

Lázaro leaned away from Tito. "Laughed?" he said as a smile slowly spread upon his face. "She laughed!" And with that, Lázaro let out a hearty laugh of his own. Tito joined in.

After a moment Lázaro handed the boy a coin and told him to run along. He called out to Marta, who had been observing the dialogue from the kitchen window. "Marta, we have a change of plan. Prepare dinner and pack it in my automobile, por favor."

Marta looked at him disbelievingly.

"I will have to approach the widow a bit differently, I believe," Lázaro offered as an explanation.

Marta shrugged. "It is your choice."

"Yes," said Lázaro. "It is my choice."

Once Marta had prepared the meal as ordered and packed the Model T with the delicacies, Lázaro drove off in a great puff of smoke, waving triumphantly to his disgusted housekeeper. *He is becoming foolish,* thought Marta. *Men are such stupid creatures!* She watched as the black vehicle grew smaller with distance. Finally, Marta turned to the task of scrubbing the kitchen, her one true domain.

As Lázaro drove over the newly paved roads of the pueblo—paved by his company at a fair but lucrative price—he thought of what he should say to Socorro. She was a proud woman, no doubt. And he had virtually ignored her after the Revolutionaries murdered her husband and took her property. Why he had, Lázaro did not know. Perhaps he wanted to forget the horror of it all and concentrate on rebuilding his life. Perhaps he felt responsible in some way. It did not matter. It was time to begin anew, a fresh start, and write the next chapter of his life.

Lázaro drove past Socorro's former home, a large structure built in the French colonial style with smooth columns and a fine, ornate balcony. He remembered many wonderful dinners there with his friends, talking of business and politics and even moving pictures. Now the house was filled with three families, all Revolutionaries, who had allowed the magnificent residence to fall into disrepair. So sad. So unnecessary.

By the time he had reached Socorro's simple home at the outskirts of the pueblo, Lázaro's mind was mired in pitiful thoughts. He shut off the motor and grabbed the basket of food. Was this a bad idea? Well, it was too late to turn back now—he saw Socorro standing at her front door, arms crossed, brow knitted. Lázaro offered a wan smile and a tip of his hat as he left his automobile and walked toward his best friend's widow.

"What is that?" she asked.

Lázaro blushed a deep crimson. But even in his embarrassment, he observed the great beauty of this woman. "Dinner," he answered. "May I come in?"

Socorro slowly and without a word stepped aside to let Lázaro pass. Inside, he noticed the humble but tidy surroundings. Despite being forced into this hovel, Socorro had made the best she could of her predicament. Lázaro nodded toward the dining table.

"Yes," said Socorro. She spoke without emotion, as if she were telling a boy to gather twigs for her. "You may put the food there. I will get everything else."

Lázaro complied. The wonderful rich aroma of Marta's cooking began to fill the modest abode, mixing with the loamy smells emanating from the red dirt floor. Lázaro allowed his eyes to roam freely over Socorro's sturdy, curvaceous physique as she set the table. Once or twice, when she leaned close to him, Lázaro filled his nostrils with her warm, sweaty, delicious scent. But Socorro did not seem to notice. She had a task to complete and she set to it as if she were alone.

Finally, she said, "Done."

Lázaro hurried to hold Socorro's chair for her. He thought he saw a bit of a smile appear on her lips, but he wasn't certain. She sat slowly, elegantly, but it could have been fatigue that made Socorro move in such a manner. Lázaro, acting as haughty as a French waiter, bowed and proceeded to serve dinner. This time a true, almost broad smile flickered on the woman's beautiful face. When both plates were full of Marta's fine cuisine, Lázaro bowed again and took his seat.

As dinner proceeded, Socorro grew more comfortable, and the conversation eased into that wistful nostalgia that only two old friends could delight in. Her anger toward Lázaro dwindled with each laugh, every shared anecdote. And Lázaro fell into the moment with such ease and joy that he forgot his great plans to propose marriage. He simply luxuriated in this woman's company without a conscious thought. When the food had disappeared and the wine bottle had long stood empty, the two old friends grew quiet. They simply looked at each other, lost in their separate, though similar, thoughts. *Why be alone? Life is so short. Why not this one?* While such thoughts were new to Socorro, they seemed new to Lázaro as well, because his abstract plan of action had been met with the power of this woman's presence.

Finally Socorro broke the silence: "So Lázaro, my dear friend. It is time you started a family. ¿No?"

Though Lázaro normally would have been shocked by both the boldness and the prescience of such a question, he was not. Rather, he leaned forward and tried to catch the scent of this woman. And he answered, simply, with a nod and a soft smile. Socorro touched Lázaro's hand, and he felt what could have been a small spark leave her fingers, travel up his arm, round his shoulder, and reach the nape of his neck in a small electrical dance. He had indeed made the right choice.

And so it was: the wedding took place one month later in the still-majestic Santa Cristina Church with an extravagant fiesta in the plaza that lasted two full days and nights. People wondered why Socorro had hidden herself away for so long, for when they saw her resplendent and smiling on her wedding morning, she was certainly the most beautiful and joyous woman within many miles.

But perhaps the happiest person in the pueblo was Marta, who knew that of all the women her master could have married, Socorro was least likely to be a burden.

Yet this was not to be so. For when the new mistress of the household moved in with her new husband, she proceeded to chip away at Marta's duties. Socorro never would sit idly as Marta cooked, cleaned, and did the laundry. No, Socorro was constitutionally incapable of being indolent. So she started to prepare the meals while Marta watched helplessly from the corner of what was once her domain. This distressed Marta to no end, but what could she say? The mistress was now her boss. Marta decided to spend more time with the housecleaning and laundry, but she still had too much free time. No problem, Socorro told her. You work so hard. Take a day off. We will survive. A day off? What would she do with a day off? She had no friends, no family, nothing to occupy herself. And if she left for even a day, Marta was certain that Socorro would start doing the cleaning and maybe even the laundry. Oh, what a horrible predicament!

One day, forced to leave the house and enjoy a day off at the insistence of Socorro, Marta wandered the pueblo like a suffering ghost. She mumbled to herself, damning the day she had cunningly convinced Lázaro to choose this woman. *This horrible, evil woman! What will I do?*

The next morning, Marta's worst fears came to fruition. She entered through the kitchen at the back of the house and found it empty except for the rich aromas of beef picadillo and frijoles cooking on the stove. But the smells made her queasy. Marta suspected something was amiss. She left the kitchen, ostensibly to see if her mistress needed anything—and to her horror, she almost stumbled over Socorro, who was scrubbing the main hallway's tiled floor!

"Mistress," Marta sputtered. "What are you doing? Are you well?"

Socorro let out a laugh. "I am very well, thank you."

"Let me do that," said Marta, sounding more like the boss than the housekeeper.

Socorro turned back to scrubbing. "No, I do not mind. In fact, I enjoy good hard work. It makes me feel alive."

"But that is my job!"

Socorro laughed again. "Feeling alive is your job?"

Marta did not welcome this joke at her expense. But she could not fathom what to do next. This *was* her mistress, after all, and Marta was at the mercy of this strange woman. So she offered a weak nod and headed toward the backyard to do laundry. Luckily there was plenty to do that day. Certainly her mistress would not take this task away. Unless, of course, she was indeed insane! For what kind of woman would voluntarily take on such toil? If Marta were wealthy, she would relax, perhaps travel, maybe tend a pretty garden. That is what a woman with money does! She does not cook and scrub floors!

On the back porch Marta gazed upon the gleaming copper

electric washing machine that sat squat on three legs. Marta hated using it. *That damn machine can never get the clothes as clean as my own two hands could!* She pumped water into a basin, sprinkled in a liberal amount of soap powder, and set the washboard at a good angle. Marta's mind felt as though it would burst. She grabbed one of Socorro's dresses from the basket and plopped it into the soapy water with a splash that wet her face. But she did not care. Marta had to calculate a way to end this lunacy. She soaked the fabric and then started to knead it up and down the washboard's metal ripples. After a few moments Marta suddenly stopped, hands clenching Socorro's dress. She stood motionless, staring at the white cotton garment. And the longer she stood there, the more her mind turned. Finally she let out a small chuckle. Yes, there was something Marta could do before it was too late, before she lost her job to this demented woman's desire to slave away at household chores when she could be enjoying her new station in life. Marta had no choice. Something had to be done. Period. But the solution had to be subtle. Nothing too dramatic and certainly nothing to bring blame upon Marta's head.

That afternoon, pretending to need additional soap, Marta offered Socorro a strained smile and headed to an encampment just outside the pueblo in search of Katrina, the curandera. The townspeople knew that Katrina was Russian and that long ago she sold her body to any man who was willing to turn over a few pesos. Now that her face and body no longer pleased, she had turned to the black arts to make her living. There was no doubt that Katrina possessed the kind of powers that no one had ever before witnessed, at least no one in this particular pueblo.

As Marta approached the encampment, she could discern several dilapidated, crudely constructed huts hugging the edge of a creek. The closer she got, the stronger the stench of this loose community grew. Disheveled men, women, and children wandered about the encampment almost in slow motion, without joy, without sound. Even a pack of mongrels lacked life as it hovered by the garbage heap to the far north of the structures. Marta entered the encampment but not a soul seemed to care: no one lifted a head, no one glanced at her. She asked a young girl where she could find Katrina. The girl offered nothing but large, vague eyes. Then, just as Marta was to give up, the girl lethargically pointed to a moss-covered hut a few yards away. Marta trudged through the muck to the hut and rapped on the piece of rotting wood that passed for a door.

"Come," said a voice that sounded more like an animal's grunt than a human response.

Though usually not a woman to be cowed by anyone or anything, Marta shuddered with dread, for she knew that there were things that could not be explained, things that could cause great harm if you refused to admit your helplessness. And rumor had it that Katrina was no less than a devotee of the Santisima Muerte, a banned saint whose cult was rooted in an Aztec goddess often depicted as a skeleton. Oh, the thought of such mysterious power shook Marta to the core. She entered the darkened hut warily and with great trepidation. Once inside, Marta squinted, attempting to adjust her eyes as rapidly as possible.

"Come," said the voice again. "I am here."

Marta turned to the far corner of the small room and beheld this woman the townspeople feared most. Marta's heart relaxed as her eyes absorbed the vision of this great curandera. At a table sat Katrina, a small-framed, fragile-looking woman of no more than forty. The curandera's long hair, which still shimmered a rich cinnamon, hung neatly away from her face and down her back. Her sharp green eyes flickered with the light of a lone candle.

"Please," said Katrina. "Come forward and sit here." She motioned with a small hand toward a stool that stood at the opposite end of the table.

So this is the great curandera, thought Marta. *I have wasted my time for certain!*

Katrina let out a low chuckle. "No," she said. "You have not wasted your time, I assure you."

Marta's eyes widened and her scalp danced.

Katrina chuckled again. "Please," she said. "Sit. It is time to talk of what you need."

Marta had no choice. She must sit and tell this powerful woman what was in her heart, though it was clear that she already knew. Marta slowly made her way to the stool and sat as directed.

Katrina smiled, leaned forward, and said softly, almost gently,

"You have come to me to regain the freedom another woman is taking from you."

As these words entered Marta's consciousness, she knew that Katrina would help her. Marta nodded and mouthed the word *Yes*. The curandera suddenly stood and walked to a small ledge that was cluttered with bottles of every size, shape, and color. As Katrina carefully examined her potions, searching for the correct one, Marta noticed that the woman was no taller than a child but moved with the grace of a dancer. Finally, Katrina emitted a soft "*Ah!*" and returned to her chair.

"Here," she said as she placed a slender blue bottle before Marta. "This will bring you freedom from that woman."

Marta reached for the bottle, but Katrina snatched it away with such alacrity that the housekeeper jumped back in fright. After a moment Marta understood. She reached into her cloth purse, produced three coins, and placed them on the table. Katrina smiled and put the bottle near the money. Marta grasped the bottle and brought it to her bosom.

"So," she said to the curandera, "I give this to Socorro?"

"No," said Katrina. "Find a way to feed it to your master."

Marta's eyes narrowed. "What?"

Katrina ignored the question. "But you must make certain Socorro is not in the house."

"How?"

Katrina again ignored the question. "Be patient," she said. "Wait for the right time."

Marta opened her mouth to ask another question, but she knew it was useless. She slid the bottle into her purse, stood, and left the hut without turning back. As Marta hurried away, she heard a small but distinct laugh follow her.

And so it was: Marta waited for the opportunity to use the magic as Katrina had instructed. She patiently watched as Socorro cleaned house and cooked every meal, leaving only the laundry for the once-busy housekeeper. In disgust, Marta also watched as Lázaro fell deeper in love with this interloper. But her patience paid off well. One morning, after Socorro had cooked but not served her husband breakfast, she called Marta to the kitchen.

"Tomorrow is Lázaro's birthday," she whispered to the

housekeeper, though there was little chance that anyone could overhear.

"Yes?" said Marta through a forced smile.

"I wish to make a magnificent dinner for him," said Socorro as she tidied the kitchen. "But I must go to town today to buy what I need."

"Oh, I can do that for you," offered Marta, knowing full well that her mistress would reject the offer.

"No, no," Socorro said, almost on cue. "This must be from me."

"Is there anything I can do to help?"

"Yes." Socorro smiled in excitement. "I have prepared breakfast for Lázaro. Please serve it right after I leave."

"Of course," Marta answered. "Anything else that I can help you with?"

As Socorro removed her apron and reached for her purse, she said, "Make certain our finest table linens are as clean as they can be. And if Lázaro should ask, confirm that I simply went out to visit with Señora Miramontes."

Marta grinned with such intensity that Socorro froze. "Are you all right?"

"Yes, yes," Marta said as she tried to control her glee. "Please go. All will be well."

As soon as Socorro left the house, Marta quickly fumbled with her own purse, which always hung by her side. When she found the bottle, she poured its reddish thick contents into the boiling pot of frijoles and stirred until not a trace was visible. Marta filled a large bowl with a hearty helping of the frijoles, placed the bowl on a silver tray, and completed the meal with pan dulce, tortillas, a pot of coffee, and a large glass of water.

"Ah!" said Lázaro as Marta carried the food to the dining room. "Looks wonderful! But where is my lovely wife?"

The housekeeper set the tray down and started to unload it. As she placed the bowl of frijoles before her master, her right hand trembled a bit, so she quickly employed her left to steady the bowl.

"Socorro had an errand or two to tend to," said Marta, not remembering what her mistress had instructed. "But she left this magnificent breakfast for you."

Lázaro's eyes glistened with hunger. After Marta had set out everything, Lázaro took a big gulp of coffee, grabbed a tortilla, tore it in half, and proceeded to devour his breakfast. His housekeeper stood back, arms crossed tightly across her narrow chest, crooked smile in place, and quietly observed Lázaro. In a short time, he had finished every bit of food.

As Lázaro drank the last of the coffee, Marta approached. "Do you desire anything else?" she asked as she reached for the empty bowl.

Lázaro nodded, placing the palm of his hand squarely on Marta's lower back. "I desire you," he said softly.

Lázaro's intimate request paralyzed the housekeeper. After a moment of silence, Marta realized what was happening. The potion! But what to do? She had not anticipated such a result.

"Well, mi amor," cooed Lázaro. "Socorro is out of the house. You and I are alone."

Before she could answer, Lázaro stood and enveloped Marta in his arms. She thought that she should scream, but she knew her own actions had brought this on. And perhaps it was the only way to get rid of Socorro without shedding any blood.

"But I am too old for you," said Marta, knowing full well that her words would not matter.

"And the thought delights me," countered Lázaro. He gently lifted Marta's chin with one strong finger. She saw nothing but adoration in his eyes.

Well! Why not? she thought. *I am not so old that I cannot enjoy myself. And if this is the only way to win back my freedom from that woman, so be it!* With that, Marta closed her eyes and welcomed her master's lips to hers. And her memory fell back many years to when her own father had kissed and embraced her in such a way. But she had been only twelve then. What did she know about what a father should not do to his own daughter? But that was long ago. She had been alone for too long. Now, as a mature woman, she could truly enjoy the love of an appropriate man without guilt.

A scream snapped Marta from her reverie. She pushed her body from Lázaro's. In the entryway stood Socorro, her expression of abhorrence so excruciating Marta had to turn away. Lázaro looked at Socorro and then back at Marta, and back again. He shook his head, blinked several times, and tried to say something, but his lips could form no words. Socorro's hands trembled before her. All three stood motionless, not knowing what to do or say. Socorro finally turned and ran from the house, emitting a pitiable whimper.

Lázaro turned to Marta. He no longer craved her. Rather, his heart was now filled with disgust and the knowledge that Marta had played with fate, though he did not know how. And Marta understood she could not escape. So as Lázaro approached her and slowly but with great passion placed his enormous hands around his housekeeper's frail neck, Marta did not scream or struggle. She merely closed her eyes and yielded to Lázaro's hatred. For she had no choice. He was her master. And the curandera, indeed, had promised her freedom. Nothing more. Nothing less.

ELIZONDO RETURNS HOME

WHEN I FIRST MET Elizondo, he lived in the small house at the back end of my abuela's property. Ana Ortiz Camacho, my grandmother and the only grandparent I had the opportunity to know, had died the week before, a life of cigarettes and Mexican food and hard work and not a little beer finally catching up with her. My mother, Abuela's only child, had died seven years ago when I was in my senior year at Reed College, so it fell on me to make the funeral arrangements and then begin the arduous task of emptying out Abuela's house and selling it.

It is at a time such as this that I realize how solitary our lives have been. Abuela's husband disappeared so long ago no one even mentioned him by name anymore. And my biological father was some unknown male who sold his sperm to a bank—we know he was (or is) "Hispanic" (the terminology used on the form he filled out) with a college degree and no known cases of cancer or other dreaded diseases in his gene pool. Oh, and he had (or has) an I.Q. of 136. And me, I'm perpetually single despite being what some might call a good-looking youngish woman with a dream job of assistant professor in the Chicana and Chicano studies department at Cal State-Northridge where I teach queer Latina poetics. I can't seem to keep a woman in my bed for longer than six months. Loners, all of us. And now that Abuela has passed on, I am more alone than ever.

Anyway, I'd thought the back house was vacant, used more as a storage space than anything else. I hadn't been to that part of the property for years—no reason to—and Abuela always kept me in the main house whenever I paid a visit, which was every month or so. But when I walked down the driveway the day after the funeral, passing the side of the main house, I could see signs of life in that little house in back: a worn but serviceable brown couch on the porch, three small planters, filled with what looked to be peonies, set perfectly along the porch's wooden railing, a classic Schwinn men's Cruiser—in beautiful shape—painted a bright, shiny red, its two large tires fully inflated and ready for a ride. And the small house itself was in better shape than I'd ever seen it. That old wood-framed structure had never been anything but in need of fresh paint, and here it was, gleaming white with dark-green trim.

As I approached, the crunch of gravel under my old Converse high-tops seemed to grow louder as my apprehension level elevated. It was almost noon and the Valley heat was just getting started. I tightened my grip on my backpack—heavy with two Norton anthologies and a binder full of student papers needing to be graded—getting ready to swing at this mystery man living on Abuela's property. But then he appeared, slowly opening the screen door, drying his hands on a dishtowel, smiling, nodding at me as if in recognition. I had twenty-five pounds on him, easy, so I relaxed. He couldn't have stood more than five feet tall, very thin, a full head of white hair cropped close to his skull. A handsome man with beautiful, brown skin, probably sixty or maybe seventy years old. He just stood there waiting for me to come up to the porch. I stopped about three yards from him and waited.

"Ah," he said in a soft, almost singsong voice. "¡La profesora!"

"You know me?" I asked as my stomach tightened.

"Your abuela bragged and bragged about you," he said, not losing his smile. "She showed me your photos many times, especially that one of you with her when you finished your Ph.D."

I knew the picture, one of my favorites. Abuela usually never smiled, especially for photos, but this time she displayed a huge grin and hugged me so tightly for the camera, I thought she was going to break one of my ribs. We're surrounded by other graduates in caps and gowns, excitement all around. She was prouder at that moment than when I graduated from Reed with a double major in gender studies and English. Abuela couldn't figure out how I could make a living wage with that. But when I finished graduate school at UCLA and told her that I'd landed a tenure-track position at CSUN the week before I was awarded my doctorate, she realized that I was going to be just fine. A steady job at a major university not too far from her home. It didn't matter that her granddaughter's focus was queer Latina lit. . .she loved me and we just didn't discuss it. What did matter was that I was educated and I had a great job, and she showed her elation in that picture.

"You know me," I said. "But who are you?"

"Elizondo," he said, his smile slowly disappearing. "Your abuela never mentioned me?"

"No, and I didn't see you at the funeral. Were you there? Did I miss you?" I asked more as a challenge than wanting to hear the answers.

He eased himself onto the couch, which let out a groan of ancient springs giving under his weight. Elizondo shook his head and averted his eyes.

"Why weren't you there?" I pressed.

He sighed. "Because I am just a tenant and. . ."

"And?"

He turned back to me: "And I could not think of seeing Ana in a coffin."

I shivered, though I'm not certain why. I seldom heard Abuela's name mentioned. . .she was simply Abuela to me. But when this strange man said her name, it carried a meaning beyond anything I knew about her.

"Have you eaten lunch?" he asked.

I wondered if he could hear my stomach rumble. I shook my head, but not very convincingly.

"Ah!" he said, standing and smiling again. "I'm heating up some lengua in a delicious soup, not too spicy, with little sliced potatoes. There's plenty."

His description of the beef tongue soup made my mouth water, and I could feel my stomach do a flip. Not until then had I noticed the wonderful scent of the soup emanating from the little house. I nodded and walked toward him. I figured he was harmless, and I needed some good Mexican food right then in honor of Abuela and to sate my hunger.

He had me sit at the small table in the kitchen. He kept the house very neat with little adornment. Pure efficiency. He moved back and forth, setting my place, filling a large glass with lemonade, ladling soup into my bowl. After he served himself, he sat, smiled, and commenced eating. I did the same.

"This is so good," I said, and I meant it.

"It is Ana's favorite."

He didn't correct himself to change the "is" to "was." And that was fine. I smiled back at him and we continued eating in contented silence, although I was formulating questions in my mind.

When we finished, he refilled our glasses with lemonade and directed us back to the porch. We sat on the couch with about two feet distance between us and sipped our cool drinks.

"How long have you lived here?" I finally asked.

He thought for a few moments. "It will be ten months tomorrow."

"Do you pay rent?"

"Por supuesto," he said, sounding a bit hurt. "I pay $300 each month, always on time. And I will pay you tomorrow because it is due."

I thought for a moment. Tomorrow was Saturday, the day I'd figured I would do the actual packing and organizing of Abuela's things. So I could come by, pick up the money, and figure out what to do about Elizondo then. I mean, I did not want to become a landlady. I'd planned to sell Abuela's property and use it for a down payment on a condo so that I wouldn't have to be a renter anymore. But today the goal was to survey Abuela's belongings, trying to determine what needed to be packed up for storage and what should be sold off. I nodded, said that tomorrow was fine, and for some reason, laid out my plans for the next two days. He asked if I needed help, but I declined. This was something I wanted to do in private.

I finished my lemonade in one big gulp, handed him the glass, and thanked him for the wonderful lunch. I headed back to Abuela's house to begin the task. I'd done the same with Mom's apartment when she died, so I kind of had a strategy for making it less onerous. I charted out each room, making lists of this and that, and then prioritized. I was always good at planning, turning big projects into manageable bite-sized jobs. Before I knew it, it was almost midnight. I wondered if Elizondo were still awake, but it would have been rather rude to bother him just in the hope of scrounging another good meal. So I hopped in my car, found a McDonald's drive-through, and ordered a chocolate shake and Angus Deluxe for the drive home.

The next morning I pulled up in front of Abuela's house. My trunk and back seat were filled with dozens of flattened packing boxes. But first I wanted to visit Elizondo, let him pay his rent, and maybe accept his offer of help. I could have used the company that day, the finality of Abuela's death finally sinking in. As I walked toward the little house in back, my Converse again offered a crunchy soundtrack to my short journey. Elizondo really had made it a nice little place, I had to admit. Even though this area of Van Nuys had not felt the full force of gentrification in recent years, it was getting there, and this property would likely bring in a tidy sum. I went up the three stairs to the porch and knocked on the screen door. I didn't hear anything. I tried to peer through the screen but couldn't see anything except shadows.

"Hello?" I said. "Elizondo?"

No answer. I opened the screen door slowly and entered the tiny living room. Everything was in place. I called out his name again, checked the kitchen. Nothing. There was only one place left to search, the small bedroom, so I made my way there in a few steps. The door stood ajar. I called his name again. Again, no answer. I slowly pushed the door open.

Elizondo lay in bed, fully clothed on top of a green bedspread, head nestled in a fluffy pillow, arms crossed. His eyes, open a bit, were lifeless, staring up at the ceiling. An empty diminutive brown bottle sat on the nightstand. As I approached the body, I bumped into a small table to my left. I looked down and saw three new $100 bills neatly lined up, waiting for me. There was a small piece of yellow paper near the bills with some writing on it. I picked it up and read: LO SIENTO. ELIZONDO

And then I noticed three women's rings and a small gold wristwatch set neatly by the money. I sighed and looked over to Elizondo. To say he looked peaceful would have been untruthful. In fact, his expression was one of mild surprise—the kind of surprise you experience when you walk in on a parent getting dressed, or happen upon two strangers kissing in public. The kind of surprise that is small, commonplace, but in the end, significant beyond its size. The kind of surprise I felt just then.

GOOD THINGS HAPPEN AT TINA'S CAFÉ

DURING WAKING HOURS Félix José Costa would never allow himself to wonder how different life would be if he were just like everyone else. Average. Common. *Normal.* In that way he was quite wise, despite his relative youth. Even at twenty-six years of age, Félix knew that it was a fool's destiny to expend energy imagining something that could never be.

But in his dreams—oh, those dreams!—he was like everyone else. In his nocturnal visions, Félix would saunter into the Spring Street entrance of the Ronald Reagan State Building and wave to the security guard, a heavyset, middle-aged man who would smile for no one but Félix. *Good morning! How about those Lakers!* And then a manly fist bump, another wave, a jaunty nod from both men. He'd then stroll along to the elevators, waving to friends and colleagues, his right hand (and sometimes his left) happily and publicly displayed for all to see: another beautiful day in Los Angeles, this grand City of Angels, Lotusland, a magical metropolis where dreams come true.

Compare reality: five mornings a week, after enjoying a cup or two of coffee at a nearby café, Félix enters his building, faux leather briefcase slung over his right shoulder, both hands jammed into his pants pockets, a slight turn to the guard so that he can see Félix's California-issued laminated identification card clipped to his jacket pocket, a silent dance without emotion, and then on toward the elevators, averting his eyes from passersby. He eventually gets to the eleventh floor, finds his barren cubicle, and begins his day as a legal secretary for three deputy attorneys general and one paralegal, employees in the Public Rights Division of the California Department of Justice.

Félix had learned the word for his "circumstance" when he was relatively young. His mother, Josefina, being quite educated and unafraid of reality, believed in truth regardless of where it might lead one, even her only child. A day after Félix's sixth birthday—after a short life filled with mockery and vicious jibes from neighborhood children and classmates—Josefina wrote the word on a piece of scrap paper and had Félix find it in the family's well-worn *American Heritage Dictionary*. Félix was very good with words and loved the musty smell of their dictionary. He flipped the pages until he came to the word his mother had written down: "pol-y-dac-tyl (pŏl'ē-dăk'təl) *adj*. Having more than the normal number of fingers or toes."

Félix rested his right hand on the page, palm on the cool, smooth paper, six fingers spread wide. There was *that* word: "normal." And he sighed. But Josefina swelled with pride because Félix pronounced *polydactyl* correctly. What a talented boy! What a handsome, promising, smart boy!

Félix's father, Reymundo, was not as educated as Josefina. No, he was a man of the old ways. He believed his son was cursed. Period. And the only way to fight a curse was through magic. One week after Félix learned the word for his condition, and unbeknownst to his wife, Reymundo took his son to visit a childless widower cousin named Tony who lived at the edge of Koreatown on Ardmore Avenue near Fifteenth Street in a rambling, two-story, wood-frame house built circa 1910 that was excessively large for Tony. But too many memories kept him in his home. Tony had what people called a sunny disposition; he was a man who never complained but spent his days appreciating the little things in life. He stayed put, thanked the heavens for his home, for the many years he had spent with his late lovely wife, Trini, and lived alone with his memories.

Nevertheless, Tony knew others suffered from loss, and he possessed a gift that could help them. Put simply, he could do wondrous things with mud and a few primordial incantations. For example, if your husband of fifty years finally succumbed to that undetected anomalous coronary artery, Tony could make a new spouse for you, complete with that little paunch and a more or less working male anatomy, out of the deep-brown mud from his backyard. Your beloved beagle got hit by a car? Presto chang-o! A new canine with the same sweet disposition and memories. . .expertly shaped out of mud by Tony's elegant long fingers. And Tony offered his talents at a bargain, too! If you were hard up, he'd take payment in house cleaning, tree trimming, or home-cooked tamales.

People said Tony was a saint, and one would be hard-pressed to argue with such an assessment. But some asked Tony why he didn't make a muddy double of his late wife. Tony would only wave the question away, shake his head, and say: "Not possible." This response could have several meanings. Some thought that he would lose his gift if he selfishly used it for himself. Others believed that Tony idolized Trini so much that he didn't know if he could do her justice with simple mud. Regardless, Tony's friends, family, and neighbors appreciated what he did for them and that was that.

So one bright Saturday morning, Reymundo told Josefina that he was going to take Félix for a hike at Griffith Park, knowing full well that his beautiful, brilliant wife did not like to perspire in public. She wished them well. Though the west San Fernando Valley had more than its share of trails that snaked up into the Santa Monica Mountains, Griffith Park sat at the eastern end of that same mountain range and boasted other attractions, such as an observatory and planetarium, not to mention the nearby zoo, the Autry National Center, and the Greek Theater. Reymundo and Félix kissed Josefina good-bye, hopped in the family's Honda Civic, and left Canoga Park for nature. But they took a detour to visit Tony, who lived just a few miles from their destination. Though Félix was puzzled when his father stayed on the 101 instead of switching over to the 134, he kept quiet and simply enjoyed the ride. When they exited at Normandie Avenue, Félix knew where his father was taking him. He figured his father wanted to chat with his cousin for a few moments just to see how he was getting along in that big empty house.

But no. Félix's father clearly had other plans. Tony came out to greet them, hands and arms covered in dark mud. Despite his equally muddy Levi's and red T-shirt, Tony could not hide his innate elegance. He had a head full of white curly hair, a countenance made up of sharp regal features. Tony could have been an actor, everyone had said, but he loved his magic too much to think of such silliness.

"Vámonos," he said through a broad smile. "Follow me to the backyard. I don't want to hug you two since, as you can see, I am a muddy mess."

Tony's yard was immense, a double lot, with a massive ancient avocado tree at its center. A grassy lawn covered most of the yard. Here and there were a few small lemon trees, a rose bush or two. Félix's eyes were drawn to Tony's shed at the far end of the yard just to the left of a thick cover of morning glory vines that twined in and out of the chain-link fence that separated Tony's property from a well-maintained fourplex apartment building. Hundreds of flowers had just opened fully to display trumpets of vibrant blues and purples, dappled with morning dew. To the right of the vines was a vast, wet pit of mud—clearly the source of Tony's medium of choice.

Tony walked toward the shed, his guests following. When they entered, Tony clicked on the overhead fluorescent lights. The loamy smell overtook Félix for a moment, making him blink and then sneeze. He had never been invited into his cousin's workspace before.

"Welcome," Tony said. He pointed to an ancient blue velvet couch and nodded to Reymundo, who obeyed the silent command to sit.

"Un momento. . .I have a little more preparation to take care of," said Tony as he walked to his workbench, where a wet pile of mud sat waiting. "Make yourself at home." He plunged his hands into the mud, humming a little nondescript tune.

Félix stood still, scanning the sparsely furnished room. Other than the couch, a lone metal folding chair stood in one corner. A muddy white towel hung from a large nail in the wall behind the workbench. Above his father's head was a single wooden bookshelf attached precariously to the wall. Félix could make out a few of the titles. *The Sculpture of Africa*, by Eliot Elisofon. Paulo Freire's *Pedagogy of the Oppressed. Aztec Thought and Culture*, by Miguel León-Portillo. He squinted a bit to discern what other books sat on the shelf but could only make out two that had the word *wrestling* in the titles. Félix's mother had always said that despite Tony's belief in magic, he was quite an intellectual who read two or three books a week on everything from art to philosophy to history. His reading material seemed to support this. Tony also seemed to enjoy the art of wrestling, and judging from the tight ropes of muscle that undulated in his shoulders and arms while he worked the mud, Tony had very likely wrestled in his younger years. Félix had tried to watch a wrestling match during the last summer Olympics, but he found it boring and nothing like he thought wrestling should be like. It seemed to him that the two men almost never touched each other, and they looked like two cats prancing on their hind legs. Yet the Cuban won the gold over the American. How? Why?

"Estoy listo," said Tony.

Félix jumped just a bit and turned to the workbench. Tony stood to the side of the mud, which he had sculpted into the shape of a small sheet cake. Félix walked slowly toward Tony, who smiled encouragingly. Finally, the boy stood in front of the workbench and looked down to see what Tony had been doing: in the mud were two perfectly formed imprints of five-fingered hands. Félix's stomach leapt.

"No tengas miedo," whispered Tony. "It won't hurt. Just fit your hands into the mud, palms down."

"But. . ."

Tony understood: "Fit your two outside fingers into the pinkies. . .the mud will give just a bit because it's still wet."

Félix turned his head to his father, who now sat at the edge of the couch, an elbow resting on each knee, hands folded as if in prayer. He nodded to Félix.

The boy turned back to the workbench and slowly placed his hands into the mud. It felt cool, moist, almost comforting.

"¡Excelente!" exclaimed Tony as he scooped up fresh mud and covered Félix's hands. When he had finished, he stepped back and admired his work. He then closed his eyes and mumbled something in a language Félix did not recognize.

"Now what?" asked Reymundo.

Tony's eyes popped open. "Now," he said as he reached for the towel, "you and I will go and have a beer in the house while the boy stands here for an hour."

"What?" exclaimed Félix, unable to hide his alarm.

Tony smiled. "Do you think great magic can happen in a minute?"

Of course. This made sense. Félix sighed, nodded, and closed his eyes.

"Good boy," said Tony. "Reymundo, I have some cold Buds in the fridge. Let's go."

Reymundo stood and walked to his son. He kissed Félix on the top of his head and inhaled deeply of the perspiration that permeated his son's thick hair. Reymundo loved his son and sincerely wanted to make his life a little easier. After a few moments, Reymundo lifted his head and looked down at the muddy magic. "It'll be over soon," he offered as Tony started to lead him toward the door. "You are a brave young man."

Félix kept his eyes closed, falling into what his mother called a self-induced trance, something the boy had mastered when he needed to escape this world.

An hour later, the sound of Tony's cheerful voice brought him back to this world. "Let's see those hands of yours."

Félix's father stood to the side, watching intently as Tony opened a battered tool chest that sat on the workbench and pulled out a mud-stained wooden stick that resembled a large broken spoon. With the sharp end, he slowly chiseled away the now-dried mud. Tony and his father kept their eyes glued to the stick, following its movements as Tony uncovered Félix's hands—first the thumbs, then moving outward toward the offending extra digits. When he finally finished, Félix lifted his hands and wiggled his fingers.

Six fingers on each hand. Félix sighed.

Tony turned to Reymundo. "Have you explored surgery?"

"The insurance won't cover the procedure, and it's so expensive."

Tony asked, "How could they not cover it?"

"Look," said Reymundo. "All of his fingers work perfectly. So they consider it merely cosmetic surgery. Elective."

"Pendejos," muttered Tony.

TWENTY YEARS LATER, Tony was three years' dead and his favorite cousin, Félix, now lived in his big house. And one Thursday morning half an hour before the workday began, after catching the bus at Pico and Ardmore, Félix sat at Tina's Café enjoying a delicious cup of Yuban, his twelve fingers wrapped around the coffee mug, and reading the *Los Angeles Times*. He felt so at home here. The other customers were not professionals but men and women who had little money and even less hope of improving their lives. Not one of them ever stared at his hands. All offered a smile and a nod, nothing more. But that was quite a gift as far as Félix was concerned.

He had discovered Tina's Café while searching Yelp for places near his office. He was intrigued by its lone three-star review written by a disheveled, confused-looking man named Barney:

> Located at 357½ South Spring Street. Founded in 2008, Tina's Café has nurtured a loyal following with its dedication to traditional coffee brands such as Folgers and Yuban. Convenient location with some of the lowest coffee prices in town. Decor has a garage sale feel to it, and the lighting could be improved, but the seating is comfortable and encourages random conversations. Unfortunately, the service is poor: owner is often distant and seems preoccupied with some other venture, but this might be an act. Also, customers must clean up after themselves or else the owner gets very cross and points a finger at the offending mess. Even so, a much better deal than the nearby Third Street Deli.

Félix had tried to speak with Tina the first time he had come in, a year ago, but true to the Yelp review, she was not responsive. She was content to pour coffee and collect money, but not much else. Was she pretty? Maybe. Young? Not certain. Félix suspected that Tina was about five years older than he, but then again, she could be two or three years younger. Was she Mexican? Probably not. Maybe she was Filipina or perhaps Native American. She did not engage any customer in conversation. Tina was Tina, and that was that.

But on this Thursday morning, after Tina poured Félix a second cup of coffee, she didn't turn to attend to other customers but instead stood before Félix as if she were waiting for something.

Félix looked up and tried to smile, but his confusion thwarted his attempt at nonchalance. Tina's face remained impassive as she stared into his eyes.

"Yes?" Félix finally said.

"You have six fingers on each hand, you know."

"Yes, I know."

"Good," said Tina before turning away. "Glad you know it."

The next morning after Tina poured Félix's first cup of coffee, she said, "I have three breasts."

Félix almost fell out of his chair.

Tina laughed. "Not really," she said. "I just made that up."

Félix looked down at the tabletop and put his hands in his lap, out of sight.

"But," continued Tina, now that the dam was broken, "I'm sure there are women out there, someplace, who do have three breasts, don't you think?"

Félix nodded.

Tina pulled up a chair, sat down with a little grunt, and put the coffeepot down on the table. "Women just love those hands, don't they?"

Félix looked up at the clock on the wall, pulled out $3, dropped the money on the table, and stood up. "Going to be late for work," he said but didn't move.

"No you're not," said Tina. "You always leave here at 8:15. It's only 7:50. Sit. You have time. I won't bother you anymore."

As Félix took his seat again, Tina stood and walked to another customer, but a minute later she came back. "I'm sorry," she said. "I was being rude. I have no right to ask such questions, right?"

"Not a big deal," said Félix. For reasons he could not understand, he hoped she'd sit down again.

"Saturday morning," she began, "I think we should meet at the base of Angels Flight. Then we can figure out what to do for the day."

Before he could stop himself, Félix said, "I'd like that."

"Groovy," said Tina. She finally smiled. "Let's make it 10 in the a.m., as my papa would say."

"Ten in the a.m.," he said. "It's a date."

"You bet it is," said Tina. "There's nothing else you could call it even if you tried."

FÉLIX STOOD at the base of Angels Flight on Hill Street. He was seven minutes early so he walked back and forth, occasionally looking up at the two orange and black funicular cars as they clacked up and down the parallel tracks. Félix checked the time on his iPhone. Five more minutes. He then noticed a small plaque and took three steps, leaned close, and read it:

> Built in 1901 by Colonel J. W. Eddy, lawyer, engineer and friend of President Abraham Lincoln, Angels Flight is said to be the world's shortest incorporated railway. The counterbalanced cars, controlled by cables, travel a 33 percent grade for 315 feet. It is estimated that Angels Flight has carried more passengers per mile than any other railway in the world, over 100 million in its first fifty years. This incline railway is a public utility operating under a franchise granted by the City of Los Angeles.

"You know they have names."

Félix tried not to show surprise but he failed. The morning sun caused him to squint into Tina's shadowed face. "What?"

"Sinai and Olivet," said Tina. "That's their names."

"Who?"

"The cars, silly."

"Oh," said Félix. "Why?"

"Biblical, of course."

"Of course."

Tina held out her right hand, palm up. At first Félix thought she wanted to hold his hand, but then noticed that she was presenting four shiny quarters. "Our funicular fare," said Tina. "We pay the kind gentleman at the top. It's 50 cents per person each way."

"I know."

"Oh, you are a wise and experienced man."

Félix blushed and turned away.

"Let's go," she said. "Time is *not* on our side."

When they got to the top and paid their fare, Tina said: "Must. Drink. Coffee."

"There's a Starbucks right over there."

"Starbucks is evil," she said. "Starbucks was created to destroy small businesspeople like me."

"Oh, sorry," said Félix. "Of course you believe that."

"Yes, you should be ashamed of yourself."

"I am."

"Good," said Tina as she started to walk toward the Starbucks. "Let's go to Starbucks."

Félix didn't move. "What?"

"Starbucks is evil but I have a hankerin' for a Caffè Vanilla Frappuccino Blended Beverage."

Félix took one step and then another after Tina. "That sounds good."

"Yes, it's delicious," she said with a smack of her lips. "And then we'll sit and talk for a bit about very important things and go to MOCA, which opens at 11:00 to look at an exhibit or two or three and then come back here and grab some Panda Express since I am already now craving orange chicken for lunch and we can talk about less important things and then we'll take Angels Flight back down and find a bar or two or three and have a microbrew or some fancy girl's drink and then find some other places to hang out because we are young and the day lies before us like a cornucopia filled with unforgettable and life-changing experiences."

Félix smiled.

"It does appear that you like my plan," said Tina.

"I think I do."

Tina stopped walking to let Félix catch up to her. "I repeat: you are a wise and experienced man," she said when he finally stood by her side.

"I guess I am," he said. "I guess I am."

AND THEY SPENT THE DAY more or less as Tina had planned, though it was Félix's idea to walk to Olvera Street to eat dinner at La Golondrina Mexican Café. They spoke of many things, whatever came into their heads, as the hours passed.

For example, at 10:31 a.m., over their blended Starbucks coffee drinks, Tina said: "You know, George Bernard Shaw wrote a scathing review of Brahms, called him a 'great baby' and said he was 'addicted to dressing himself up as Handel or Beethoven and making a prolonged and intolerable noise.' Can you imagine? Brahms? A 'great baby'? Craziness!"

And at 12:57 p.m., as they stood in line at Panda Express, Félix said: "Did you know that Panda Express executive chef

Andy Kao is widely considered the creator of orange chicken? And they sold over 60 million pounds of it last year. Amazing."

And it was at precisely 2:13 p.m., as they rode Sinai back down to Hill Street, that Tina offered this: "Wilshire Boulevard was named after Henry Gaylord Wilshire, who was from Cincinnati and was known as a bit of a flirt and a definite rabble-rouser. At least that's what I read in a book by this guy named Kevin Roderick."

It was 6:39 p.m. as they strolled along Olvera Street toward La Golondrina for dinner when they said absolutely nothing—not a peep—which was just fine by them.

Their day ended at 10:03 p.m. at the base of Angels Flight, just as it had started. They stood facing each other, swaying in the cool evening, bellies full, heads a bit woozy from microbrews and lady drinks.

"One kiss?" asked Félix.

"One kiss it is," said Tina.

And they kissed, bodies apart, faces turned in, lips tentative, a flicker of tongue. After a few moments, they pulled back in unison.

"I assume you will come by the very famous Tina's Café on Monday morning," said Tina.

"I'll be there," said Félix.

"I know you will," said Tina.

And they went their separate ways.

It was a foggy Monday morning as Félix stepped off the bus and walked toward Spring Street. He had had all of Sunday to think about his day with Tina. The chilled air allowed him to see his breath. Félix tried not to smile but he couldn't help himself. He would soon be in Tina's Café having a hot cup of Yuban poured by Tina herself.

Félix walked past a storefront with its name, MIKE'S USED FURNITURE, in old-fashioned golden script emblazoned across the plate glass. Below the name was: EST'D 1962. He was a few steps beyond the store before the realization hit him, so he stopped and walked back. He checked the address: yes, it was 357½ South Spring Street. But this was not Tina's Café. The lights were out, the store not yet open for business. Félix pulled his hands from his jacket pockets and cupped his eyes, leaning forward to the window and squinting into the darkened interior. Instead of Tina's Café, he saw bureaus and chairs and tables and loveseats neatly arranged and ready for sale.

Félix pulled back, placing his palms onto the plate glass, unable to catch his breath. He closed his eyes and tried to conjure Tina's face in his mind's eye, but he couldn't. His legs began to buckle and it took every bit of concentration to keep from falling down to the cold sidewalk. After a full minute, Félix opened his eyes and focused on his splayed fingers. He blinked once and then again and then once more. Five. *Five!* Five fingers on each hand. He brought his hands away from the plate glass, turned toward the street, mouth open like an empty wallet. And at that moment, every memory of Tina slipped from his mind.

He closed his mouth into a tight smile. And with a little laugh, Félix José Costa raised his perfectly normal hands to caress the cool Los Angeles morning.

DON DE LA CRUZ AND THE DEVIL OF MALIBU

DON JESÚS REYMUNDO DE LA CRUZ slept with the Devil. No, this is both too genteel and inaccurate. Don de la Cruz screwed the Devil, fucked the Devil, but never slept with the Devil. La Diabla. As most of us know, the Devil who lived in Southern California was a female so she was La Diabla, not El Diablo. Because the Devil is legion, the Devil resides in most towns and cities and may be a man or a woman. It all depends on what is needed. So in Southern California, the Devil is a woman. In New York, a male. Anyway, Don de la Cruz was La Diabla's sex mate and as payment for that, he gained great power and wealth.

La Diabla lived in Malibu. But this is not the Malibu that you're imagining right now. No, she did not live in the Malibu of Johnny Carson and Olivia Newton-John and Gladstone's and the Pacific Coastal Highway that was used for the opening credits in the 1960s sitcom with Sally Fields, *Gidget,* before Sally Fields was the Flying Nun and Norma Rae and before everyone *really* loved her. No, this was the Malibu of 1822, long before any of that bullshit. But I get ahead of myself. First, a little history. Because without history, stories cannot settle in a place that elucidates and adds shadows and meaning. And, as the Devil well knows, without a sense of history, holocausts are repeated and the Devil wins another battle.

In case your fathers and mothers have not already taught you, here is the lesson. Forty-four poor Spanish settlers founded El Pueblo de Nuestra Señora la Reina de los Ángeles de la Porciúncula on September 4, 1791. The pueblo eventually became known simply as Los Angeles. The Spanish settlers converted the native Indians, known as the Tongva, who had already occupied the region for thousands of years, to Catholicism. When Mexico severed its ties with Spain in 1822, Los Angeles became an important Mexican colony and would remain so until, twenty-four years later, the United States waged war on Mexico after gold was discovered in California. President James Polk called it "Manifest Destiny." But that's a different story.

In 1822, Don de la Cruz was a wealthy man of thirty-two. For twelve years he had fucked La Diabla and, as I said earlier, she paid him well for his services. Don de la Cruz owned and operated the largest bank in El Pueblo de Nuestra Señora la Reina de los Ángeles de la Porciúncula. Through very little effort, he held one, two, sometimes three mortgages on most of the town's prime and not-so-prime properties. He lived in a thirty-room mansion built in the French style, and ten servants met all his needs. Don de la Cruz dressed impeccably and he looked handsome, with a trim figure, white skin, and black hair. He said he was Spanish, not Mestizo—not an ounce of pinche Indian blood ran through his veins, he said. When he walked the streets, people bowed and lowered their eyes and Don de la Cruz felt important, like a king.

But at the age of thirty-two, Don de la Cruz grew bored and weary of his success. Not that his success was not earned. Oh, no! Fucking La Diabla was a painful and ugly chore! She had a voracious appetite for Don de la Cruz. Though La Diabla was as beautiful as any creature that walked this Earth, her various orifices let out the rank stench of rape, mayhem, torture, and all things horrible and terrifying. And when Don de la Cruz inserted himself into La Diabla, a burning, gut-wrenching pain traveled up through his lower intestines, up into his stomach to his heart, which the pain wrapped itself around like the clenched fist of a drowning man. And La Diabla would squeeze Don de la Cruz with her beautiful thighs and scream such hideous screams that Don de la Cruz had to shut his ears and close his eyes and put his mind someplace else far from this atrocity that he fucked.

All this happened in La Diabla's home under the rocks of Malibu in a cave—lined with the souls she had conquered—just out of sight of the wandering Chumash Indians, for they were the

Malibu people, different from their relatives in town, the Tongva. And it was one day in April 1822, after fucking, that Don de la Cruz lay by La Diabla and broached the subject of his boredom.

"I need a challenge," Don de la Cruz began slowly, knowing that La Diabla had a horrible temper and reacted with lightning speed to anything resembling a threat to her power.

La Diabla turned to the man who lay near her in her bed of seaweed. "I'm not challenge enough?" she hissed.

"I mean," continued Don de la Cruz, "my wealth and power within the town doesn't mean much to me anymore. It's too easy. Do you know what I mean?"

La Diabla smiled. Of course she knew what he meant. She had expected this day to come and so she had planned a response to his plea. "In one month you will have a challenge."

Don de la Cruz jumped in anticipation. "What will it be?"

La Diabla smiled and grabbed her man's penis, squeezing until Don de la Cruz almost screamed.

"You will know it when it presents itself to you." And with that, La Diabla mounted Don de la Cruz and fucked him again. "And in order to prepare you for that day, you will not share my bed during that time. So, my love, fuck me so that I can remember what you feel like!"

And after they were done, Don de la Cruz got dressed and went to his thirty-room mansion built in the French style with the ten servants who met all his needs and he waited for his challenge.

Throughout the month of April, Don de la Cruz wondered who or what his challenge would be. A warrior, perhaps? A natural disaster? What, he wondered, did La Diabla have in mind?

As he thought and the days passed, Don de la Cruz noticed subtle changes in his town. Slowly, one by one, the landowners paid off their mortgages and withdrew their money from his bank. And, as Don de la Cruz walked through the town, people no longer bowed and lowered their eyes as they had before—instead they whispered and pointed and sneered and showed no respect for the great Don de la Cruz. Finally, the greatest insult occurred: each and every one of his servants left his mansion. There was no one left. No one to cook for him, to dress him, to keep the horses brushed and fed, no one to care for his every need.

And Don de la Cruz grew angrier and angrier and angrier.

But he dared not go to La Diabla. He knew better. So he waited. The twenty-second day, the twenty-third, and finally the thirtieth day arrived, a sunny spring morning. And Don de la Cruz rose from bed and bathed and dressed and cooked for himself a big bowl of menudo—for he had taught himself to cook because he no longer had any servants!—and he drank much brandy and waited.

At 10 in the morning, he still sat at his dining table after finishing three bowls of the tripe and hominy soup and a whole bottle of brandy. And he sat and waited.

"¡Bastante!" he finally yelled and shoved his bowl and glass and bottle and candelabra onto the hardwood floor and stomped toward the front door of his mansion. He took in a long breath through his narrow Spanish nostrils to prepare himself, grasped the large brass doorknob with his powerful pistol hand, and threw the door open. Don de la Cruz marched out of his mansion with all the resolve of his brave stallion but then suddenly froze in mid-stride, in the dead center of his grand porch.

Standing before Don de la Cruz was the entire population of the town. Just staring at him. All he could hear was their breathing, in unison, and not one bird or other creature dared make a sound. He stood on his porch, frozen in mid-stride, for one full minute as his brandy-soaked brain tried hard to absorb what faced him at that moment.

And then he noticed her. A little girl, maybe thirteen or so, standing in the middle of the crowd. She looked like—no, I can't describe her; that would be impossible. But let me say that to Don de la Cruz, she looked like everything that La Diabla was not. And she wore a simple brown dress and her skin was brown as well, like the Indian that she surely was, and she wore no shoes. The girl carried a large wooden box and Don de la Cruz could see that carved on the box was an eagle with a serpent in its beak and the eagle was perched on a cactus.

Ah! thought Don de la Cruz. Pistols! La Diabla has sent her challenge to me.

"Little girl," he said. "Are you my challenge with your box of pistols?"

The little girl said nothing but motioned to a man next to her and the man quickly brought a table and then two chairs and put them between the girl and Don de la Cruz. She set the box on the hardwood table and opened it. And she said: "No pistols. Dominoes."

Don de la Cruz stood on the porch. He started to shake and the crowd murmured in confusion. And then he started to laugh. And he laughed with all the strength of his body. "Dominoes!" he yelled. "That is my challenge!" And he laughed some more.

The crowd remained dead silent. And the girl threw down the challenge: "If I win, you will leave this town forever."

"And if I win, mija, what do I get?"

The girl smiled. "Whatever you want."

Don de la Cruz thought for but a moment before exclaiming, "¡Tú! I will have you and you know precisely what I mean, mija!"

The crowd let out a gasp, a sound of revulsion and fear.

"Yes," said the girl. "Yes, that is a bargain." And she sat down and poured the dominoes out onto the table and they made a rattling sound like the sound an old man makes when he dies and lets out his last breath.

Don de la Cruz walked slowly down the porch stairs, his beautiful black boots making a loud and majestic pound with each step. And he sat down and said, prompting another gasp from the crowd: "I can't wait to take you to my bed, mija."

The girl did not blush, nor did she betray fear. She simply said: "Choose your dominoes."

So the man and the girl chose their dominoes and each lined them up and examined their choices. "You may go first," said the little girl. And the crowd laughed.

"No!" yelled Don de la Cruz. "I will not be embarrassed by a pinche little Indian girl! You will go first."

The little girl shrugged a little shrug and complied. She put down a double six. Don de la Cruz's face turned as purple as a ripe fig. For, as any child knows, the person who picks a double six always goes first. So! he thought, she was trying to humiliate me!

"¡Puta!" said Don de la Cruz through his perfectly aligned white teeth. "You will lose and you will be mine!"

The game lasted for two full days. Piece by piece, the pattern of dominoes grew into an angular snake with many eyes.

The girl remained calm, but an uneasiness slowly crept into the heart of her opponent.

At one point, hours into the game, Don de la Cruz remarked: "Mija, you look familiar. Who are you? Do you live near our pueblo?"

"We have never met before," she said and put down a domino with a one and a five on it. "Never before."

And Don de la Cruz shrugged and continued the game.

It was the first day of May when finally the little girl put down her last domino and there were no more to pick from the pile that had once sat on the side of the table. Don de la Cruz's eyes widened. He felt ill. He was hungry and he had to piss and crap, but he had not left his chair for two days. And now he had lost to a little bitch of an Indian girl! He grabbed the table, almost hitting the little girl's face with its edge, and threw it to the ground. The crowd held its breath.

She stood up and said: "I win. You lose. You know what to do!"

The crowd drew near so Don de la Cruz decided not to pull his gun. "Okay, mija. I may be many things, but I never cheat when I gamble. I have lost. And I will honor my part of the bargain." And he went into his mansion and shut the door.

The crowd stared at the door, hoping that Don de la Cruz would come out with supplies and then ride off on his stallion, leaving the town forever.

Instead he put his pistol into his mouth and blew the back of his head off.

And as the crowd realized what had happened, loud cheers filled the air and the townspeople carried the little girl on their shoulders to the plaza to commence a wonderful fiesta that lasted two weeks.

And what happened to that little girl? Well, she eventually was given the honor of running Don de la Cruz's bank and she grew wealthy and powerful and eventually held one, two, or maybe three mortgages on most of the town's prime and not-so-prime properties. She lived in Don de la Cruz's thirty-room mansion built in the French style, with ten servants who met all her needs. She also dressed impeccably and she looked beautiful, with a trim figure, brown skin, and black hair. When she walked the streets, people bowed and lowered their eyes and she felt important, like a queen.

And she laughed to herself when she remembered how Don de la Cruz had thought she looked familiar. She had not lied. They had never met. But she looked familiar to Don de la Cruz because she was his daughter—the result of Don de la Cruz's many years of fucking La Diabla. She was born fully formed that month when the Devil and her lover were separated.

And La Diabla continues to run El Pueblo de Nuestra Señora la Reina de los Ángeles de la Porciúncula, which today is known simply as Los Angeles. And she still lives in Malibu. But not in the rocks by the ocean with all that seaweed. No. La Diabla submitted a building permit application with the California Coastal Commission in 1986 so that she could build a luxurious townhouse not far from Johnny Carson's beautiful home. The Coastal Commission stipulated a few conditions, but her application was granted. And La Diabla very much enjoys life in Malibu at the beach.

SEÑOR SÁNCHEZ

Señor Sánchez lived a rather nice life in our little pueblo of Dos Cuentos. He sat most days in the plaza by the statue of our pueblo's founder, Don Antonio Segoviano, and waited, eyes closed, lips pursed in a constant little hum, with his dog Chucho panting by his side. You see, people came to him to hear him talk. They paid a few pesos, dropping them noisily into an empty Maxwell House tin that sat between Señor Sánchez and Chucho. With each clank of the heavy coins, Chucho's ratty little ears would pop up, frisky and alert, and Señor Sánchez would smile as he leaned back into his weather-beaten foldout chair. He held his elegant, unusually small hands draped over the brass head of his cane, and he laughed, always asking the same question: "What is it you want to hear?"

And the customers would tell him.

"A sad story," said Señora Cruz, a widow for these last ten years.

"A very funny joke," offered our priest, Padre Olivares. And he tipped his shaggy head at Señor Sánchez, smiling. "One I can tell in my sermon next Sunday."

"Will I ever find a wife?" asked poor, lonely Simón, the carpenter.

One day the mayor visited Señor Sánchez. I was sitting not far away at the Bar Americano, drinking my usual lunch of two (or perhaps three) bottles of Tecate beer, and I was eager to hear what the great man wanted. No noise came from the Maxwell House tin: the mayor dropped a nice fat wad of paper bills into the till. The sun hit my face, hard and true, and I put my cool bottle down with a little clink and waited for Señor Sánchez to ask his usual question. But he did not. What did he do? He smiled. That is all. And Chucho slept.

The mayor stood, frozen, for a moment or two. And then he spoke. "Speak to me as my son would," he said, "if he were still alive."

My heart beat hard in my throat. The whole pueblo knew of the horrible tragedy of Mario's death in April, three months ago. It had rained so hard for six days that no one ventured out. Finally, on a Sunday, in the afternoon on the sixth day, the sun peeked out from behind the dark clouds. Some of us went out to inspect the roads and it's there that we found him, head deep in muddy water, by the side of Calle Verdad. Mario's body was so bloated we assumed that he had been dead for several days. And, of course, it was clearly an accident. The mayor fell into a dark sadness at the loss of his only child.

So on that day the mayor went to Señor Sánchez, I tried to listen. I saw him smile at the mayor and then I saw his lips move slowly, but although I strained and strained I could not discern a word. Señor Sánchez's thin, almost blue lips stopped moving. The mayor jumped back as if struck hard in the chest. And for a moment the birds did not sing, the wind did not blow. I glanced at my watch and noted that the mayor did not move for a full three minutes! Finally, he straightened himself, brushed nonexistent dust from his fine blue suit, bowed slowly and elegantly, and turned on his heel. Within a few seconds he was out of view.

The odd thing was what happened afterward. When the mayor left the plaza, Señor Sánchez sighed and shook his head. Slowly he stood, folded his chair, patted Chucho's head, and wandered off. Chucho, for some odd reason, stayed put. As he walked away, Señor Sánchez turned, ever so slowly, and caught my eye. In my embarrassment, I waved and then turned to my newspaper. He disappeared within a few moments.

Señor Sánchez never came to the plaza after that. A month later we learned that he had died in his bed. Padre Olivares said that he had lived to be 125, according to the church's baptism records. And according to some of the older citizens, Señor Sánchez had been talking in the plaza since he was twenty years old. That is a long time to be speaking. ¿No?

DRIVING TO VENTURA

It's not dramatic, not really. Not in the least. Not like the movies or TV. It's kind of small and gnarled but swift as a sparrow, with a pitiful muffled sound of *pam! pam! pam!* And then there's this silence except for a ringing that's far off, like it's coming from some other room, but I know that can't be true because we have a one-room apartment, not counting the bathroom, so the ringing must be coming from the upstairs neighbor. Or maybe from the people who live right under us. So I push my ear down hard against the orange shag carpeting because I'm on the floor now. And I listen, listen hard. I hear his breathing above me and I want to shush him but I don't. I try harder to hear where that ringing is coming from. But it's not coming from that nice couple below. It's right here. Right in my head.

I should have known the first time we went out. Three years ago this May. We were both broke so we went to Tommy's on Topanga Canyon Boulevard, near the Beef Bowl, and got these big greasy chili burgers, each with a tomato slice the size of a deck of cards, chili-cheese fries, and king-size cups of Coke. We actually laughed a lot as the chili dripped from our fingers and chins and onto the table and our clothes. The Santa Ana winds were blowing hard so it was a warm night. The stars kind of twinkled, just a bit, their energy being sucked up by the city lights. During a lull in the laughter, Mike leaned toward me, his blond mustache carrying bits of chili, and he said, "You want to be my little Mexican bitch?" I blinked hard, trying to understand what he said. He leaned closer. "Well, do you?"

I LOVE THE VENTURA FREEWAY. Especially when I'm driving north. Away from the Valley. There's this point when you pass Canoga Park, West Hills, and then Calabasas, and you know you're on your way. It doesn't matter where. But you're on your way because you can feel it.

MOMEE WAS PRETTY MUCH LIKE ME. Or is it the other way around? Anyway, she fell hard for the good-looking ones without regard for anything else. Take Pops, for example. Handsome as all get-out. Kind of looked like a young suntanned John Wayne, but way better looking. No crooked smile like Wayne's. Actually, no smile at all. He and Momee used to yell at each other but Pops never hit her. She said he went with other women. Usually she called him names and he called her names, and then she'd leave with a bang of the door to stay with Grandma. It happened a lot when I was five or six. Pops used to sit and drink in the dark when she left and I'd lie there listening to him mutter. And then one time, he came to my room and lay down next to me. I pretended to be asleep. And he cried, shaking like a small jackhammer, and smelled my hair. And I pretended even harder to be asleep.

I LIKE DRIVING TO VENTURA. It's a good, clean drive. This time it's not just a drive. My bag is packed and sits right behind me in the back seat. This time is different in every way. After the *pam! pam! pam!* I heard a crack. Cheekbone, left one, just caved in. He never broke a bone before. But that was it. When he drove me to West Hills Emergency, the doctor asked me how this had happened. Mike shot me a look like he's saying, *Okay, it'll be okay, just lie for me this one more time.* But he knew the look I shot back at him said, *No, not this time. I will not lie.* And I didn't. That was two weeks ago. He'll end up serving time because I'm pressing charges. I like my lawyer. Cool lady. She says, *Elena, time to begin a new life. What do you want to do?* And I think. It doesn't take long. So now here I sit, in my old Toyota, listening to B. B. King and driving to Ventura. I'm on my way.

FRANZ KAFKA IN FRESNO

FRANZ KAFKA HATED HIS FATHER. And he had good reason to. Specifically, Franz could not forgive his father for insisting that his only child be named Franz. Franz understood that his father was very proud that he likely was related to the great writer whose surname he shared. However, with a name like Franz, Carl Kafka virtually guaranteed that his son would be beaten up every day of his life from kindergarten through high school. Fresno was not a hospitable place for a slender, overly intelligent, German-Mexican kid named Franz. Franz wondered why he couldn't have been named after some relative on his mother's side. The Gamboa family possessed many fine names from which to choose, such as Alfredo, Eloy, César, and even Kiko, although that last one was really a nickname. Sometimes, when he was nursing a black eye given to him by a bully, Franz would daydream about who he could have been. The possibilities made his young head swim in a giddy swirl. Can you imagine it? Kiko Kafka! Who in his right mind, even in Fresno, would mess with a boy named Kiko Kafka? But, alas, he was named Franz. And so it was: Franz hated his father.

The day Franz's father died, Franz had made a vow never to speak to his father again. Enough is enough, he reasoned. If you hate someone, why waste time speaking with them? Unfortunately, Franz made the vow before he got the call that his father had died, and he felt a great pang of guilt. How could a son hate his dead father? It was not right.

So Franz drove up to Fresno from Los Angeles and made certain that Carl had a fine burial. With his mother long gone, Franz was now officially an orphan at the age of thirty-one.

"Good-bye, Papá," said Franz as the coffin slowly creaked down into the fresh grave. "I didn't mean to hate you." The few people in attendance looked away, and the priest offered nothing more than a grunt.

As Franz started toward his car after the service, an old man stopped him, placing a large heavy hand carefully but insistently on Franz's shoulder. "I knew your father well," said the man.

"Who are you?" asked Franz.

The old man smiled. "Just a man," he said. "Nothing more, nothing less."

They stood there in silence. With each second that passed, Franz's uneasiness grew. Who was this man? Franz felt as though his head might explode. "Well," Franz finally said. "Thank you for coming. I'm sure my father would have been happy you made the effort."

The man let go of Franz's shoulder. "I doubt it," he said with a chuckle.

With that, the man turned and walked off. Franz noticed that the man was almost a giant, certainly seven feet tall if he were an inch. Franz let out a sigh and continued toward his car. Why would a sardonic giant be attending his father's funeral? And why had Franz bothered to show up? What possible benefit could be derived from his presence at the funeral of the only man he hated? Nothing good could come of this.

There was only one solution. Franz needed to find a Starbucks. Since moving to Los Angeles ten years ago, he had become addicted to the brilliant concoction known as the Iced Caramel Macchiato. It was his only addiction and he fed it liberally. Franz wondered if Starbucks had made any inroads into Fresno. He then laughed because to ask such a question was to admit to a great ignorance as to how the world worked. Franz drove into the nearest gas station and, after filling up his Ford Taurus, he asked the attendant for directions to the nearest Starbucks.

"On Cedar," the man said brusquely. "Just south of Shepherd Avenue." He pointed with his right thumb over his left shoulder.

"Thank you," said Franz.

"Okay," said the man.

As Franz was about to get into his car, he suddenly froze. On the outside of the driver's side window crawled a plump, gigantic cockroach. For obvious reasons, Franz had developed an aversion to all vermin, in particular cockroaches. His shiver was so deep it went down below his heart. Franz took a tremulous breath, averted his eyes, and got himself into the car. Once safely inside, he looked for the cockroach, but it had disappeared. And for reasons he could not fathom, Franz at that moment missed that cockroach more than his father. He sighed. He needed an Iced Caramel Macchiato now more than ever. Franz imagined the gas station attendant's thumb pointing toward Cedar and aimed his car in that direction.

The moment Franz entered the Starbucks, his heartbeat and breathing slowed, his brow unknitted, his hands unclenched. Ah! Starbucks. He stood without moving, absorbing the calm, the familiar coffee smells and sounds. Franz looked around his second home. A few young, beautiful people chatted in one corner; two old men played chess over by the wall; a mother and her two children laughed and joked over their frothy drinks. What a perfect place. Franz walked to the counter—and there stood the most magnificent example of young womanhood he had ever seen. Her name tag said MARÍA and she did indeed look like the Madonna, the Virgin, La Virgén de Guadalupe, with long black hair spilling out from under a perfect Starbucks cap.

"May I help you?" she smiled.

Franz had never seen such a beautiful smile. His hands shook and his tongue had trouble finding the right position to put itself to form a word.

"Sir?" she asked, still giving him the most exquisite smile Franz had ever witnessed. The young woman's eyes then brightened with an idea. She offered: "¿Puedo ayudar usted, señor?"

Oh, God bless her, thought Franz. She thinks I speak only Spanish. What a wonderful, thoughtful, empathetic creature she is! He noticed that she did not wear a wedding band and wondered how such a perfect woman could still be unmarried, even taking into account her obvious youth. Fresno men just don't get it, he figured. They just don't know how lucky they are to have such a perfect woman in their midst.

"Sorry," said Franz, trying his best to offer a smile that expressed the joy that filled his heart at that moment. Instead he merely confused the young woman.

"Why are you sorry?" she asked.

Franz coughed and felt the beginnings of flop sweat on his upper lip, the kind that would have made Richard Nixon proud. "Iced Caramel Macchiato, please," was all he could get out.

The young woman nodded. "Size?"

"Oh, yes," he said. "Sorry."

She stood there offering nothing but a gentle look of understanding. She certainly had seen all kinds.

"Grande," said Franz thinking that he should pace himself and not order a larger size cup.

The young woman keyed it into the cash register with a few beeps and grabbed a cup from the counter. "Name?"

This was the only part of the Starbucks experience Franz hated. Because he had ordered a bar drink, the young woman would have to write his name on the cup and hand it to the barista, who would then make the drink and, when finished, call out the name printed on the cup. Inevitably, Franz would be misspelled as Frank and it was just too much trouble to offer a correction.

"Frank," said Franz.

The young woman nodded, smiled, and printed "Frank" on the cup before handing it to the tall earringed young man who worked the bar. The barista annoyed Franz, though he wasn't quite certain why. After paying, he waited by the bar to observe how his drink was being put together. This seemed to bother the young man, or at least that's what Franz surmised. He wondered if this poor excuse for masculinity was sleeping with the young woman.

Such thoughts made Franz feel a bit ill, so he shook his head and tried to think of happy things. But he couldn't think of any happy things. His mind kept falling back to the dream he'd had last night as he slept in his old room, his family's house quiet except for Franz's breathing. In the dream Franz admired a beautiful black fish swimming in a small round bowl that sat on the kitchen counter in his parents' house. Oh, what an elegant fish it was! It swam slowly, regally, showing off its almost translucent flowing fins. But then Franz noticed that the water was growing dirty. And soon the fish was swimming in muck, gasping for oxygen. He quickly poured some of the water out of the bowl and refilled it. But the water grew dirty again, and although Franz changed it numerous times, each time the water turned back into a noxious brew. Suddenly Franz's long-deceased black cat, who was named Blue, leapt from seemingly nowhere and snatched the fish with a lightning quick paw. Before Franz could do anything, Blue gulped down the fish whole. Franz shook a finger at Blue and said, "Blue, give me back the fish." Blue did what cats do so well: he smiled but did not obey. After a few more scoldings from Franz, Blue leaned back upon his spine and made a loud mewing sound. Franz looked closely at Blue's hind legs, which were spread wide open. With another mew, Blue quickly gave birth to the fish. Franz should have been a bit surprised because Blue was a male. But no matter. Franz said, "Thank you, Blue," and put the fish back in the bowl. The fish happily swam about, and the water looked cleaner than it had before. Franz then woke.

Franz wished he knew what the dream meant. His mother had been an expert dream interpreter. She had inherited the skill, she always said, from her grandmother, who was a famous curandera from Las Vegas. But his mother was dead. So all Franz could do was be haunted by his dream's disturbing images.

Suddenly the young man behind the bar yelled, "Iced Caramel Macchiato for Frank!" although Franz was the only person waiting so there was no reason to yell. Franz reached for his drink, nodding his thanks. The young man's face broke into a smile that was nothing short of angelic. With a few movements of a facial muscle here, another there, this dreary, bored-to-tears teenage boy became a seraph, an exquisite celestial spirit. Franz smiled back. How could he not? Franz took a sip while keeping his eyes locked on the barista. Perfect! He had never tasted a better Iced Caramel Macchiato.

"Thank you," said Franz.

"You're very welcome, Frank," said the young man, still looking like an angel.

Franz nodded and started to walk away.

"It's funny," said the young man.

Franz stopped and looked back. "What?"

"Your name."

Franz now offered a laugh. "What's funny about 'Frank'?"

"Oh, no, that's not what I meant." The young man wiped his brow with the back of his hand before continuing. "Not the name. It's just kind of funny because it's almost my name."

"Almost?"

The young man pointed to his name tag. Franz squinted to read the letters. When he registered exactly what it read, his mouth opened slightly, making a small smacking sound. The name tag said FRANZ. Franz Kafka blinked once, and then again. He could feel his heart beating hard within his chest. Franz moved one foot, and then the other. He turned quickly from the bar, accelerating further as he passed the young woman at the cash register. The young woman said, "Bye!" but Franz didn't acknowledge her. He opened the glass door and the midday Fresno sun quickly counteracted the Starbucks air-conditioning. Franz found his car, got in, placed his Iced Caramel Macchiato in the cup holder, and started the engine with a *vroom*.

As he eased his car out of the parking lot, Franz thought about his father, who now lay in a box under fresh, wet dirt. And he knew then that he could not hate Carl Kafka even if he tried. He breathed deeply and tried to impose calm upon himself. After a few minutes, Franz took a sip of his drink and savored the coolness within his mouth. It was without question the best Iced Caramel Macchiato he had ever tasted.

THE FABRICATOR

RIGOBERTO SAT on the large cold boulder. His eyes rested upon the lake's calm surface, discerning no more than a ripple at the base of the partially submerged tree twenty or so yards from where he sat. Probably a happy family of waterbugs enjoying the safety of the root, he thought. He noticed another ripple in the middle of the lake and imagined that a Loch Ness-type monster would languidly rise out of that small aquatic disturbance once Rigoberto had walked away, out of sight. But this was not the Scottish Highlands. No. This was a carefully planned gated community in the suburbs with a man-made lake carved out in the middle of it all, for the recreation and esthetic enjoyment of its residents.

Rigoberto rubbed his hands together and then cupped them before blowing warm breath into his palms, making an almost whistling sound. The lake made him remember Mrs. Lewis, his favorite English teacher in high school, who once lectured on Virginia Woolf. He recalled how he chuckled when she described how Woolf committed suicide, filling her pockets with heavy stones and then walking slowly into a lake. Which lake? Someplace in England. Right? He couldn't remember. Time dims memory. And Mrs. Lewis had lectured to him over twenty years ago. But Rigoberto remembered the odd look Mrs. Lewis threw in his direction when she heard him chuckle. It wasn't an angry look, but it stopped him in mid-chortle—his face had grown hot and red and he'd felt stupid. At the time he hadn't known how to describe that look. But now as he sat on the boulder, the stone's coolness seeping through his thick woolen slacks, he could finally describe it. It was a look of disappointment. Nothing more. But it was enough. Just enough. Too much.

"Mi cielo" were the words that pulled him from his reverie. "Mi cielo," she said to Rigoberto. "What are you doing here?"

Rigoberto didn't turn around. He blew into his hands again. She walked over to him, making a crunching sound on the well-raked gravel.

"Sonia," said Rigoberto, still not turning in her direction. "Hola, mi amor."

Sonia lowered herself onto the boulder, almost leaning into Rigoberto. But not quite. He could feel her warmth travel the quarter inch of empty space to his shoulder and arm. Rigoberto took in Sonia's scent, a whirling mix of cigarettes, coffee, and lemon shampoo. He thought of Mrs. Lewis. Her face. White, perfect complexion. Six months' pregnant at the end of the school year. Beautiful, peaceful face. Except for that one look of disappointment.

A willet appeared out of the shrubs and walked gingerly to the lake's edge. Its gray-brown feathers reminded Rigoberto of his favorite tweed jacket, the one he'd worn on his and Sonia's first date. He couldn't believe that this remarkable woman, this published poet—an award-winning poet—would agree to go out with him. Even for coffee. But she did. After she'd read from her second book of poetry at Barnes & Noble. He'd been in the audience because his girlfriend asked him to go. Arlene. Poor Arlene! She had dragged her boyfriend to a poetry reading and he ended up asking the poet out for coffee afterwards. And the poet had said yes. And Arlene didn't know what to do so she slinked away, into the New Releases section. Six years ago this September. And he couldn't believe it when Sonia said yes to his marriage proposal a mere five months after their first date. This beautiful, brilliant woman. And he wondered if Mrs. Lewis were still alive. And whether the child she had carried was now a young man or woman, in college perhaps, falling in love, living a separate life from the lovely, disappointed Mrs. Lewis. And he wondered if he and Sonia would ever decide to have children.

"Catherine called," said Sonia.

"My sister?"

"No," she said. "Kabayashi."

"Oh."

"She needs you to come a bit early this morning."

The willet pecked at something hidden under the water's surface. Rigoberto finally turned to his wife. He caught his breath, forgetting how exquisite this woman, this poet, was. "Why?" he whispered.

Sonia leaned into him. "Several last-minute bodies."

"Oh," he sighed. "Oh."

"She said you'd be happy. The artist in you and all."

"You're the only artist in this family," he offered.

Another willet appeared from the shrub and approached the first. The morning's sun began to warm Rigoberto.

"You should go," said Sonia. "Catherine sounded a bit panicked."

"Yes, of course," he said.

Rigoberto stood and his movement startled the birds. They looked up suddenly, in unison, but didn't fly away. Then Sonia stood. This time the willets took flight.

"I'm surprised there aren't more birds here," she said.

Rigoberto reached for Sonia's hand and kissed it. Without a word, he turned and headed toward their house.

"YOU SHOULD BE ABLE TO FINISH THEM," said Catherine as she scratched her left ear with long, gleaming red nails. "So don't start panicking."

"I never panic," said Rigoberto.

"I know, I know."

Rigoberto walked to the first table and lifted the sheet. Perfect, he thought. Wonderful job. "Castro Brothers?"

"Of course," said Catherine in a calmer voice. "They do beautiful work."

"Makes my job easier."

Rigoberto dropped the sheet and scanned the other three draped tables. "Four in one day," he said. "All Castro Brothers?"

"No."

"Don't tell me."

Catherine sighed. "Sorry. One is from Gretsch Mortuary." She pointed to the table at the far end of the room.

Rigoberto went over to inspect. He lifted the sheet. "Damn!"

"I know," said Catherine.

"No life at all."

"I know. I'm sorry."

"Forces me to use too much imagination." Rigoberto dropped the sheet. "Sam Gretsch embalms the way I cook."

"Yes. Sorry."

"Do you know what I wish?" said Rigoberto.

"Wish?"

"I wish I could make a mold. Just in the hard cases, you know. Just once."

Catherine walked over to him, her heels clicking on the tiled floor. "Don't even think of it," she said.

"I know. I just. . ."

"We'd be prosecuted if anyone found out. That's in the statute. This has to be a hands-off process. Artistic."

"You don't have to lecture me," he said. "I helped write the damn law. Testified before Congress, you know."

"I know, but you make me nervous when you talk about making molds."

Rigoberto rubbed his hands together. "Well, I guess I have to get started." He looked around the room. "I'm in a grandmotherly mood. Any sweet abuelitas here?"

Catherine looked about the room. She pointed to a table. "I have a nice old aunt for you. But no grandmother."

"Good enough. Let me see the file."

Catherine clicked over to a large metal desk across the room and riffled through a pile of files. She said, "Ah!" and plucked out a manila folder. She brought it to Rigoberto, who had already perused the aunt. Without looking at Catherine, he took the file, flipped it open, and scanned the several pages' worth of information. "Looks good," he murmured.

"Yes. It's an easy position."

"Yes," he said, looking at Catherine. "Sitting."

"On a living room couch."

Rigoberto smiled. "Dear old Tía Raquel will never leave us," he said.

"No. Never."

"How much time to I have? Before they pick up the bodies?"

Catherine looked away.

"How much time?" asked Rigoberto, this time a bit louder, a little tenser.

"Well, they all have to be picked up tonight."

"What?"

"That's why I called you at home," said Catherine, trying to keep her voice from trembling. "We've never had this happen before. It must have been that interview you did."

Rigoberto shook his head. "I told you we shouldn't have let them in here and ask me questions. I told you."

"But it's a lot of money, getting four in one day, don't you know? A lot of money."

Rigoberto walked over to his workstation and grabbed a camera. "Then you should hire another fabricator."

"There aren't enough to go around," she said through a forced smile. "The state only gives ten licenses a year, you know?"

"I know," he said as he took a few shots of the aunt. He removed the sheet completely and continued to take pictures. Catherine turned her head. "Remember, I helped write the law." He lowered the camera and admired the aunt. "Pretty good body for sixty-seven, eh?"

Catherine didn't respond but she turned to look at the aunt. He was right. She did look pretty good. Rigoberto took a few more shots. "That should do it," he said. "Now for some sketches."

He walked to his workstation, returned the camera, and searched for a sharp pencil and a new tablet. He found them, pulled a chair over to Tía Raquel, sat down, and started to draw.

"All of their personal effects are here," said Catherine, pointing to a stack of labeled plastic boxes by the desk. "Clothes, jewelry, everything."

"Thanks."

"You can start the fabrication tomorrow," she said. "Just focus on the pictures, sketches, and measurements today. The bodies will be picked up around 6:00 or so."

"Who's going to fabricate me when I die?" said Rigoberto as he penciled in more detail.

Catherine admired Rigoberto's easy strokes. The aunt's face was already taking shape. "Sonia might not want such a reminder of you when you leave this world," she said as she patted Rigoberto's shoulder. Catherine could feel his muscles tighten under her touch but she didn't remove her hand. "Memorial fabrication isn't for everyone."

Rigoberto stopped sketching and looked up at Catherine. He wondered why she'd gotten into this business in the first place. She had little stomach for the bodies, and she possessed paltry compassion and even less artistic sensibility. But Catherine, he guessed, had seen the opening and appreciated its potential. A way to make good money once the memorial fabrication law passed. But was she only about the money? Didn't she want to fall in love? Maybe get married? Was she even interested in anything romantic? Rigoberto never felt comfortable enough with Catherine to ask. So he'd probably never know.

"I need to work alone," was all he said.

"Yes, I'm sorry. Yes."

Catherine lifted her hand from his shoulder and stood there for a moment. Rigoberto turned back to the aunt and Catherine clicked out of the room. When she closed the door behind her, Rigoberto stood with a crack of his knees. He walked to his workstation and turned on the ancient CD player, the one his father had bought him when Rigoberto graduated from middle school. You can't buy a new CD player anymore. But he refused to give up his old CD collection, which he liked to say sounded better than the new technology: nothing beats the warmth, the depth of a CD. He laughed to himself because that's what audiophiles used to say about vinyl records, a technology he'd only seen in old movies. John Lee Hooker's "Boom Boom" came on. Rigoberto smiled, got into the beat, and returned to his seat.

THE HOURS PASSED. One, two, and then three bodies were completed: photographed and sketched, with measurements put into the computer for Sylvia to start designing the basic body structures, to be refined later by Rigoberto. He stretched, rubbing his eyes. He noticed that the CD player was silent; when the music had stopped he didn't know. Rigoberto wanted to push on, finish well before the 6:00 deadline.

He walked to the last body and pulled down the sheet. A boy. No more than eight, maybe nine. What a shame, he thought. Rigoberto checked the file. Fernando Torres. Age nine. In the personal information section all that was written, in a tight, controlled hand, was the name of the boy's favorite book: *My Friend Fernando*. Rigoberto opened the personal effects box. A red shirt, blue shorts, a pair of Nikes and white socks. And the book. Rigoberto picked up the book, pulled up a chair, and sat down by the boy. On the cover was a smiling, playful, floppy-eared brown and white puppy. The pages curled at the edges like the boy's tousled hair; the book had obviously been read and reread during his short life. Rigoberto turned the first page and saw the copyright year: 2003. So long ago. Before the boy was born. Before *Rigoberto* was born. The pages were almost brittle. He turned another page and read aloud: "*My Friend Fernando* by María Elena Menes." Rigoberto touched the boy's hair. It didn't feel real: too soft, not of this Earth. He sighed, looked at his watch, and sighed again. Rigoberto cleared his throat, turned the page, and began to read the book in a soft bedtime voice: "This is the story of my friend Fernando, who is the best friend anyone could ever have."

The book was not long. It had bright pictures on each page. When he reached the end, Rigoberto closed the book and said, "The end." He looked at the boy. Of course this was his favorite book. A book with his name in the title. A silly little story about a talking puppy who becomes friends with a butterfly. But it was his favorite. Rigoberto stood and walked over to his workstation. He plucked a fresh pencil out of a smudged ceramic mug and picked up a drawing tablet. He walked back to the small body.

"So," said Rigoberto. "Let's begin, my boy. Let's begin."

RIGOBERTO SWIRLED the cream in his coffee slowly, with calculation, as Sonia read the newspaper. Yesterday had sucked his energy; his neck, back, and arms hurt and each movement took great effort. He suddenly turned his eyes up to Sonia, and even that small movement came with an ache. "Why?" he asked.

"¿Cómo?

"Why here?"

Sonia put down the paper. "What?"

"Why do we live here? This state? It's not home. It's not L.A." As Rigoberto said this, he kept his spoon moving steadily in his coffee, the only movement he could tolerate. The morning sun came in brightly, happily into their kitchen.

"Well," she ventured slowly, "you went to college here."

"And?"

"And then you stayed."

"And?"

"And then you met me."

"Oh."

"And I'm from here."

"Oh."

Sonia pulled her chair closer to the table. It squeaked as she moved it. "¿Por qué?"

"I mean, you know, this state. This state. It's hot. Hot. Too hot."

Sonia scratched her nose. "This is about weather?"

Rigoberto put his spoon down on the napkin. He watched the cotton soak up the coffee, creating a small but steady bronze stain. "Never mind."

Sonia looked at him for a few moments. Her eyelashes fluttered and she took a deep breath. "Okay."

"I mean," said Rigoberto, "I don't have to be here. *We* don't, I mean. You know?"

"But California hasn't passed the fabricator law."

"I know. I helped write the federal law that allowed for states to opt in."

"Yes, of course. Anyway, my state has passed it. And Massachusetts. Texas, too."

"Yes," he said. "I know. And New Hampshire. But I'm not from any of those states."

"Yes," said Sonia.

"California almost passed that proposition."

"Almost."

"Proposition 40859."

Sonia frowned. "You remember the number?"

"Yes. It was easy."

"Odd number," she said. "I mean, strange. Hard to remember."

"No," said Rigoberto. "It's my grandfather's birthday. So I remember it."

Sonia's eyes widened. She coughed, a forced cough.

"What?" he asked.

"You," she said.

"I what?"

"You never mentioned that to me. About your grandfather."

"April 8, 1959. His birthday. I told you."

Sonia stood up. "No. No you didn't."

Rigoberto wiped his forehead. "Yes I did."

"No." She walked to the sink and looked into it.

"I know I did."

"Why?"

"Because it's important to me. That's why."

Sonia turned on the water and rinsed a cup. "I know."

"To me."

"I know," she said. "Forget it."

"It?"

"Yes," said Sonia. She turned off the water and looked out the window. She saw a bird, not a willet, by the lake. It pecked at something in the grass. "Forget it," she whispered.

"What?"

"Nothing."

Rigoberto gazed at Sonia's back, his eyes moving slowly from her short black hair to her sharp shoulders and then her small waist, sliding around her pleasant wide hips, down her long legs, and finally resting at her small feet. He didn't want to talk about yesterday. But he had no choice. "One of the bodies was a boy," he said. "Young."

Sonia turned, not quickly, but she moved with a deliberation that startled Rigoberto. "Boy?"

"Yes."

She walked back to the table and sat down. "Who would want to have a child fabricated?"

"Actually, you'd think children would be the most common," he said softly.

"I don't *know* that."

"But they're not," he said, growing more animated, as if he were lecturing. "It's usually older people. People you've grown used to so that it would be hard not to have Uncle So-and-So sitting on the couch with everyone else while the TV buzzes away."

"Yes," said Sonia. "I understand that."

"Yes. Me too."

They sat without speaking for a moment, the hum of the air-conditioner offering a constant white noise.

"What position?"

He looked at her but didn't answer.

"Position?" she asked again.

He cleared his throat. "Standing."

"Where?"

He cleared his throat again. "In the backyard. With a ball."

Sonia reached out and touched Rigoberto's arm. "Outside?"

"Yes," he said. "Yes."

"Outside?" she said again as she moved her hand from Rigoberto's arm to her lap. "More coffee?" she finally went on, reaching for his cup.

"No," he said. "Tomorrow."

"Tomorrow?"

"Tomorrow I begin the fabrication."

"Oh."

The air-conditioner clicked off. They sat staring at his empty cup.

THOUGH HE MISSED L.A., Rigoberto appreciated the night sky here. The heat of the day had ebbed into a comfortable, slightly breezy evening, and the stars—God, those stars!—almost frightened him with their brilliance. He stood, frozen, at the beginning of the red brick walk, head angled back, admiring the celestial bodies, ignoring the bustle of partygoers coming and going from the two-story house.

Sonia slid her arm around his waist. "Ready, mi cielo?" she asked.

Without turning away his gaze from the sky, he said, "Funny you call me that."

"Why?"

"Am I really your heaven?"

Sonia nestled in closer and leaned her cheek on his shoulder. "Cómo no."

"¿Verdad?" Rigoberto said, now turning to her.

"Of course. Time to go in. Meet some of my friends."

"But it's so beautiful outside."

Sonia lifted her head and started to lead Rigoberto toward the house. "Yes, but we agreed this would be good for me. For us. To get out."

Rigoberto let Sonia lead him toward the house. "But I've met these friends of yours before."

"You don't meet people once so that you can be done with them. This is called socializing. And when you get some friends of your own, we can socialize with them."

Rigoberto stopped walking. "But you're my friend."

Sonia patted his chest. "Yes, of course I am your friend. Y tu esposa. But it's nice to get out."

"If these fun folks were dead, well, it'd be more fun."

Sonia laughed. "Don't talk about dead people all night."

"What else can I talk about?"

"Movies."

"Movies?"

"Yeah," said Sonia. "When I was about twelve or so, I'd argue with my father. I wanted to see all kinds of scary movies. Like *The Birds*. I wanted to see *The Birds*." Sonia reached into her jacket pocket and pulled out a pack of cigarettes. She lit one and blew the smoke away from Rigoberto.

"So?"

"So he streamed it for me. After I bitched and moaned for a whole week. And then we watched it. And it scared the hell out of me."

"*The Birds?* Almost a hundred years old. Pretty tame stuff. Compared to now."

"No, not really. Watch it sometime."

"Okay."

"No, really," she said. "I couldn't even get to bed without my father staying close by in the study. It really freaked me out."

"So he was right."

"Yes."

They stood in silence as happy people walked past them. Sonia nodded toward the house. "Time to go in," she said.

"One question first."

Sonia let out a little groan. "Yes, mi cielo, what is it?"

"How much do you love me?"

Sonia laughed and leaned into him. "I don't love you. I hate you."

"Oh," said Rigoberto. "I thought so."

"In fact, I hate you more than I've ever hated anyone."

"Wow. I'm pretty important."

Sonia closed her eyes and slowly puckered her lips. Rigoberto responded, slowly, and let his lips rest on hers. After a moment, they pulled apart.

"I hate you with all my heart," said Sonia.

Rigoberto grinned. "Yes," he said. "I thought so."

Once inside the house, Rigoberto scanned the scene, looking for the bar.

"Mi cielo, get me a white wine," said Sonia. "I'll find Barbara."

"Okay," said Rigoberto as he headed toward the kitchen. "I smell booze coming from over there."

Sonia let out a little grunt as her eyes landed on the hostess, Professor Barbara Klein, at the far end of the living room holding forth with other members of the English department. Over the past fifteen years as department chair, Professor Klein had recruited most of the professors and assistant professors who stood around her laughing at every little joke she made. With a toughness that did not match her petite frame, she had turned an average department into one of the highest-ranking, most prestigious in the state. Though approaching sixty, she smiled and moved with the exuberance of a high school girl. Wearing a Guatemalan poncho, she resembled a multicolored exotic bird flapping its wings. Her eyes met Sonia's and she threw out her arms. "My favorite poet!" she exclaimed. "Give me a hug!"

Sonia almost skipped over to the professor, who immediately encased Sonia in her wings. The other instructors retreated a bit, almost in unison.

"Barb," said Sonia. No one in the department called Professor Klein "Barb." "You look so goddamn good!"

Professor Klein pulled back and pinched Sonia's cheek with her left hand. "You can afford to gain some weight, young lady!"

"My own private Jewish mother."

Professor Klein let out such a loud guffaw that she startled even herself. "Where's that handsome husband of yours?" she was finally able to get out.

"Getting the booze," said Sonia, nodding in the direction of the kitchen. "He's so good at that."

THE KITCHEN BUSTLED with so many people Rigoberto had trouble getting to the makeshift bar by the sink. Professor Klein believed in good alcohol and plenty of it. She had hired a pert brunette student to act as bartender but she seemed overwhelmed. Perspiration covered her clear, almost glowing face, and her green eyes widened in panic with every new person who entered the sweaty, noisy kitchen. Rigoberto reached over the counter had patted her hand. "It's okay, it's okay," he cooed as if trying to calm a baby. "They're all too drunk already to notice if you make a mistake."

She smiled and her eyes sparkled at Rigoberto. "Thanks," she mouthed. "Thanks."

"So," he said, feeling good about himself, "I have a simple order: a glass of Chardonnay and a bottle of San Miguel."

She smiled again and turned to get the drinks.

Suddenly Rigoberto felt a small, sticky hand slide into his. He turned, thinking he'd find a child who'd wandered into the kitchen, but instead his eyes rested upon a diminutive woman who could have been anywhere from twenty-five to forty years old. She kept her eyes averted, looking down. "I'm Kimberly," said the woman as she squeezed Rigoberto's hand.

"Hi," he answered, hoping the drinks would come and he could excuse himself. He pulled his hand away.

Kimberly leaned into him. She stank of smoke and booze. "I don't usually dress this way."

This comment made Rigoberto notice what Kimberly was wearing: a tight one-piece minidress, black stockings, boots. "Oh?" was all he could offer.

"Someone made a bet with me," she explained. With this, she looked up. Rigoberto almost jumped. Kimberly's eyes were like two empty black holes.

The bartending student put Rigoberto's drinks before him with a clink.

"God bless you," smiled Rigoberto. He reached into his pocket, pulled out a $20 bill, and stuffed it into the tips glass. "Here." The student smiled and nodded. Rigoberto grabbed the drinks and started to move away from Kimberly. "Gotta go," he said.

"Wait," said Kimberly. She pulled in close, too close.

"What?"

"You can hit me if you want," she whispered. "If that's what *you* like."

A chill ran through Rigoberto. Who was she? *What* was she?

"My wife is waiting for me," he said as he slid past Kimberly. "Bye."

Out of sick curiosity more than anything else, Rigoberto glanced back at Kimberly as he left the kitchen, half expecting that she'd be looking back at him. But she had already found someone else's hand to hold and ear to whisper into; this time her new friend was a surprised older woman who reminded Rigoberto of his tía Anita. He let out a sad sigh and turned his attention back to his mission. Avoiding several collisions with the odd mix of young college students and older faculty—all of whom had been enjoying the well-stocked bar—Rigoberto finally made it back to Sonia.

Professor Klein clapped her hands when she saw Rigoberto. "Ah, your handsome husband is here!"

Rigoberto tried to smile and was half successful in his attempt. "Happy juice," he said as he handed the drink to Sonia. "Drink up."

Professor Klein placed her right hand on Rigoberto's shoulder. "I am so happy to see your face."

Rigoberto now had no problem smiling. He had forgotten how easy it was to be in Professor Klein's presence. "And I am *delighted* to see your face."

Professor Klein let out a guffaw. She turned to Sonia. "Do not lose this beautiful man, do you hear me?"

"I promise," said Sonia.

Professor Klein pulled back her hand. "So Rigoberto, how is business?"

Rigoberto didn't answer for a moment. He gazed into the professor's sharp gray eyes. He imagined sketching that fine lived-in face. "Things are busy," he finally offered. "So many bodies, so little time. And how is business with you?"

Professor Klein let out another loud laugh. "The education business? Well, the laws of supply and demand don't really affect me. Tenure, you know."

"I was thinking the other day about one of my favorite teachers," said Rigoberto.

"Ah!" said the professor. "Someone who influenced you? Someone who changed your life?"

Sonia quickly turned to Rigoberto, wondering what this was about.

"Well, sort of." He hesitated. "Something about one of her lessons. About Virginia Woolf."

Professor Klein clapped twice and grinned wildly. "Virginia Woolf? How wonderful!"

"Yes," he responded. "Tell me: where did she do it?"

"It?"

Rigoberto coughed. "You know. Kill herself. With the stones in her pockets."

The professor grew serious. "Well, around noon on March 28, 1941, she walked down to the river near her weekend house in Sussex."

"Yes," said Rigoberto.

"To the River Ouse, to be precise. She put stones in her sweater. They didn't find her body for about a month or so."

Rigoberto sighed. "Yes. That's it. I remember it now. Ouse. Strange name."

Rigoberto closed his eyes and breathed deeply. He could detect Sonia, her smells, the smells he knew so well. And he took in the other scents around him, of Professor Klein and the now-silent timid junior faculty who hung in an insecure circle around them. Too many different perfumes. Booze. Cigarettes. Too much. And he remembered Mrs. Lewis's scent. Clean. Soap. Zest, he believed. And some kind of gentle perfume.

Rigoberto opened his eyes. "The River Ouse," he whispered.

"Yes," said Professor Klein. "But it should not be confused with the River Ouse in the north. It's an easy mistake to make if you're not familiar with the country. That River Ouse is the main waterway to York from the Humber and North Sea. It provided the main access to the city for the Vikings and Romans."

"Vikings," mused Rigoberto. He let the word roll around in his mind. Professor Klein could be lying or just wrong on the geography, but it didn't matter to Rigoberto. Sonia watched her husband carefully, not certain what he could be thinking.

Professor Klein grew animated. "Many believe that the name 'Ouse' comes from the Celtic word for water."

"What else?" asked Rigoberto, who could listen to Professor Klein for days and days.

"Well, if we are to assume this derivation from the Celtic is correct, then its name is nothing more than tautology, because we are really calling it 'water river.' And that would be, well, just a bit silly. But a rose is a rose is a rose, no?" The professor smiled, remembering something. "I love that part of the world, you know. Samuel and I honeymooned near there."

"He was a fine man," said Sonia.

"Yes," said Professor Klein, without hesitation. "He wasn't perfect. But he was indeed a fine man. And I loved him."

"El amor quita el hambre," whispered Rigoberto. Sonia's eyes narrowed.

"What?" asked the professor.

"Love takes away hunger," said Sonia before Rigoberto could answer.

"Yes," said Rigoberto. "An old Mexican saying. A dicho."

"Ah," said Professor Klein. "So true. So true."

"I think it's time to go, mi amor," said Sonia.

"What?" said the professor. "You just got here!"

Rigoberto studied Sonia's face but he couldn't figure out what she was thinking. He didn't have the energy to argue. "Yes," he said. "I have a lot of work to do. Must get up early."

"What a shame," said Professor Klein.

"Yes," said Sonia. "It is a shame."

They said their good-byes and left the party in silence. Sonia unlocked the car and got behind the wheel. Rigoberto glanced back at the house before getting in. Without a word, they started the drive home. Rigoberto couldn't read Sonia's face. Just when he felt ready to ask her what had happened, his phone beeped. Sonia glanced at him for a moment, neither frowning nor smiling, then turned her eyes back to the road.

"Hello?" said Rigoberto. He listened for a bit. "Must I?" Sonia looked at him again. "Okay, Catherine, okay. Don't worry. I'll be there in about an hour. Okay?" Rigoberto slid the phone back into his coat pocket.

"Tonight?" asked Sonia.

"A body came in and Catherine has to catch a plane tonight," he said. "They need to get the body back by the morning for the services. Last-minute decision to fabricate, apparently. Besides, we're not doing anything now, right?"

"Sorry about that," said Sonia. "I just suddenly lost the mood to party."

"That's okay, mi amor. That's okay."

"Want me to drop you off? I can pick you up when you're done."

Rigoberto looked out the window to the brilliant night sky. So many stars, he thought. "That would be great," he finally answered. "Gracias."

THOUGH HE HAD BEEN around bodies for years, Rigoberto preferred not to work at night when no one else was around. At night his imagination could play tricks on him. Nothing big. Usually just some kind of movement caught in his peripheral vision that would make him jump and jerk his head around to see what it was. And it was always nothing. Just a moth or perhaps a fly. He entered the workroom and immediately turned on every light he could find.

The body lay on a table at the far end of the room. "Coffee and music," Rigoberto said to himself. "Coffee and music." He trotted to the coffee maker and spooned great mounds of French roast into the filter, quickly poured distilled water into the machine's back, and flicked it on. As the sound of its gurgling started to fill the otherwise silent room, he riffled through a precarious stack of CDs and found what he needed. Within seconds, Coltrane joined the coffee maker's symphony.

"Perfecto," he whispered. Rigoberto pulled two rubber gloves from a dispenser and snapped them onto his hands. He walked over to the draped body. The embalming fluids let off a pungent odor, more so than usual. "Okay," he said. "Let's see what's what." Rigoberto pulled the sheet back. His eyes widened in disbelief when he saw the familiar contours of the face. "What?" he mouthed. "It can't be."

But he knew the face. He knew it well. Rigoberto had touched that face each day of his life. He had shaved it carefully since he was fourteen. But no, it wasn't quite his own face. It was older, had more wrinkles. But Rigoberto knew that he gazed upon himself. There was no question.

He searched for the personal effects container, but found nothing. Rigoberto walked back to his workstation. He touched the camera but quickly pulled his hand away. No pictures. Rigoberto reached for a new pencil and slowly sharpened it. He then retrieved a fresh drawing tablet. The coffee smelled good, so he filled a large mug almost to the brim. Rigoberto eventually got himself settled in front of the body, perched on a metal stool, steaming coffee nearby. "Let us begin," he said.

And as he started to sketch, Rigoberto remembered how his grandfather, shortly before he died, lost his ability to speak anything but Spanish. That is when Rigoberto first heard the dicho "El amor quita el hambre." His grandfather had whispered this to him late one afternoon after waking up from one of his many daily naps. He had said it to Rigoberto apropos of nothing. But Rigoberto had appreciated it. It was a little gift from a grandfather to his grandson. "El amor quita el hambre," Rigoberto said aloud as his face began to emerge on the sketching paper. "El amor quita el hambre."

EURT

Side A ~ October 15, 1989

PATRICK, BOY, IS THIS THING ON? I can't tell. They get smaller all the time. Let me see that. Don't worry, I won't hurt it. Toshiba? Japanese? Used to be that when something didn't work, we'd say it was made in Japan. Not anymore. What? Oh, yeah. Where do you want it? Okay. Should I lean into it when I talk? No? Okay, Patrick. What do you want me to talk about for this—what do you call it? Oral history? You kids sure like those old stories. I know it's for a grade, but admit you like this shit. Oh, sorry. I'll watch it. Okay, which story do you want? No, not that. Too personal. What else? Really? The St. Francis Dam? Sure. Suit yourself. Don't know what kind of grade you'll get, but I'll oblige because you're my favorite grandchild. Don't laugh. It's true.

Okay, here goes. As I've told you before, not many of us know why Eurt's mother named him Eurt. Strange name. Pronounced "yurt," like the word "hurt" but with a "y." Certainly not a name you could find in the Bible, nor is it a name befitting a Mexican child. Well, actually, part Mexican. Because Eurt's mother was not Mexican but some kind of white, maybe with a little Pueblo Indian mixed in her, or so some of us figured. The viejas who knew Sarah said she came from New Mexico. She had these high cheekbones and Asian eyes and she was topped off with glistening red-blond hair that she kept in two tightly wound braids cascading like a waterfall down her back. So the viejas said she must have Pueblo blood mixed in with maybe Irish or English or maybe even Swedish or German. Too beautiful and strange for her own good, the viejas claimed. And the men. Shit. Oh, sorry. I mean "shoot." Better?

Anyways, the men couldn't get enough eyefuls of Sarah. All the men. White, Negro, Chinese, Mexican. All the men. But only one man, Alfonso Villa—a distant cousin of the great Pancho Villa—made any kind of impression on Sarah. Which is a shame. Because if Sarah had fallen in love with any other man, even me, she'd probably be alive today. She'd be as old as me. But you know, women live longer than men, usually. And that whole horrible incident with Eurt never would've happened. But you can't rewrite history, and you never can figure when one act, one innocent and even good act, might set in motion a series of happenings that end up creating an evil result. Evil. That's the only word for what happened.

It was May 1927 when Alfonso and I first saw Sarah. We were working the farms near the Santa Clara River, around Saugus, not too far from the San Fancisquito Canyon—Six Flags Magic Mountain is around there now, I think—and we were living in a makeshift camp set up cheap for us workers. Mostly Mexican and some Chinese. Could see the St. Francis Dam from where we slept. Smelly place. And goddamn dusty. Sorry, but there is no other way to say it. Goddamn dusty. You can edit that later, Patrick. Anyways, though I'm white, I lived for almost ten years in Chihuahua when my papá dragged me and my older sister Elsie out of Dallas away from my crazy mother. Papá just wanted to get us the hell out of the state, out of the goddamn country because Mamá was dangerous, and who knows what she would have done to her two children? See this scar here? Mamá put the edge of a hot frying pan there just to teach me not to talk back. Well, that was the last straw. So Papá saw fit to take us away.

The years passed—ten, to be exact—and Papá fashioned leather goods for a living. And me and Elsie lived just like the Mexicans. Even went to school run by priests, although we're Protestant, at least by tradition. After we got word that Mamá died, sometime in spring of 1924, we came back north because Papá just missed this country. But he wanted something new. So we settled in California by the Santa Clara River. Poor Elsie died a year later of influenza and Papá followed her just a half year after that with cancer. There was just me. And I didn't give a good goddamn what I did for a living as long as I made enough to eat, drink, and to buy some time with a good whore now and again. Sorry. Edit that if you want.

When Alfonso and I first saw Sarah, I'd been working the Fredrickson farm for almost three years. Seasonal work, you know. But it kept me with the right amount of money for my needs. I was nineteen and he was twenty-one or -two. Anyway, Alfonso and I had worked a long day and we were having some good beer at this little bar with this big sign over the front door that said THE TIN ROOF. It mostly catered to us farm workers but a lot of other folks came on in because it had good prices and some decent food, too. Alfonso and I had hit it off pretty good the year before because I'd lived in Chihuahua, like I said, and he had lots of relatives on his mother's side who still lived there. My Spanish was good and his English was even better. So we were as close as we could be, not being related or anything. We were drinking to that Lindbergh fellow, who'd landed in Paris two days before. Everyone was so proud even though most of us couldn't figure how what he did could help us in any way. All the Mexicans and Chinese toasted him. So we lifted our glasses and said *To Lindy,* which is what they were calling that young man. The papers said his mother was so proud that she couldn't find words to express her joy. And President Coolidge sent some kind of congratulations through that embassy in Paris saying how the flight crowned the record of American aviation, whatever that means.

The funniest thing, though, the part I like because I remember how hot and dirty I used to get back then—even sixty years' distance hasn't made me forget—the newspapers said that Lindy was escorted to the embassy after landing and then fighting the crowds. He was in real need of a bath. So the American ambassador's son took Lindy to a room at the embassy where a hot bath waited. Before dipping into the tub, Lindy drank some port and then some milk. Papers said Lindbergh relaxed for a real long time before he got out, combed his hair, put on a pair of silk pajamas with flowers all over them, a silk bathrobe, and—I like this part—Moroccan leather slippers. All this compliments of the ambassador's son. And he gave a few newspaper interviews dressed just like that. I will never forget that story.

Patrick, need a drink or something? Diet Coke, the kind you like? Okay. Just offering.

So anyways, here it was Tuesday night and we were hot and tired and getting a little drunk and toasting Lindbergh's landing in Paris, and in walked this woman through the front doors. Beautiful. Alfonso's head swiveled so fast I thought it was going to come off. He had a nose, he did. Almost like radar. Beautiful woman within striking distance, Alfonso had his eyes trained on her within two seconds. Goddamn amazing skill, that. We stood at the bar which, if truth be told, was nothing more than a wide board set on bricks on either end with a white tablecloth thrown over it to make it look nicer than it was. She came in and quickly glanced around. Sarah looked in a hurry or something. Nervous. I know why now, but then all I knew was that she looked as though she had lost something and needed to find it pronto.

Well, eventually she looked over to the bar and spied me and Alfonso. I kind of pushed my hair back off my forehead and straightened up some. I was foolish for women back then. Too old now. Alfonso? Well, he was a cool character. He was handsome and he knew it. Looked like his cousin, the great Pancho Villa, except even more handsome, with smooth brown skin like a baby's butt. Thick head of black curly hair. Neat little mustache. I'm no queer or nothing, but he was the handsomest man I'd ever seen. So Sarah eventually rested her eyes on him and it was over, I tell you. I had no chance in hell. She suddenly looked calmer, like she found what she was looking for, even though Alfonso never saw her before in his life and vice versa. Sarah sauntered on over to us, smiling now, and sidled up to Alfonso. She ordered a Coca-Cola and then just stood there waiting for the inevitable. Alfonso gave me a little wink and then turned to Sarah.

"How are you?" he asked her in almost perfect English. And she didn't even turn to him. Can you believe it? She looked the other way at the window or something and she didn't answer. Alfonso gave me a quick glance and smiled this little sly smile. This is going to be fun, he was thinking. I could tell he was going to play the game. Now, Sarah was wearing this very pretty Mexican dress. You know, the long white cotton ones with pretty embroidery. It was a little loose on her but she looked beautiful.

Her hair was perfectly braided and it glistened in the lamplight. Other men and even the women started to notice her.

Anyways, Alfonso tried something else. He said, "Señorita, let me introduce myself and my friend. I am Alfonso Villa and this is my very fine friend, James O'Hara." Alfonso always became real formal when he got nervous.

She turned and smiled with these white teeth and I could see Alfonso's knees buckle just a little. Sarah's beauty could make even him get weak.

She said, "I'm Sarah Garcia. But people call me Tootsie." Funny, isn't it? Tootsie! Like that goddamn movie with that little actor, what's his name? Yeah. Hoffman. But that's what she said. And we both smiled like idiots. So we kind of. . .what? Oh. Okay. Turn that tape over and I'll go take a pee, if that's okay with you, Patrick boy.

Side B ~ October 15, 1989

¡HÍJOLE! LIFE'S SIMPLE PLEASURES! At least I'm not wearing diapers like some of my buddies. Okay, where was I? Yeah, that's right. So we all started having a nice little conversation. Sarah was asking a lot of questions, mostly directed to Alfonso but a few for me, and we answered them real fast just to make her happy and stay. She was real curious about our circumstances, you know. Money, women, stuff like that. And we talked and talked the whole evening. And then we both walked Sarah—can't bring ourselves to call her Tootsie—to the little boardinghouse she lived at. Women only. Nice place. She said just before we left her that she cooked at this little café called Hanson's down on the main street and that they served up a real good Sunday breakfast. Said we should come by that weekend and that we'd not be disappointed. Well, goddamn, we were there that Sunday, me mostly to keep things from getting awkward for Alfonso, which he appreciated. He'd done the same for me.

Anyways, their courtship started then. And it only lasted a month! They'd go on walks and Alfonso would buy her little things, he didn't have much money, but he was thoughtful about what he got her. And she smiled and patted his arm and called him Al, which he thought was funny because it sounded so white, you know? Sometimes I'd tease him and call him Al too. During that time he looked more relaxed than I'd ever seen him before. What few creases he had on his forehead melted away like butter in a hot skillet whenever Sarah was around. Anyways, it all went pretty well so I wasn't too surprised when they decided to tie the knot. They married in a civil ceremony—Sarah hated churches and Alfonso was not such a religious man—and then moved into a larger boardinghouse that took couples. Alfonso started working both the farm and any other side job he could find. He got goddamn respectable! But they seemed so happy. I couldn't complain if I saw less and less of him. He was a family man now.

Well, things got a little strange after a bit. See, Sarah got pregnant right away, which made Alfonso real proud. But she started showing real early. Too early. And Alfonso got a little quiet, real lost in his thoughts, you know. He'd not hear whatever I was saying. But eventually, when Sarah's belly was sticking out almost to Nevada, Alfonso seemed to accept things. After all, she was beautiful and good to him. Things could be worse.

So Sarah goes into labor one night in January 1928 during the off season when Alfonso was home a lot. I'll never forget that night. I was having a drink at the Tin Roof and Alfonso came in looking pale. His hands shook and he was soaked through with sweat. He wore no jacket, just a thick shirt, and I yelled at him that he was going to get pneumonia or something. He walked up to the bar and asked for a brandy and he just stared straight ahead. When his drink came, he threw it back and asked for another. He was making this little strange, squeaking sound with his mouth. His teeth, I guess.

"Hombre," I said. "¿Qué pasa?"

He threw back the second shot and asked for another. After finishing the third, he said, "The baby was born tonight."

I smiled and hit him on the back. "Wonderful!" I yelled. "You're a father!" But he was not smiling. "What's wrong?" I asked.

And then he told me. Slowly at first. It was a horrible story. Are you sure you want this for your report, Patrick? Okay. Here goes.

When he came home that night from working at the McPheeter's ranch with the horses, Sarah was already in labor. This was seven months after they married. Anyways, she was in horrible pain and Alfonso said he wanted to get someone to help but she screamed "*No!*" She saids it's too late. He'd have to help her. Well, he realized there's no way out so he went and washed up and made her as comfortable as possible. But she was in real pain and she was burning up with a fever and yelling weird things. That's when Alfonso first heard her scream out "*Eurt*!" He didn't know what she was saying. But he put a wet cloth on her forehead and tried to calm her. She kept on yelling: "*Eurt*! *Eurt*! *Eurt*!" And then she calmed down suddenly and the baby came without much warning at all. It turned out to be an easy delivery. Except for that one thing.

Alfonso described that baby to me real slow. A boy. Overall handsome, with lots of dark hair. Dark skin. Could've been Alfonso's. But one thing wrong. His right hand. He had only one finger, the index finger. The rest of his hand was smooth and narrowed down to the wrist. Looked kind of like a wriggling snake, Alfonso said. And when the baby moved that one finger, chills went down his back. He said that when he showed the baby to Sarah, she didn't react at all. Not a smile, not a scream. She just reached for him and put his little mouth on her breast. Alfonso stood there, bewildered, and then the baby started to play with Sarah's other breast with that snake of a hand and Sarah didn't mind a bit. That's when he said he had to go get things for the baby but instead came right to the bar to talk to me.

What did I say to him? Well, what would you say? I lied. I said it didn't matter. Plenty of kids are born without body parts and that's just life. At least the baby had one good hand. Said Sarah was one beautiful and kind woman and he was luckier than most men. This little speech and the booze seemed to calm him down some. I told him that his wife and son needed him right then and that he should go home. He nodded slowly and had one more drink before leaving. But despite my words of comfort, I felt sick. I knew something bad was going to happen. And, sad to say, I wasn't wrong.

As far as I know, they never baptized that baby. And Sarah insisted on naming him Eurt, that weird word she kept yelling when she was in labor. Alfonso couldn't deny his wife anything, so he agreed. Shit! What a name! Anyways, I tried to be a good friend and visited them as much as I could. But Eurt gave me the creeps. He was a handsome boy, but that hand and that stare! He'd stare at me like he was reading my thoughts. And he never smiled. I swear to God! I mean, *that* is not natural. You were a happy, smiling baby when my daughter brought you into this world nineteen years ago. Most babies are. But not this one. And Alfonso saw it too. Only Sarah didn't seem to care. She cooed and sang to that baby like nothing was wrong. She loved that baby more than Alfonso, I'd say.

In March 1928, I was staying in the men's boardinghouse because it was the off season so I couldn't live in the camp. Had three or four odd jobs to keep me going until picking started again in a couple of months. One night, just before I went to sleep, Alfonso came to visit. He looked sick. Pale, deep purple circles under his eyes, hair matted and greasy.

I asked him, "What's wrong?"

And I couldn't believe his answer: "They're killing me. Slowly killing me."

What the hell did that mean? So I said, "Who's trying to kill you, Alfonso?"

And he looked at me with eyes going wild: "Sarah and Eurt. And I think it's Eurt's idea, too."

Now, what could I think? Alfonso's gone off the deep end? So I said, "Calm down, boy. No one's trying to kill you. What are they doing to you?"

And then he closed his eyes and I suddenly realized that he looked like a skeleton. He was so thin. Finally, after a few moments of silence, like he was listening to some voice, he said, "Poison. They're poisoning me."

"How?" I asked, feeling more than a little shaky. "How?"

"The poison is everywhere. In my food, my drink, even in Sarah's kisses. And Eurt is behind it!"

Well, Patrick, I didn't know what to say except he certainly looked like he was moving from the land of the living pretty fast. I started to say something but he put his hand on my shoulder, looked deep into my eyes, and said, "I'll kill both of them before I let them kill me."

And I knew he meant it. So crazy or not, how could I stop him? What could I do? I had to think. So I said, "Alfonso, boy, I've been thinking of moving out of this town. Maybe go up to Frisco. Good jobs up there. And not so goddamn hot. Come with me. Okay, hombre?"

He looked at me for a minute. Just a minute. And he said, "Yes, I will. Let's go tonight."

Shit! I hadn't really planned on going up north but I figured I'd better go with the flow, as you kids say nowadays. Because if I didn't, my friend would commit a double murder soon. So we packed. Yep. We had very little. Alfonso put a few dollars in a handkerchief and left it by the door of their boarding room. See, he still loved Sarah. He still had a heart. And then we left. We stole a couple of horses from the ranch Alfonso worked at and started north.

After about an hour or two, we heard something awful strange. First it was just a low rumble. Couldn't figure what it was. Then it got louder. And we turned to look over at the river, in the direction of St. Francis Dam. We could see the outline of the structure, designed and built by William Mulholland, you know. He was L.A.'s chief water engineer back then. Built that dam to hold two years' worth of water in case an earthquake split the aqueduct. So we thought maybe this is an earthquake. But what we saw made us lose our ability to breathe at that moment. The dam started to shift and break apart and crumble. The noise of the water—two years' worth, mind you—shook our bodies and the horses' too. Then we saw it. A wall of water, ten stories high, going into the valley—and some toward us. I yelled, "Shit! Let's get out of here!" Alfonso just stared at the water, frozen. I could see that he was thinking about Sarah. I yelled again and he finally seemed to wake up and hear me and we made those horses run faster than they ever had before.

We rode until morning. About five hundred people died that night, though maybe more did because a lot of the migrant farm workers weren't accounted for. We learned later that the water washed away whole towns like Castaic and Piru and anything near the river. Sirens and phone calls tried to alert people to outrun the water. Some made it. Many did not. Three hours after the dam broke, the town of Santa Paula, which pretty much evacuated, got hit, destroying three hundred homes. And Santa Paula was forty-two miles downstream from the dam! Saugus got hit so bad. Totally destroyed. Sad stories, too. Like the fact that forty-two children at the Saugus Elementary School were washed away.

Anyways, the names of everyone who died, or at least everyone they could identify, were listed in all the California papers the next few days. Alfonso and I saw Sarah listed, or so we thought. A woman by the name of "Tootsie Garcia" was there, listed on the front page of the *Los Angeles Times*. We don't know why they used her maiden name. Anyways, Eurt was not there. Maybe because he wasn't baptized so there was no record. And Alfonso didn't bother telling the authorities otherwise.

Well, you know the rest. Alfonso and I got up to Frisco, finally, and got pretty good work right away. He eventually married again. Nice woman. Not so pretty. But they had five kids and twelve grandkids. Me, I married your grandmother, Hanna, God bless her soul. Had my three kids and seven grandkids, including you. Alfonso died ten years ago. Cancer just like his papá. His wife followed him a year later. Heart just stopped. Her name was María. A good, honest woman, that.

Anything else? Isn't that enough, Patrick? Well, let me think. Yes, I guess there was something else. About four years ago I was watching the CNN on that TV. And there was this story about a preacher in Bakersfield. He had this huge following. People said he could heal. Everyone who was healed swore by this man. They showed him preaching. Good-looking fellow. Looked a lot like Sarah. About sixty or so. Thick gray hair and a fine mustache. And I stared at him. Then he lifted up his left hand. It was a nice hand, long and well manicured. Then he lifted the other. And my eyes almost burst from my head. The other hand was only a finger. Like a snake. Wriggling and pointing as he preached about hell and God's wrath. He used that hand to heal, they said. He went by the name of Veritas. Story ended and I just sat there for about ten minutes, not moving.

Well, Patrick. Good enough for your report? No, I don't have any explanations, and I'm afraid to even try to come up with some. Sometimes, in life, there aren't any. At least, none that you'd care to accept. You're young still. You'll see. Right now, while things are more black and white, I'd recommend that you just enjoy yourself. And I'll tell you one thing: wish I'd gone to college. Sounds like you're having some fun, interviewing old farts like me. Want a Diet Coke? Got plenty in the fridge. Okay, okay. Thought I'd be a good host. You are my favorite grandson, you know.

THE FOX

A WOMAN LIVED at the far end of a peninsula in a modest adobe hut and she appeared to be quite happy living all alone. The woman was no older than twenty, sturdily built, dark like the other Indians and Mestizos who inhabited the other end of the peninsula and, by the standards of the time, very handsome. She had all she needed to live very comfortably. The woman owned one goat that gave a great deal of rich milk. Furthermore, fruit trees grew all around her hut so that she never wanted for juicy purple figs, sweet crisp apples, and tangy fragrant lemons. Though many colorful birds and energetic rabbits lived among the trees and shrubs, the woman did not have the heart to kill anything. So she lived on fruit as well as on goat milk which, by her skillful hands, she made into very rich cheese and butter. All in all, the woman's world was as complete and serene as she ever could have wished and she seldom had to enter town to supply her needs.

The people who lived at the other end of the peninsula viewed the woman with great suspicion because she needed no one else to make her happy. "Who does she think she is?" they grumbled. And some said, "She will learn someday that she needs more than herself to live in this world!" Still others wondered, "How could she not want to mingle with us? Are we not good people? Do we not offer warm company?"

They were not so simple as to imply that the woman was a bruja or that she had some alliance with a darker power. No, the people on the other end of the peninsula were not stupid. Quite simply, they let jealousy do their thinking. And their jealousy led to griping about the woman. Other than this griping, however, the people left the woman to her own method of living.

To the north of the woman's hut was a small but plentiful pool of fresh water that ran down the nearby mountain that the people of the peninsula dubbed El Zorro, which means The Fox. No one knows why it was so named because the mountain did not resemble anything—let alone a fox—nor did foxes populate the area. The water tasted sweet and all the people of the peninsula drew from the pool for their daily needs. It was on these trips to the pool that the people saw the woman working around her hut, tending her goat and making butter and cheese. The people stared at her but she simply went about her business singing a cheerful song in her native Indian tongue rather than in Spanish. This, of course, merely angered the people even more.

The water that ran down from El Zorro into the pool made a constant rushing sound that was pleasant, though loud. The sound encouraged the woman to do her chores at a steady pace and it helped her sleep soundly each night. One morning, after being lulled into a deep sleep by the water rushing down the mountain and into the pool, the woman awoke and, as was her daily custom, she went to feed her goat. She took a few steps to the small wooden table at the other end of her hut and pulled from beneath it a burlap sack filled with grain. The woman picked up a battered though functional bowl made from a gourd and filled the bowl with grain. She pushed the bag back to its place and headed to the door, humming a pleasant and ancient melody. As the woman attempted to step out of her hut, her feet struck something soft, though substantial. She looked down and her eyes widened. A sudden shock of horror ran throughout her limbs, making her drop the goat's food. Before her, at the entrance of her little hut, lay her goat, its body slit from throat to belly. The goat was drained of its blood, which made a sea of red interrupted only by the soft white of the goat's rich, thick milk that swirled within but did not mix with the blood.With a cry, the woman ran to the pool and threw herself to the ground by its edge. Where does such cruelty come from? she thought. And she lay there for hours, not knowing what to do or what to think. The people from the other end of the peninsula saw her as they came to draw their daily water. They looked at the carcass of the goat and back at the woman and just shook their heads and said nothing to the woman.

When the woman finally pulled her emotions and thoughts together, it was almost midday. She realized what she had to do, but this realization only made her feel ill. The woman knew that she had to get another goat, but that meant she had to go to town and barter for one because wild goats no longer roamed freely on the peninsula or on El Zorro. She stood up and went to her hut, turning her eyes up to the sky so as not to see her slain goat. The woman took some of her finest cheeses from a shelf and put them into a large cloth sack. She then pulled a little tin box from under her bed and gathered into her small but strong hand exactly 10 pesos. That tin box had once been filled with many pesos, but over the last five years, since the death of the woman's mother, the little treasure had slowly shrunk. But this was a necessary withdrawal. Prepared to barter, the woman left her hut, carefully avoiding the sight of her slain goat, and headed to town.

As she entered the main street, she kept her eyes ahead of her to evade the stares of the people. They muttered, "Look, she needs us now." But they did not interfere with the woman's mission. The woman remembered how, long ago, her mother had taken her to town to buy the goat that now lay dead by her hut. The goat seller had a small adobe structure with a large fenced-off yard where he kept his goats. The woman remembered that it was near the end of the main street, off a little street called Calle de las Máscaras. She remembered the name because, as a young girl, she had wondered why you could not buy a mask from the goat seller when, after all, the goat seller's adobe sat on the Street of the Masks. She also remembered that the goat seller was quite old, smelled of dirty leather, and had grinned a foul grin at her. But she enjoyed the memory of that day because she had been with her mother and she was allowed to choose which goat they were going to barter for.

By and by, the woman arrived at the goat seller's adobe and approached its large wooden double doors. The woman could hear goats bleating and smelled the pungent but not unpleasant odor of fresh dung. She lifted the large iron knocker, let it drop with a solid pound, and waited for a response. The woman looked to the left and then to the right and noticed that some of the townspeople slowed their pace as they passed the adobe.

She heard muttering and clicking tongues that she tried her best to ignore. Within a minute or so, she heard footsteps, light and energetic, advance on the other side of the doors. Not the footsteps of an old man, she thought. And she was right. For when the right door moved and its shadow revealed the person on the inside, the woman saw a young man, perhaps her age, with tousled black curly hair and skin as smooth and white as sand. The man smiled a smile that was crooked like a dead spider's leg, but he otherwise had the most handsome countenance the woman had ever seen.

After a moment, the woman said, "I would like to barter for a goat."

"I know," said the man, to the woman's astonishment. "I have already heard of the tragedy. The townspeople who went for their daily water at the pool saw what had been done to your goat. Come in through my home and we can look for a replacement."

The man led the woman through his simple home toward a large door at the other end that led to the yard. As she walked, the woman observed each object in the two rooms through which they had to pass and noticed that the adobe was well kept but sparsely furnished, with only a few chairs and a table or two. Not a thing adorned the walls except for several bookcases with shelves stacked with large, beautiful books. She also noticed a large painting of the old goat seller whom the woman remembered from long ago. The painting hung in an ornate gilded wooden frame. The old goat seller's eyes stared down at the woman as if lust still filled his heart.

"Where is the old man?" she asked.

"My father," said the man, "has long since left this world. I now sell goats in his place."

The woman could not help but smile at this new knowledge. She liked this young man.

When they arrived at the large door at the end of the adobe and entered the yard, more than twenty goats gamboled up to the man and bleated a noisy hello. Dust filled the air as the goats kicked their hooves up in excitement.

"Which do you want?" said the man as he patted one of the goats.

The woman held up her bag of cheeses and the 10 pesos and said, "What quality of goat can I get with these?"

The man laughed. "No need to barter. Choose one that you like."

The woman grew angry. "I am not a pauper. I can pay for what I need." And she held up her cheeses and 10 pesos even higher to make her point more emphatically.

Realizing that he had insulted the woman, the man said, "You are right. With what you have brought, you may have that goat," and he pointed to the largest animal in the yard.

The woman looked at the goat and then back at the man. "I will take this one," she said, pointing to the smallest goat that her eyes could discern from among the noisy and rambunctious herd.

"It is a deal," said the young man, realizing that it was no use to argue with this strong-willed woman. "But on one condition," he added. "You must let me come and visit it each day because that one is my favorite."

The woman smiled and said, "Yes, it is a deal." She handed the man the sack of cheeses and put the 10 pesos gently into his left hand. She then pulled a small rope from her belt, tied it to the little goat, and left through the gate at the end of the yard. The man smiled his crooked smile as he watched the woman leave, leading her new little goat. One lonely cloud cleverly found its way to the vibrant sun and the goat yard suddenly grew dark. The man laughed and went back into his adobe.

So, as they had agreed in their barter, the man visited the goat every day. And each day the woman asked the young man about his life and about the town. The townspeople gossiped and wondered if the old goat seller's son could actually bring this woman to her senses so that she would move to town as a new bride. After six months of the man's visits, the two did indeed marry in a large boisterous wedding at the town's large old church. The woman moved to the man's adobe, bringing her little goat with her.

At first the man and woman lived a happy life full of laughter and love and warmth. The goats sold well, and eventually the couple added two more rooms to the adobe and put a little hut in the yard for the new maid to live in. The woman no longer made cheese and butter so she had to buy such things in town. Over time she began to mingle with the townspeople on her trips to the marketplace and they grew to enjoy the woman's company. And the townspeople felt vindicated in their belief that the woman was now finally and truly a whole person.

Except for one thing. Despite a full year of sharing their wedding bed with her husband, the woman did not bear a child. The man was, at first, very patient. But in the second year of their marriage he grew cold, and slowly his anger replaced the love he once had for the woman. By the third year, anger permeated his every thought, every movement, and every prayer. And the townspeople began to laugh behind his back and spread ugly gossip about him. The woman grew lonely as her husband stopped speaking to her. The man eventually stopped sleeping in their bed as well, instead sleeping on a bench in the yard with the goats.

The only joy left for the woman was her daily visit to the pool for water. She would see her little abandoned hut and remember the peaceful and full life she had once led, caring for her goat and making cheese and butter from the goat's rich milk. She thought about her mother, who had taught her the Indian ways and songs and stories. The woman's joy vanished when she realized that she had to go back to town to her husband's house.

One morning, as she returned home from drawing water from the pool, she saw her husband in the yard speaking softly to their maid. Their bodies did not touch but she saw a familiarity between them that she recognized. The woman turned her head and went into the adobe.

In the fourth year of their marriage, the maid gave birth to a handsome boy with tousled black curly hair. The townspeople gossiped and the maid became surly and refused to work. The woman grew even more silent and accepted her circumstances. The man gave up the charade and moved his things into the maid's hut.

One night in the fifth year of their marriage, the woman lay awake in her bed looking out her opened window. The moon lit her bedroom with the light of twenty candles. The woman thought that she had been less lonely when she lived by herself under the shadow of El Zorro. While wrestling with this truth, she suddenly noticed that the light of the moon had dimmed and the dark figure of a man stood at the window. The woman remained still. She saw that the man wore the mask of a canine—a dog, a fox, or a wolf? She could not tell from this distance. The man slowly lifted his left leg over the windowsill and entered the room. She could hear his breath echo within the mask as he came close to the bed. The man lifted his right hand and revealed a long and shiny knife.

As the man plunged the knife into the woman's soft brown neck, she saw that the mask was indeed that of a fox. And her mind fell back effortlessly to memories of the mountain called El Zorro and of the cool sweet water that ran down the mountain and into the pool by the hut she once lived in. And she noticed the exquisite red-brown paint shining on the mask's surface and the glossy dabs of raven black glistening at the fox's eyes and nostrils. The woman listened calmly to her breathing as it slowed.

And as the man unhurriedly dug the knife deeper into the woman's neck and then dragged it down toward her belly, he remembered how, long ago, the woman had looked so beautiful and peaceful tending to her daily chores when she lived alone near El Zorro. The man also observed how the knife he now held in his hand felt no different than it had the night he had used it on the woman's goat all those years ago.

BELÉN

BELÉN STUMBLED and fell hard on her knees in the middle of the dirt road. A chicken clucked in front of her, not seeming to care that this fifteen-year-old girl's dress was ripped in three places and that dried blood mixed with bits of straw and grime covered her thin legs. Belén knew this stupid chicken. It sported a heart-shaped spot on its left wing and had escaped her uncle's coop three months ago. Tío Normando believed that this unnatural mancha was a bad omen so he didn't bother looking for the bird. Besides, ever since its disappearance, his other chickens gave more eggs than ever before. Now, Belén discerned that the fugitive chicken had grown skinny, filthy, and ragged, but the heart shape miraculously maintained its rich brown shimmer.

"Get away from me," said Belén.

The chicken stopped, cocked its head to the left and then to the right, blinked four times at Belén, and then clucked its way to the other side of the road.

"Stupid chicken."

Belén slowly got to her feet. Her groin hurt but at least the blood had stopped dripping out of her. The sun began to set, filling the sky with brilliant reds and purples. She needed to get home before dark. Belén only had another half mile to go but the pain kept her from moving any faster than a shuffle. Her parents would be angry. But Belén could do nothing to avoid the inevitable screaming from her mother, the slap from her father.

"Stupid chicken," she muttered again as she hobbled forward.

As Belén got closer to home, the light emanating from the other houses helped to illuminate the way. These structures could not compare with the one her father had built—most were nothing more than wooden shacks with tar-paper roofs—but they made Belén feel safer, as if they stood sentry just for her.

By the time Belén could see the silhouette of her house, the day's heat had dissipated and a chill began to creep into her bones. She smacked her lips and tried to make saliva but couldn't. Belén shivered and thought how magnificent a drink of water would taste right then. Something so simple, so perfect. She closed her eyes and imagined the water on her lips and tongue, and then slaking her parched throat. She'd let some dribble down her chin and then she'd swallow a little and then gulp the rest all at once. That was her plan once she got home, if she could stay awake.

Her feet seemed to sink into the dusty road, deeper with each step. Belén heard an owl—*hoot-hoot-hoot*—and then a woman's voice—was it her mother?—call her name. She tried to answer but her lips were now sealed dry and tight. And as she fell toward the voice that called her name, Belén believed that she would land safely on her mattress so that she could enjoy a long nap first, saving that cool drink of water for when she awoke.

"SOMETHING LIKE THIS wouldn't have happened when Cárdenas was president!"

Belén recognized her father's familiar rant against President Manuel Ávila Camacho. Even though he spoke angrily, the sound of her father's voice comforted Belén. She kept her eyes closed and enjoyed the soft mattress.

"Why does it always come down to politics?"

That was Tío Normando. Oh! Belén should tell him that she saw his stupid runaway chicken today but she couldn't bring herself to stir or even open her eyes.

"Because politics is everything," said her father, barely controlling his voice. "Politics has turned Mexico into Roosevelt's bitch, that's why. Our good men are moving north to work the fields so Roosevelt can send his men to fight Hitler."

"So?"

"So because of politics, our daughters can't walk freely in this town without being molested by some stranger who feels that he can swoop down and take what he wants."

"Who said it was a stranger?"

Silence. Just the sound of three people breathing somewhere above her.

And then, slowly: "Because anyone who knows she's my daughter would know that I'd kill him for this."

This last comment from her father sent a shiver through Belén's entire body. Her eyelids fluttered uncontrollably and she coughed.

"She's awake!" Belén heard her mother yell.

Adolfo ran to his daughter but stopped short of touching her. He turned to his wife. "Mónica, wipe her forehead with a wet cloth," he said.

Mónica complied. The cool dampness refreshed Belén. She opened her eyes and looked at the concerned faces that encircled her.

"Mija," said Mónica. But she couldn't get another word out so she continued to wipe her daughter's forehead and cheeks.

Adolfo came a step closer. "Who did this to you?" he said.

"Not now," pleaded Mónica.

"Now," said Adolfo. "Was it a stranger or someone you knew?"

Belén thought of that chicken, the one her tío Normando didn't miss at all. But she figured he would be amused by her telling of their meeting earlier on the dirt road when she fell. That stupid chicken looked so ridiculous and skinny and ragged. Yes, that would make her tío laugh his special deep laugh. ¡Ay! He was so handsome! Her mother was always saying that some lucky girl would steal his heart away. Why couldn't it be Belén? She needed to tell him about the chicken so he could see how clever and funny and observant she was, even though she was only a girl and he was a grown man.

"Tío," Belén began, but her throat caught and she broke into a coughing jag.

"Who?" howled Adolfo.

Mónica let out a gasp. She and Adolfo turned to Normando.

"You don't think. . . ," Normando stammered. "Hermano, that's crazy."

Belén gained control of her voice. She so wanted to tell her uncle about the stupid chicken. "Tío," she began again, but before she could say anything else, her father leapt across the room and pounced on Normando.

Mónica screamed, "Esposo, it's not possible!"

Normando slipped from his brother's grip. Adolfo stumbled over his own feet and reached for the small wooden table that still held their supper's dirty dishes. The table stuttered and then gave way under Adolfo's weight, collapsing and coming down in a crash that made Belén's ears ring. Normando took advantage of Adolfo's confusion to scamper to the door and rush from the house.

Adolfo finally got to his feet. "I will kill him," he said as he wiped beans and rice from his shirt and pants.

"Why?" asked Belén. "He's my tío."

Mónica let out a whimper.

Adolfo shook his head. "No need to protect him, mija. Brother or not, he will pay for what he did to you."

All Belén could say was: "Tío."

Her parents looked at each other and sighed.

BELÉN'S UNCLE was many things, but he wasn't one who took unnecessary risks, and he knew too well his older brother's temper. It didn't matter that Normando had not touched his niece or that he secretly desired men instead of women; it was not possible to calm Adolfo. So that night Normando disappeared into the darkness. No one knew where he went, though several neighbors had seen him gather a few things from his shack, unlock the chicken coop, saddle a horse, and head north. When Adolfo showed up later that night with a loaded rifle, he was met by a dark, empty house and clucking chickens roaming happily in the yard. Six months later rumors made it back that Normando had sold his horse when he reached Ciudad Juárez and then he'd crossed the border, eventually settling in El Paso, maybe for good. But no matter. Normando was out of Belén's life, so he might as well have been killed by her father.

In the meantime Belén's belly grew. At first her mother tried to hide it by making dresses one, two, and then three sizes too big for her daughter. But just when their neighbors started to spread chisme about this unmarried girl's apparent condition, Belén awoke one night drenched in her own blood. The doctor from the Instituto Mexicano de Seguro Social came to finish what nature had started and *poof!*—no more pregnancy, no more gossip. Belén wept at the death of her baby girl, so tiny, so perfect, but without a chance.

Mónica tried to comfort her daughter with promises of future babies made within the sanctity of marriage, blessed by the Church, as it should be. "It's God's plan, mija," said Mónica as she braided Belén's long, sleek hair.

Belén nodded because her mother would know such things. She herself had lost five babies—two before and three after Belén—and had long accepted such deaths as part of a sacred plan. God let many seemingly evil things happen because that was His way. God even let Adolfo confuse what Belén was trying to say to Normando and through such confusion, her favorite tío had to flee for his life. In fact, God later told Belén in a dream that she shouldn't even bother setting the record straight. "What's done is done," said God. At least, Belén believed that it was God, despite the fact that He took the form of that stupid runaway chicken. "And besides," God added with a cluck, "the identity of the true perpetrators must be kept secret."

"Why?" Belén asked God.

With another cluck, God said: "Because it is part of my plan."

Belén could do nothing but accept God's pronouncement, though she did feel a bit odd each time her mother served chicken posole or chicken with rice. But she figured if she could eat the body of Christ at Mass, she wouldn't be punished if she ate chicken in all of its delectable manifestations.

The next year Belén started to fill out the oversized dresses her mother had made to hide the pregnancy. Her legs were no longer skinny but had become round and muscular, burned a deep brown from her constant running through the fields. And her bosom—well, something had to be done!—so Mónica bought two sturdy brassieres when they made a special trip to the Federal District. But what surprised her most about Belén was not her rapid development (for this had happened to Mónica suddenly in her sixteenth year as well) but her daughter's remarkable good nature and cheerfulness despite that horrible event of the year before. Ah, no matter. That was all in the past and best forgotten. No doubt Belén would find a good man, marry, and provide Mónica with loads of fat, squirming, happy grandchildren.

But, gracias a Dios, Mónica never learned that her daughter had started slipping out of the house at night to meet Francisco, the young butcher who lived down the road. While Francisco fell in love with this wild young woman, all Belén was trying to do was fill a hole that could never be filled. Those trysts ended after a few weeks—the butcher's heart torn to pieces—and Belén grew hungry for something else.

ONE MORNING as Belén walked to the mercado for her mother, she decided to take the long way so that she'd pass by her tío's abandoned shack. As Belén approached the tiny structure, she squinted and imagined seeing Normando puttering around the front yard, tending the coop, whistling a happy tune. She marveled at the power of her imagination because she could almost see him there, stooping and picking something up, standing again and taking a puff on a fat cigarette. . . but her uncle didn't smoke! Belén's eyes popped wide open and she froze. Could it be him? Was he back from El Paso with a new smoking habit? She broke into a trot. It was a man, a young man. Could it be Normando?

But as she approached, Belén could see that he clearly was not her tío. Unlike Normando, this man kept his hair cropped close to his skull, and he stood at least six inches shorter. His face and forearms gleamed a smooth and hairless bronze. So unlike Normando, who boasted a large mustache, hairy arms, and fair skin; he'd always asserted that he and his brother had much more Spanish blood than Indian, something Adolfo confirmed with well-preserved family photographs of Belén's grandparents.

On the other hand, this stranger reminded Belén of the Indios who lived in the hills and spoke their ancient language instead of Spanish. A few worked at the Velasco ranch with her father, but the boss always gave them the dirtiest, worst-paying jobs. And they wore their traditional clothing and sandals, which did nothing but separate them even further from the town's social fabric. But this Indio, he was different. He wore a plaid work shirt with sleeves rolled up to his elbows, jeans, and pointy-toed boots.

The man looked up and caught Belén's eye. She stopped,

blinked, and stood immobile, five yards away, not knowing what to do or say.

"Señorita," he said with a polite nod.

Belén blinked again.

"Do you speak Spanish?" asked the man.

Belén nodded. She coughed and regained some composure. "Why do you live here?" she finally asked.

The man laughed and took a long drag from his fat cigarette. "To protect me from the heat, the cold, the rain," he said.

Belén took a few steps closer and then stopped. "No," she said, impatient with this stranger. "Why *this* house?"

"I moved from Cuernavaca," the man said, maintaining his calm demeanor. "Now I work at the Velasco ranch. I needed a place to stay so I rented this humble home."

"From my father," blurted Belén, more as an accusation than a statement of fact.

The man smiled, revealing straight teeth. "I see the resemblance," he said.

They stood for a moment in silence, sizing each other up. If it weren't for his boot heels, Belén estimated that they would stand eye to eye if she came right up to him. The man kept his cigarette tucked in the left corner of his mouth, making his left eye squint from the smoke.

Finally Belén walked up to him. "May I have one?" she said, pointing to the man's cigarette.

The man nodded, pulled out a small bag of tobacco and a small, square piece of paper from his shirt pocket, and started to pour.

"Make it fat like yours."

The man chuckled and added more tobacco. He returned the bag to his shirt pocket, gingerly licked one edge of the paper, and rolled a neat but bulging cigarette. He presented it to Belén with a flourish and a bow. She took it, put it between her lips, and leaned in toward the man. He lit it with the glowing tip of his cigarette. "You need to draw on it," he said.

And she did. Belén puffed away for a few moments without grimacing or coughing. "Very nice," she said. "I like it."

Without another word, Belén walked past the man and entered

the shack. The man followed. When he entered, he found the girl sitting on his cot. "Close the door," she said.

"But your father. . ."

"Don't worry about him."

"But you don't even know my name."

Belén dropped the cigarette into a glass of water that sat on the nightstand. It sizzled, making a sound that pleased her. She slowly slipped off one shoe, then the other. "I'm waiting," she said.

"For what?"

"For your name."

"Celso."

"Good. Now close the door, Celso."

He stood motionless, thinking about this order coming from such a young beautiful woman.

"I'm not asking again," said Belén.

After a moment, Celso nodded and then obliged.

ADOLFO AND MÓNICA could hardly object to the engagement of their daughter to Celso. After what had happened to Belén, they were lucky that any man would want to marry her. Adolfo was far from happy with Celso's deep-brown coloring and his Indio features, but at least he was a hard worker, spoke perfect Spanish along with his native tongue, and abstained from alcohol. True, Adolfo's future grandchildren had a fifty-fifty chance of looking like Indios, but he knew that worse things happened in life. He also knew that he could trust this Indio, which, in this world, accounted for much. Despite his temper, Adolfo was more or less a pragmatist.

Seven months after the wedding, Belén gave birth to a chubby girl whose skin color seemed to be a perfect blend of her parents' shadings. Adolfo sighed in relief when he saw the baby: though darker than his family, she possessed Spanish features, which would make her life easier. Mónica paid no attention to such things. She simply thanked God in all His glory that this baby was as healthy as can be. Belén and Celso named her Concepción, but they liked calling her Conchita. And Belén almost forgot what had happened to her when she was fifteen. Now, as a mature woman of seventeen years, she could get on with her life as a mother and wife. Her new husband tore down the old shack and built a larger home for his family. Belén believed that her life was on a perfect road, free of the past.

But the past has a way of finding us no matter how we try to hide from it. One night as Celso and the baby snored in unison, Normando appeared to Belén in a dream.

"Oh, Tío," she said to him. "I've missed you so much. Will you ever come home?"

Normando slowly shook his head. This filled Belén with such grief that she began to weep in her sleep.

She woke to find herself in Celso's strong embrace. "Mi amor," he said as he pulled Belén close. "Why do you cry?" But she didn't answer. Within moments, Celso was asleep.

His bride hoped that Normando would visit her dreams again. And he did. The next night, as she slept, Normando appeared, but this time he sat at a wooden table holding the runaway chicken in his lap. The chicken was no longer scrawny and dirty—it was plump and displayed abundant healthy feathers. That heart-shaped spot looked as if it had grown in both size and brilliance. Normando ran his right palm over the chicken's puffed-out breast and cooed softly to keep the bird calm.

"So," said Belén, "you finally found your bird."

"Yes, she's been waiting for me."

"I thought you were happy to see her go."

"No," said Normando between coos. "I believed that this mancha was bad luck but I always missed her."

Her uncle seemed so content holding the chicken. That bird gave him peace. Belén suddenly felt a pang of guilt for calling it stupid. But wait! Hadn't God spoken to her through this chicken? And here was Tío Normando holding God on his lap and cooing to Him.

"Does God want you to do that?" she asked.

"Why wouldn't God want me to hold my chicken?"

"Because God spoke to me through that bird."

Normando's head popped up, a grin spread across his face, and he let out a chuckle. "My, this is a special chicken," he said and continued to pet the bird.

Belén shifted from one foot to the other.

"What did God say to you through my chicken?"

Belén opened her mouth but then stopped short.

"What did He say to you?" he pressed.

With the question, Belén's mind fell back to the day of the rape. There were two men, men she knew by reputation because of who their fathers were. And God had told her not to divulge their identity, not to set the record straight. And the more she thought about it, the more Belén realized that He was right. If her father had learned the truth, he would have killed these men. And there was no doubt their fathers would have retaliated ruthlessly.

"Not much," she finally answered.

"Well, if God went through the trouble of appearing in your dream, I imagine that He'd have something important to say, ¿no?"

Before she could answer, Belén woke to Conchita's wailing. She opened her eyes and saw Celso fully dressed for work, holding their baby.

"She's hungry," said Celso.

"Why didn't you wake me earlier?"

"I thought that I could calm her but I don't have what she needs," he said as he handed the baby to Belén, who quickly put Conchita to her breast. "You looked so peaceful."

The room grew quiet except for the baby's happy suckling sounds.

"Oh?" she asked, feeling her face turn red.

"You were even smiling much of the time, except just before you woke," he said.

Belén looked down at Conchita.

"She's beautiful, like you," said Celso.

Belén looked up.

"What's wrong?" he asked.

Belén smiled. Celso leaned down to kiss his wife and touch the baby's puffing cheeks. "Must go," he said, leaving Belén alone with her memories of Normando as Conchita fed happily at her breast.

"I've been waiting for you."

Again in her dream she found Normando sitting at that little wooden table, holding the chicken. Belén sat down across from him and the bird. "Do you wait all day while I'm awake?" she asked, truly puzzled.

"In a way," he said, looking thoughtful.

Belén hesitated to ask her next question, but she had to know: "Are you dead?"

The chicken clucked loudly, flapped its stubby wings, and jumped out of Normando's hands.

"There, you've upset her," said Normando in mock concern.

"Lo siento."

"No matter," he said. And then he paused before answering: "Yes, I am now a spirit."

Belén lost her breath. Normando reached over and stroked her arm in the same gentle way he had been petting the chicken. "I'm fine," he said. "No more worries."

The chicken pecked at the ground, not wanting to move too far from Normando.

"How did you die?"

"My brother kept his promise."

"No!"

Normando smiled. "I would have done the same."

"But that's not the point," she said. "You never touched me."

Normando nodded in agreement. The chicken came close to his feet and pecked near the toes of its master's shiny boots. Normando reached down with a little grunt and returned the chicken to his lap. The bird clucked contentedly and gave Belén a look that seemed to say: *Ha, ha! He's mine!*

"I must go," she said, standing.

"Of course," agreed Normando.

Belén hesitated for a moment, took a deep breath, leaned down, and kissed her uncle on his cheek. The chicken clucked loudly and flapped its wings. Belén woke to Conchita's hungry cry.

Later that day Belén set out to the mercado while her mother watched the baby. Normally this was her time to chat and share chisme with the other women of the town. But today, as she haggled half-heartedly with the vendors, Belén was in no mood to gossip. She merely nodded to her female friends or, when forced to, offered nothing more than one- or two-word answers to questions about Conchita and Celso. As she walked home, bags heavy with meat, cheeses, and fruit, Belén's thoughts were gripped by Normando's revelation. Deep in her heart, she'd suspected it, but to be told that her father had killed his own brother based on a misunderstanding filled Belén with an almost paralyzing guilt. She needed to talk to her uncle further about all this, but she'd have to wait until bedtime.

Belén stopped under a tree to rest. She rolled a fat cigarette as Celso had taught her. Belén's mother thought smoking was unladylike. But her father was, despite himself, a bit impressed by his daughter's talent at rolling loose tobacco. As Belén smoked, she let her eyes wander. She took great pleasure in this portion of the road between home and the mercado. The town's pine trees were thickest here, mostly standing in clusters of five or six. On either side of the dirt road thick grasses grew tall, covering the ground like a thick fur all the way to the foot of the mountains to the east. For reasons she couldn't fathom, the townspeople hadn't built houses here. Belén would, if she could, move her home to this spot.

As she pondered the possibility of this, she noticed something moving along the road. She squinted. Some kind of small animal, she figured. Belén puffed on her cigarette, keeping her eyes on the creature's slow but steady progress. "Ay Dios," she whispered when she realized what approached her.

Belén took one last drag on the cigarette, ground it into the dirt, picked up the bags, and resumed her trek home, realizing that she would soon come upon Normando's runaway chicken. Unlike the bird of her dreams, this chicken was as skinny and grimy as when she'd last encountered it. Belén had assumed that the bird must have died to keep Normando company, but she could now see that this was indeed the bird with the heart-shaped mancha on its wing.

As they approached each other, Belén realized that the chicken had been clucking softly to itself. The bird suddenly became mute when it noticed the girl, but it kept moving forward, though warily. Soon they stood toe-to-toe. The chicken seemed to mock Belén by its refusal to be frightened off the road. How could Normando care for such a spiteful creature? she thought. Perhaps her tío could see the good in it. With that idea taking root in her mind, Belén reached down to touch the heart-shaped mancha, which still maintained its deep-brown luster despite the rather mangy feathers that surrounded it. The chicken eyed Belén's advancing hand suspiciously. "Good bird," she cooed as her hand drew closer.

The chicken blinked wildly. As Belén's hand came within an inch of the mancha, the bird emitted a loud cluck, pulled its ragged head back, and then plunged its cracked but sharp beak into the back of the girl's hand. Belén yelped, stood, swung her right leg back, and kicked the chicken with all her strength. The bird let out a bizarre muffled cackle as it sailed through the air, over a clump of bushes, and directly into a large pine. The chicken bounced off the tree, dislodging a bit of bark upon impact, and finally plopped upon the soft grass, motionless.

"¡Ay!" Belén exclaimed, shocked by her violent reaction. She ran to the chicken, hoping that it was merely stunned. But the unnatural angle of the bird's scrawny neck drained all hope from Belén. "Oh, what will Normando say?" she whimpered as she fell to her knees.

And then she remembered that God had spoken to her through this bird. Belén knew that she had to do something to show respect for this life she'd taken. She snapped a sharp branch in half and used it to dig a small grave at the base of the pine. Belén couldn't bring herself to touch the chicken so she gently nudged it with her foot to the edge of the miniature grave and then let the bird fall lightly to the bottom. She kneeled and filled the hole with dirt, patting it as flat as possible. Belén stood, solemnly hung her head, and said a prayer. After a few moments of sacred contemplation, she picked up the bags of food and resumed the walk home.

Throughout the rest of the day Belén clung to the hope that the chicken would be in her dream as usual, comforting her tío. And to her thinking, now that the bird was as dead as Normando, there should be no reason why it wouldn't be there. However, that night when Belén went into her dream, Normando sat at his usual place but his lap and hands were empty, the chicken nowhere in sight. Did he know what had happened? She approached slowly, then sat across from her uncle. Normando stared at his empty hands, which rested limply in his lap.

"Tío," said Belén softly, "how are you?"

"I have something to tell you," he said without looking up.

"I'm sorry," she said.

Normando lifted his head and met his niece's moist eyes. "No, I'm the one who is sorry for what I'm about to reveal."

Confusion rolled over Belén in waves.

"It's time for you to know," continued Normando.

"What?" was all she could say.

"The identity of the man who took my life."

Belén's confusion grew deeper. She already knew, didn't she? It was her father who had killed Normando. "But I know," she said. "I've accepted that. It's been easier because I can see you in my dreams."

Normando shook his head. "My brother was indeed responsible for my death, that is true."

"But?"

Normando turned away, shifted in his chair, and coughed. They sat in silence. Suddenly Normando's eyes widened, a smile spread across his face, and he raised his hands. "My little bird!" he exclaimed.

Sure enough, the chicken was slowly making its way toward Normando, clucking softly, periodically casting a glance at its murderer. Belén blushed and sighed deeply. She watched as the bird finally reached Normando's feet. He lifted it and placed it on his lap. "Yes," Normando cooed to the bird, "rest right here."

To Belén's surprise, the chicken didn't look any the worse for its death. In fact, it appeared to have grown plumper and even healthier than the last time she'd seen it in her dream.

"Tío," she said, attempting to hide her annoyance with this intrusion and forgetting her own guilt. "What is it that you want to tell me?"

Normando looked up, still smiling with the joy his chicken gave him. "My brother hired a man to kill me."

Belén fell back in her chair. She could easily imagine her father's anger leading to violence, especially when it came to harm visited upon his family. But a cold-blooded planned murder with payment made to complete the job?

"This can't be!" she screamed, standing up so quickly that her chair teetered back and rocked until it steadied on its own.

"Why would I lie?"

Belén thought for a moment. Of course he was right: there was no reason to lie to his niece. She pulled the chair back into place and sat, defeated.

"Little one," said Normando. "In the end it doesn't matter."

"Then why are you telling me this?"

"Because sometimes the truth will teach us something about ourselves." The chicken clucked in agreement.

Many questions came to Belén's mind. But Normando knew this. "You may ask me only one," he said.

"But. . ."

"Lo siento," said Normando. "Only one."

This agitated Belén. She vowed that when *she* died and visited the living, she wouldn't be so mysterious. No, she would avoid such games. But at that moment she had no choice. Belén had to play by her uncle's rules now. She thought for a minute. "All right," said Belén. "I've chosen one question for you."

"Yes?"

"Who actually killed you?"

"I always knew you were a smart girl," said Normando with a smile.

Belén remained serious, resolute. She crossed her arms tightly across her chest.

Normando grew serious as well. "My brother hired a man, un Indio, from Cuernavaca to track me down and. . ."

A shock ran through Belén but she remained quiet to hear everything.

". . .you know this man."

Belén nodded. For some reason, it made sense to her and she accepted it as she would the color of the morning sky or the smell of her baby's skin. They sat in silence for a long while. Eventually Normando put the chicken down, smiled, stood, and then walked away, disappearing into the shadows. The bird clucked loudly and then followed its master until it too was gone.

Belén woke to a kiss on her cheek from Celso. "Mi amor," he whispered. "Are you all right?"

Belén sat up and rubbed her eyes. Celso didn't rise but kept his head nestled into his pillow. "Were you having a bad dream?" he asked.

She looked at Celso. The morning sun began to fill the

bedroom with a soft light. Conchita snored softly in her crib in the far corner. Belén strained to see Celso's features clearly. He gently touched her cheek. She wondered how he had killed Normando. Did he use a gun? His bare hands? Belén would never know.

"I'm fine," she said.

Celso pulled her down and she settled into the crook of his arm. Belén listened to her husband's heartbeat. His strong chest rose and fell with each breath. She could feel his limbs grow slack as he drifted back to sleep.

"I'm fine," Belén said again. "I'm fine, mi amor."

THE HORNED TOAD

THERE WAS A MAN who lived in a small Mexican fishing village with his wife and three children in a two-room wooden house not far from the shore. The man was not a fisherman like the others. Rather, he made the fishing nets that were used by the fishermen. He had long delicate fingers that were put to good use tying the tiny knots of the nets he made. His nets were the best in the village because they could withstand heavy catches and he earned a good living selling them to the fishermen. The man lived a quiet but loving life with his wife of ten years and his children: ages one, three, and five.

The man's daily routine was set early on in his marriage and he veered from it only in emergencies, such as when one of his children got sick or when a terrible storm blew into the village. Each morning his wife served the man strong black coffee and two pieces of pan dulce. He would eat his sweet bread and drink his coffee at their too-crowded dining table while his children played more than they ate and his wife attended to her never-ending chore of cleaning. After eating, the man would kiss his wife and children, take his little bag with his lunch, and head off to his little shop, which was about ten minutes away by foot. When he got to his shop he would open all the windows and sit down to his work of making fishing nets.

The man had a view of the ocean from his little shop. To rest his eyes, he would look up from his work every so often and focus on the waves as they hit the sand. Sometimes he would be mesmerized by the waves and lose track of time. After finishing a full day of making and selling nets, he would pack up his empty lunch bag and walk home to his family.

One day as the man sat in his shop looking out the window, he saw a rowboat sitting on the sand. He had never seen it before and had not noticed who had put it there. He put aside the net he was working on and went out to inspect the boat.

It was a simple boat with both its oars set inside. There was no net or any personal belongings in it and no name on its side. The man looked around and saw no one. The sun shone brilliantly as it hung at its highest point, even making the man's dark Mestizo skin burn hot. He looked out to the ocean and saw the little island the people called El Lagarto Cornudo, which means "The Horned Toad." It was called that not because horned toads populated the island but because its silhouette resembled one.

The man had often wondered what was on El Lagarto Cornudo. He had heard that getting there was very difficult because of the crosscurrents that had to be navigated. He thought for a moment about his wife and three children and his little shop. The man then turned and walked back to his shop, retrieved his lunch, and walked back to the rowboat. He looked around again and, without hesitation, he pushed the boat to the edge of the water, got in, and started rowing in the direction of El Lagarto Cornudo.

The man enjoyed the broad movements of his arms as he rowed. It was in contrast to the delicate work he did each day making fishing nets. He breathed deeply of the ocean smell. Rowing was easy and pleasing without any fight from the notorious crosscurrents he had heard about. Several white egrets flew by the boat and landed in the water nearby. The man rowed with his back to the island and the egrets stayed alongside the boat, hoping the man would throw them some bread. The man looked over his shoulder and saw El Lagarto Cornudo in the distance.

After a half hour of rowing, the man stopped to eat. He opened his bag, pulled out a tortilla filled with carnitas, and he ate it slowly, enjoying the feel of the tender meat in his mouth. The man then opened his bottle of red wine and drank deeply. He wiped his mouth, put the bottle away in his bag, and started to row again. The island was much farther than he had realized.

Eventually the man grew tired because he had entered the crosscurrents, which made it harder to row. Suddenly, without warning, the boat jerked and started to twirl and spin and the oars flew in every direction. The egrets flew away helter-skelter.

The man tried to stay calm and gain control over the oars, but to no avail. Every few seconds, as the boat went round and round, the man could see El Lagarto Cornudo which, by now, was only about one hundred yards away. But the man could not control the boat: one of the oars flew up and hit the man hard on his forehead and he fell to the bottom of the boat.

The man felt himself slip from this world into the next. His soul left his body and stood over the still figure lying on the bottom of the boat. The man looked so small to himself. The water became calm and the boat eventually was at rest. The egrets flew back and landed by the boat. The man's soul looked at the island. With one movement of his outstretched arms, the man's soul rose into the air. He aimed himself toward the island and flew around it. It was a beautiful island, with many trees and plants and waterfalls. The sand of its beaches gleamed a white different from the darker sand of the mainland.

After surveying El Lagarto Cornudo, the man turned toward the mainland, passing over the little boat where his body lay. He then glided over the shore and his little shop and eventually he found his little house.

The man entered a window and found his wife working in the kitchen. She could not see him but she looked up momentarily when he came close to her. The man noticed that his wife was indeed quite beautiful and had lovely brown skin and gleaming black hair. He used to notice such things but with time he had forgotten how to look at her.

The man then went out the back door and entered the yard where his children would be playing. And they were there, as he had anticipated, playing loudly and joyously. He watched them move and yell and laugh, and his heart filled with a love that would have made him cry but he was a spirit so he could not cry. The man looked up into the sky and before he knew it he was floating again, heading back to the boat.

Again over the boat, he looked down upon his still body. Without warning, the man started to fall, fast and silently. All went dark.

"Mateo," said a voice. "Are you all right?"

The man opened his eyes. He lay at the bottom of the boat, which now sat on the shore. Several fishermen looked down on him. "Did you try to go to El Lagarto Cornudo by yourself?" one asked. "What a dangerous thing to do with such a small boat," said another.

The man rubbed his forehead, realizing that he was not dead but very much alive. He thanked the fishermen and after gaining his strength, he walked home. It was almost sunset.

The man entered his little house and saw his wife. She said hello and they gave each other a little kiss. His wife noticed the bruise on her husband's forehead but said nothing. His children came in, ran to the man, and hugged him. That night they had a very good dinner of fish and vegetables and bread.

The next morning the man's wife served the man strong black coffee and two pieces of pan dulce. He ate the sweet bread and drank the coffee at their too-crowded dining table while his children played more than they ate and his wife attended to her never-ending chore of cleaning. After eating the man kissed his wife and children, took his little bag with his lunch, and headed off to his little shop, which was about ten minutes away by foot. When he got to his shop he opened all the windows and sat down to his work of making fishing nets.

After an hour or so, the man looked out his window and saw the same little rowboat he had seen the day before. He set his work aside, grabbed his lunch bag, and walked to the boat. The man looked around and saw no one. He put his lunch bag in the boat and pushed it to the edge of the water. He looked around again and, without hesitation, he pushed the boat into the water, got in, and then started to row in the direction of El Lagarto Cornudo.

Several white egrets flew by the boat and landed in the water nearby. The man rowed with his back to the island and the egrets stayed alongside the boat, hoping the man would throw them some bread. The man looked over his shoulder and saw El Lagarto Cornudo in the distance. The sun was hot and the man smiled as he rowed toward the island.

CHOCK-CHOCK

VINNIA SITS CROSS-LEGGED and spreads her dark blue skirt around her on the linoleum so she looks like an inverted morning glory. But it's too late: bright yellow pee has already escaped the protective cover of the pleated cotton and now flows uninhibited toward the base of the oven. Chock-Chock is too vigilant to miss this. He narrows his eyes and juts out his lower lip just like a soldier planning an attack.

"That's bad to pee yourself," says Chock-Chock.

Vinnia turns away and focuses on the gleaming chrome toaster. She pats her skirt flat against the floor and tries to hum a tune but it comes out like a moan.

"You heard me, Vinnia?" says Chock-Chock. "A bad thing to pee yourself. Very bad. Your mother will be very mean to you now."

Vinnia's head snaps forward. "Don't lie to me," she says. "You're a liar. And you're not even family, really."

Chock-Chock walks toward Vinnia and stops at the edge of her skirt. He holds his arms out from his body like a crucified Jesus, closes his eyes, and slowly steps onto Vinnia's skirt.

"Stop it!" she yells. Vinnia tries to stand but falls back down with a little grunt. "Let me up!" Vinnia tugs at her skirt but Chock-Chock weighs almost 120 pounds, much too much for a sixth grader, and twice what Vinnia weighs. Chock-Chock keeps inching forward, feeling his way blindly but purposefully.

"Stop it!" Vinnia now pleads. "You're hurting me!"

Chock-Chock stops, opens his eyes, and lowers his arms. "I'm stopping now," he says. "See? Stopped in my tracks just like that," and he snaps with the fingers of his left hand.

Vinnia wipes her cheek.

"Just like that," Chock-Chock says again with another snap. "On a dime."

Vinnia smiles. "Thank you," she mouths.

"What?" asks Chock-Chock.

"Thank you," she answers, this time in a louder voice.

Chock-Chock crosses his arms across his chest and breathes through his mouth as if he's winded. "You are very welcome, little lady," Chock-Chock says after a few seconds. He pulls his lips into a smile, revealing small white teeth and a pink tongue. "Yes, very welcome indeed."

A key slides and clicks at the front door. Chock-Chock steps back from Vinnia. The door opens to the accompaniment of a happy *Hello!* as Vinnia's mother struggles in with grocery bags.

"Hello, Tía," says Chock-Chock.

Mrs. Vargas smiles and walks toward the kitchen.

"Look what Vinnia did," he says, pointing down to the yellow streak of pee.

Mrs. Vargas puts her packages down on the counter. A box of raisins falls out and bounces into the almost-empty sink.

"Oh, Vinnia," she says to her daughter. "Vinnia, Vinnia, Vinnia, what are we going to do with you?"

Chock-Chock smiles and catches Vinnia's eye. He nods just a little. Vinnia snorts. "Sorry, Mamá," she says, keeping her eyes on Chock-Chock. "Sorry."

"You're too old for this," says Mrs. Vargas as she reaches for the roll of paper towels. "Too old, mija, too old."

Chock-Chock says, "I can help."

"You're such a little gentleman, Carlos," says Mrs. Vargas.

Vinnia quickly stands, startling the others. "But Chock-Chock was mean!"

"Don't call him that!" says Mrs. Vargas. "It's an ugly name. Carlos is who he is. Not Chock-Chock. Why do you call him that?"

Vinnia looks at her feet.

Mrs. Vargas turns to Chock-Chock and coos, "Carlos, sweetie, let me go change and if you can start cleaning, that would be a huge help to me." She hands him the paper towels and tells Vinnia not to move until she comes back. Vinnia nods and her mother leaves.

When they hear the bedroom door click closed, Vinnia leans into Chock-Chock. "Clean my pee," she whispers. "Clean it, Chock-Chock."

Chock-Chock stops moving, doesn't know what to say. Vinnia leans closer. "Clean it," she says in a hiss.

Chock-Chock steps back. Looks around. His mind goes blank. He hears Mrs. Vargas in her bedroom humming like she's not mad at Vinnia anymore. Vinnia laughs. Chock-Chock walks to the sink, wets the paper towels, kneels by the pee. He wipes at the puddle near Vinnia's shoes. Then he stops suddenly and looks up at Vinnia. She stares down at him, smiling. "Clean it," she almost sings. "Clean it now."

VINNIA SMELLS LIKE SOAP and her hair glistens wet from the bath. She tries to keep up with Chock-Chock as they head to the Sav-on Drugs. Chock-Chock clutches a $5 bill in his left hand.

"Slow down!" says Vinnia.

Chock-Chock glances over his shoulder but doesn't slow down. Vinnia looks so clean now in a crisp white Hello Kitty blouse, red shorts, white Keds. No smell of pee. He turns ahead again and squints so that he can see the big Sav-on sign. And then he hears it for the first time: "Vaya a casa."

Chock-Chock stops and lets Vinnia catch up.

"What?" he asks.

"I said you shouldn't walk so fast!" Vinnia's upper lip shines with perspiration. "My legs aren't as long as yours!"

"No," says Chock-Chock. "That other thing you said."

Vinnia wipes her lip with the back of her hand. "That's what I said! To wait!"

Chock-Chock lets out a whistle from his narrow nostrils and starts his trek again to the store. This time he walks slowly enough for Vinnia to keep up.

"Sorry I said you weren't really family," says Vinnia, trying to get Chock-Chock to say something.

"Yeah," he says.

"I mean, you *are* adopted. That's no secret."

Chock-Chock grunts.

"And even if you weren't," reasons Vinnia, "we would only be cousins. And besides, it's not my fault your mother is sick."

"Vaya a casa," the voice says again. This time Chock-Chock knows it's not Vinnia. The glass doors of Sav-on are so close that he can feel the air-conditioned air pour out when an old man leaves the store. But it's not the old man talking. The voice sounds soft, like a woman's. Chock-Chock hands Vinnia the $5 bill. "Go in and get the Cokes. I'll wait here."

Vinnia's eyes widen with excitement. "Yes!" she squeals as she snatches the money and runs into the store.

Now Chock-Chock can look around to find out who's talking to him. He narrows his eyes, wrinkles his nose, and slowly scans the perimeter of the parking lot, beginning with Ralphs at the left, then All-American Karate Studio, Pizza Hut, Alfonso's Chiropractic, Dollar Tree, and finally Sav-on. "Come out," says Chock-Chock. "I know you're around here somewhere."

But there's no answer. He notices Vinnia waiting in line struggling with a six-pack of Coke. Chock-Chock figures he should help his cousin but then he notices a woman in the shadows of the purified water machine near the store's entrance.

"Vaya a casa," says the woman.

Chock-Chock shades his eyes so he can see her better. She reminds him of his mother, who has been sleeping for almost two months at a hospital in El Paso. They called the sleep something else but he can't remember what. The woman smiles and motions gently, slowly with her hand for Chock-Chock to approach. He smiles back at her and takes a step forward but stops. She isn't pretty but the face is kind and brown like his mother's. A floppy straw hat almost hides the woman's dark eyes. She gestures again. Chock-Chock takes two more steps and stops. He notices for the first time that the woman hugs crutches under her arms and only one leg peeks out from under her white cotton skirt. A too-large man's shirt—blue like the sky—hangs on her thin frame and billows where she has tucked it in carefully at her waist.

"What are you doing?"

Chock-Chock's head swivels in response to Vinnia's voice.

"Nothing," he says trying to sound bored.

"Well, I got the Cokes!" she says triumphantly.

"Good. Give me the change."

Vinnia hands over two balled-up $1 bills and a few coins. "Let's go home," she chirps. "It's hot!"

Chock-Chock shoves the money into his pants' pocket and takes the Cokes from Vinnia. As they start to leave, Chock-Chock turns to see the woman again. The sun is bright and he squints. He's not certain if she's still standing by the water machine.

"Hurry!" says Vinnia. "The sun is burning me!"

"Okay," says Chock-Chock. "Okay."

CHOCK-CHOCK PULLS the blanket up close to his chin and tries to get comfortable on the sofa. He misses his bed back in El Paso but his aunt is nice and the sofa is the best she can do. His eyes are now used to the dark so he can discern the china cabinet across the room. It's filled not with china but with Mexican dolls made of brightly painted papier-mâché. He can make out the fat lady on the horse, the group of mariachis that are really grinning skeletons in costume, several doves, the Virgin of Guadalupe. There are others hidden in the shadows but he knows they're there: dancing dogs, a beautiful mermaid, a bloody heart, a smiling devil, a dappled tortoise, a long-tailed cat.

Chock-Chock's eyelids flutter and he yawns. He tries to remember how his mother smells but he can't. His mind wanders to the woman on crutches. How did he hear her from so far? Why did she keep telling him to go home? And which home? El Paso? Here with his aunt and cousin? Chock-Chock shifts to his side as his questions keep running through his mind: How did she lose her leg? Did she have a son? Why didn't Vinnia see her?

And then it comes to him like it should have long ago. The woman was magic and only he could see and hear her. Chock-Chock remembers stories about such magical people but he thought they only lived in Mexico. Maybe she made a special trip just for him because he needed help. The woman's soft words go round and round the boy's head. He listens to his breathing grow heavier and he feels safe and warm. Chock-Chock's last thought before he falls asleep are the words *Vaya a casa*. The words are soft and round and dependable. And they come from a magical woman who traveled very far just to speak to this special boy.

THE NEXT DAY Chock-Chock goes to Mass with his aunt and Vinnia. But the priest's words drift in and out as the boy thinks about the woman at Sav-on. His aunt mistakes Chock-Chock's absorption for piety and she reaches over to pat him softly on the shoulder. She smiles at him and he offers a smile back. She leans past Vinnia and whispers, "Are you praying for your mother?"

"Yes," he mouths.

But it's a lie. All he can think about is getting back to the store to hear what the woman has to say to him. And he has his chance: his aunt wants a copy of the Sunday *Times* and they sell it at the Sav-on. She says he can go on his own after he changes out of his good clothes. Vinnia doesn't want to go. That's good, thinks Chock-Chock. That's good. I can see her alone.

CHOCK-CHOCK FEELS liberated from the scratchy, starched church clothes. His feet almost bounce in his New Balance shoes. His elbows, knees, and neck rejoice in freedom as he heads toward the Sav-on. What will she say to him today? More advice? Will she explain what she meant when she told him to go home? And then he sees her! Right by the purified water machine, just like yesterday. And she wears the same hat, shirt, and skirt. Her lips move but Chock-Chock can't hear anything yet. He squints and then quickens his pace. The woman sees him and smiles through whatever words she's uttering. Chock-Chock is no more than twenty yards away.

The store's automatic doors suddenly slide open and a man wearing a Sav-on vest walks to the water machine. Chock-Chock stops and waits, hoping the man will walk past the woman. But he doesn't. He goes up to the woman, places his hands on his small hips, and says something to her. The woman stops smiling, stops talking. Her eyes lower and she shakes her head. The man keeps on talking, and now he's pointing at a large bundle on the ground that Chock-Chock has not noticed until now. This can't be good, the boy thinks. But I'll wait. The man will get tired of bothering the woman and then I'll get my chance to hear what she has to say.

But the man does not get tired. In fact, he seems energized the more he talks. He raises his voice and starts to yell something at the woman. The words are not nice and Chock-Chock doesn't know what to do. The woman starts to shake and then the man does something that makes the boy jump: he looks to the left and then to the right. No one is around other than the boy but the man doesn't look behind him so he doesn't know Chock-Chock stands there. Then he kicks the woman's left crutch and she falls to the ground, quietly, in slow motion. The straw hat falls off and bounces on the cement, revealing the woman's black shaggy hair.

Chock-Chock wants to help but he doesn't move. He can't. The woman hangs her head as the man turns on his heel and goes back into the store. She sobs and shakes. And then she stops and looks up. Her eyes are sharp and dark. Chock-Chock can't move his eyes from hers. The woman wipes her nose with the back of her hand. And then she speaks. And this time Chock-Chock can hear the words. She says them slowly. And then she repeats them. She speaks them to him. The words are different from yesterday. But the words are meant for the boy. He listens to them and he understands what they mean. His face burns, not from the sun but from shame. Chock-Chock turns from the woman and starts to walk. And the walk becomes a trot. In seconds, the trot becomes a full run. And he runs faster with each step. Faster away from the woman. Down the street, as the woman's words echo in his ears. Loud and clear. A special message. Just for him.

THE PLUMED SERPENT OF LOS ANGELES

I KNOW YOUR PARENTS, being good Mexicans, taught you that although Columbus came from Italy, the Spanish crown commissioned his voyage to El Nuevo Mundo, and so his three ships sailed under a Spanish flag. Then, a bit later, Spanish conquistadors and missionaries with names like Hernando Cortés and Friar Bartolomé de las Casas and Álvar Núñez Cabeza de Vaca came and, as that son of a bitch Cromwell did to the Irish, they liberated the native people from their "barbarian" pagan beliefs and gave them Catholicism. Or so the Spanish conquistadors and missionaries thought. For, as we say in Spanish: "La zorra mudará los dientes mas no las mientes." A fox might lose its teeth, but not its nature. In other words, although the Spanish may have banished the old Aztec gods so that the people had to worship in churches, they forgot to ask the gods if they wanted to leave. Therefore, because the Spanish forgot their manners, the old Aztec gods hung around and did what they could to make mischief in the lives of the Mestizos—the new people of mixed Spanish and Indian blood—so that they would never forget who were the true ruling powers of the land.

The same is true in Ireland: the ancient gods still rumble through the night or pop up on a spring morning and cause mischief on that beautiful green island. I know this because, believe it or not, I have traveled throughout Ireland. When I was much younger, I hitchhiked through most of that wonderful island (I stayed in the Republic of Ireland because I was too nervous to deal with the shooting in Northern Ireland!), and on more than one occasion I saw the mischief of the old Celtic gods. Little things, sometimes. Like when I was having a beer—a nice pint of

Guinness—at a pub in Galway on the western coast and I looked up at the wall by the dartboard and saw a painting. It was a typical painting of Ireland's patron saints: John Fitzgerald Kennedy, his brother Robert, and the pope. Well, just as I was staring at the painting, admiring its workmanship, in a blink, the painting changed! Now, instead of John Fitzgerald Kennedy, his brother Robert, and the pope, I saw, clear as day, John Fitzgerald Kennedy, his brother Robert, and *Muhammad Ali!* The greatest boxer who ever entered a ring! Float like a mariposa, sting like an abeja! I looked around the pub but no one else was looking and I wanted to yell, "¡Chingao!" but I just stood there, mouth agape like a pinche pendejo, clenching my pint of Guinness. But there he was, clear as an Arizona morning, Muhammad Ali, the former Mr. Cassius Marcellas Clay, smiling that little sly smile of his and looking at me with that twinkle in his eyes that he used to have—before he got sick and started shaking—you know, when he used to appear on *The Mike Douglas Show* and tease him something bad because it looked like he didn't know how to act around Black folk. That magical transformation of the painting on that pub's wall in Galway—that, mis amigos, was the work of a pinche Irish god!

Well, the old Aztec gods are just as bad. No, worse! ¡Ay Dios mío! Don't get me wrong. They won't kill or anything. But their idea of a joke can sometimes include a little physical and emotional pain. And they don't care who their next victim is. So, when the Spanish came the old gods went underground and hid during the daylight, but when it got dark they came back up to play their tricks on the Mestizos and Indians. And this is where my story begins: the most pissed-off Aztec god was, who else? Quetzalcoatl. Just like Ali, he was simply the greatest, and he ruled the Aztecs and the Toltecs with an iron fist. His fame continued even into the twentieth century when D. H. Lawrence—one of my favorite writers; you know, he's buried in Taos, New Mexico—wrote a novel and called it *Quetzalcoatl.* But his publishers were worried that with such a strange title the book wouldn't sell, so they changed it to *The Plumed Serpent.* Because that's what Quetzalcoatl was: a snake with many beautiful feathers surrounding his face. Few would condemn me for saying that Quetzalcoatl was probably the greatest god the Americas have ever known.

Now, Quetzi—as his friends called him because, let's face it, even for gods, "Quetzalcoatl" is quite a mouthful—Quetzi was a grouchy son of a bitch because, well, you would be too if you were a great god and then the Spanish tell your people to worship Jesus Christ and they do—can you believe it!—they do. This Jesus, fumed Quetzi, doesn't require human sacrifices! Hell, he let *himself* be sacrificed! What kind of god does that? And then, to top it off, other people, pale people, come and take over the land you once ruled.

Now, most of the other Aztec gods took on human form—the way you would if you were in their position. Gods with names like Huitzilopochtli, Chalchihuitlicue, and Tlacahuepan became José, María, and Hernán. They looked at the human population and found the best-looking examples of humanity that they could. Sometimes they mixed and matched different features. Then they transmuted into these beautiful hombres y damas! The best-looking faces and legs and arms and man-oh-Manischewitz! They were the loveliest Mexicans you ever saw, with skin as smooth and brown as polished Indian pottery, with raven-black hair that glistened in the sun! And at night—only at night, well after midnight—they changed back into their original forms and flew through Mexico playing their evil tricks on the poor, unsuspecting, Jesus-worshipping Mestizos and Indians.

But Quetzi was so angry that he left Tenochtitlán—you know, Mexico City—and wandered without purpose for almost three hundred years. He eventually headed north until he found a little one-room hut far from his home in a place that would eventually be called El Pueblo de Nuestra Señora la Reina de los Ángeles de la Porciúncula, now known simply as Los Angeles. You see, he had suffered greatly once before and this latest insult was too much to bear. It is a painful and embarrassing story, but you must know it to understand why Quetzi could not live in his home of Tenochtitlán anymore. Centuries before the Spanish came, the god Tezcatlipoca disguised himself as a great hairy spider and offered Quetzi his very first taste of pulque, which—as I'm sure you know—is more dangerous than tequila because it goes down so easily. Oh! That shit will get you borracho! And Quetzi loved the feeling he got from the pulque and drank so much that, in a drunken heat, he had his way with his sister, Quetzalpetlatl!

The *shame* of it! So Quetzi banished himself and wandered the land for many generations.

But this Spanish conquest thing, that was too much for Quetzi to stomach. So, as I said, Quetzi left Tenochtitlán and eventually ended up in old Los Angeles living in a little adobe hut. And in his disgust, instead of choosing a beautiful body to transmute into, Quetzi borrowed the looks of the first person he saw after the Spanish banned the Aztec religion. Unfortunately, the first person he laid eyes on was a broken-down old borrachín who was bald as a mango with a large pot of a belly that hung below his belt. But Quetzi's anger blinded him so that he didn't care.

One day poor old Quetzi left his little adobe to look for something to eat. Yes, he now suffered from hunger of the human type. So he headed to the little hut owned by this vieja, an old Indian woman who bartered with anyone who wanted good Mexican comida and who had something she might want. But as he scrambled down some rocks to avoid taking the long way on the foot-worn dirt road, the stupid Aztec god tripped on his own feet and landed with a *thump!* right in the scrubby bushes. You see, the drunkard that Quetzi had turned into had these goddamn big Godzilla-like feet, so it was easy to trip just walking.

As he lay there with a spinning head, Quetzi noticed a woman standing over him. A beautiful woman! And for a moment his bitterness and grouchiness melted away and he felt a little joy in his rock of a heart.

"Quetzalcoatl?" the woman said.

¡Híjole! Quetzi thought. This beautiful human knows my name!

"Quetzalcoatl?" the woman said again, this time with urgency in her voice. Before he could answer, the woman went on, "We need you. We need you now!"

"Who?" said Quetzi rubbing his nalgas as he stood up with the help of the beautiful woman.

"We do. The old Aztec gods. We need you!"

And at that moment Quetzi recognized the beautiful woman's eyes. The rest of her face he did not know, but he knew the eyes of his sister, Quetzalpetlatl, the one whom he had disgraced so many years before. But he grew angry and growled, "Get away from me, puta!" He dusted himself off and carried on down the main dirt road.

But she followed him. "Please, O great Quetzalcoatl! Our way of life is being threatened and we need all the power of the old days to survive, to win! Please don't run from me!" The beautiful woman had great tears falling from her eyes as she almost ran by Quetzi's side.

Quetzi stopped abruptly and turned to the beautiful woman. His face burned a deep red and he sputtered, "Where were my compañeros and compañeras when the Spanish came to banish us? Huh? Where?"

Quetzalpetlatl looked down, ashamed.

Quetzi continued: "You did not fight then, did you? I asked you all to fight but you weaklings just hid and let Jesus and Mary and Joseph and all those pinches santos replace us! You cowards! Leave me be! Do I look like a pendejo to you?" And with that, Quetzi started to walk on with a quick gait, kicking up dust and rocks.

Quetzalpetlatl thought for a moment and then, in a panic, she said, "If we win, you can rule all of us again! I promise!"

And this, my friends, made Quetzi stop and think. Oh, to be the highest god again! Could he even remember how it felt? Quetzi looked out to the clear Los Angeles sky. He trained his eyes on a hawk circling in the eastern horizon.

Quetzalpetlatl saw that her brother was considering the possibilities. So, to up the ante, she added, "And I will forgive you, and you will no longer carry shame in your heart."

Oh, joy! thought Quetzi. Can I have it all again? Is it possible? But it has to be done the right way. So Quetzi said, "Let's go and get some food, mi hermana, and talk about what is needed."

They made their way to the little hut owned by the old Indian woman to get something to eat. Quetzi's sister offered the vieja beautiful stones and, in exchange, received two wooden platters of pollo in a thick mole sauce and a large steaming pile of corn tortillas wrapped in a moist towel. They then found a nice place to sit under a large pine tree so that Quetzi could learn what was afoot.

Quetzi's sister explained that the Christian god of evil, Satan, had decided to set up shop in various cities and towns of the Americas. Satan, being legion, sent parts of himself throughout the land to lay the foundation for a revolution to displace Jesus and rule the human race. But in order to topple Christianity, he also had to purge the land of the Aztec gods. He wanted a clean slate, a complete coup. And the first place Satan was going to go was El Pueblo de Nuestra Señora la Reina de los Ángeles de la Porciúncula. You see, Satan appreciated irony, and what better place to begin than a pueblo named after Jesus's mother? As I told you, Satan is legion, so he sent the female part of himself, La Diabla, to plan the war against the old Aztec gods. La Diabla found a little cave in Malibu by the ocean and there she plotted.

"So," said Quetzi as he wiped mole from his round face with his already filthy sleeve, "all we have to do is kill La Diabla. Right?"

His sister thought for a moment and then said, "No, La Diabla cannot be killed. But she can be weakened. She can be taught a lesson. La Diabla can be seduced." As she said this last thing, she looked down and blushed a dark red-brown.

"Ah," said Quetzi, purposely ignoring his sister's embarrassment. "We must be clever." And then he laughed. "Why don't we use that pulque trick Tezcatlipoca pulled on me all those years ago and get La Diabla muy borracha!" Quetzi let out a big laugh and then a loud fart—not caring because, after all, he had lived as an anchorite in his little hut for so long that his manners were atrocious.

"Perhaps," said Quetzalpetlatl, covering her nose as nonchalantly as possible. "But we must get you in shape first."

Quetzi looked down at himself and saw what she meant. He had chosen a poor example of a human form. But it was good to feel needed again and he said, "I'll do whatever you want me to do!"

So it began on that day. Quetzalpetlatl became her brother's own personal trainer. For two months she made Quetzi run and eat small meals and lift large stones in the heat of the desert day and stop drinking booze. And at the end of two months, Quetzi's belly had become flat and strong, his face burned a nice healthy brown, and his arms and legs developed bands of pulsating muscles. And, my friends, while the two were getting Quetzi in shape, they started to develop a plan, step by step, always keeping in mind La Diabla's psychology.

In getting Quetzi in shape, his sister couldn't do anything

about his bald head—he was a total pelón! But Quetzi allowed his beard to grow and his sister then trimmed it into a fine mustache and goatee. Quetzalpetlatl helped her brother find beautiful clothes to show off his new physique. She stood him in front of a mirror in his little hut and they both admired his new physical power. Poor Quetzalpetlatl felt ashamed because she admired her brother in all his manliness, but she shook herself from within and said, "You are now ready to seduce La Diabla and save us!"

As I've told you, La Diabla could not be killed but her power could be limited, tied in knots. And she loved bargains. It's funny. La Diabla is vicious and evil but she always keeps a bargain. The trick, though, is to lure her into a bargain that will backfire, and to do that you have to rely on her own failing: her pride. Remember, pride led Satan to be cast from heaven in the first place. And as they say in America, you can't teach an old dog new tricks! So they hatched a plan whereby Quetzi would challenge La Diabla to a duel of sorts. A duel of gods. If La Diabla won, the Aztec gods would leave this world without protest. But if Quetzi prevailed, La Diabla would leave the Americas forever and confine her playground to the rest of the world.

But first Quetzi had to go to Malibu where La Diabla lived. His sister bargained for a great stallion and a fine saddle and Quetzi prepared for his twenty-six-mile trek to the coast. When all was prepared, Quetzalpetlatl helped Quetzi mount the magnificent horse. She said, "I love you, my brother."

"And I you," said Quetzi. He felt proud as he dug his spurs into the horse and headed west.

Now, the Chumash Indians still lived by the beach, they called Umalido, meaning "where the surf is loud," which eventually became Malibu. As Quetzi came within a few miles of La Diabla's cave, the Chumash looked up from their daily lives and stared in amazement at the striking figure cut by the newly minted hero-to-be. As he neared La Diabla's home, Quetzi's nostrils filled with the stench of evil and his horse became skittish.

"There, there, my beauty," said Quetzi soothingly as he patted his horse's muscular neck. "All will be well." The horse slowly calmed and continued its march toward the profane shelter. When they reached the mouth of the cave, Quetzi could see nothing but black, so he dismounted, pulled a lantern from the side of his saddle, and lit it. Slowly, wary of the rocky ground, Quetzi entered the cave. He walked, one foot gently placed in front of the other, for almost an hour. What the hell am I doing? he thought. What will become of me? The darkness of the cave almost swallowed the flickering light of the lantern. What will become of me?

Suddenly Quetzi stopped short with a crunch of gravel under his shining boots. He sensed a presence, though no figure appeared.

"What took you so long?" said an unseen woman.

The skin on Quetzi's bald head danced with fear. He sucked in as much air as possible and said, "It is I, the great Quetzalcoatl! Come out so that I may see you, Diabla!" But only silence answered him. Oh, poor Quetzi! What had he gotten himself into? As no response came, he continued to walk deeper into the cave. After about ten minutes he stopped and called out again, "It is I, the great Quetzalcoatl! Come out so that I may see you, Diabla!"

And this time he got his wish. Without a sound, La Diabla appeared before Quetzi. I cannot describe her other than to say that Quetzi's eyes had never rested upon a creature more beautiful and seductive. He could not speak.

"Oh, great Quetzalcoatl, please, come and share a drink with me. I am honored to be in the presence of such a great god." With that, a grand oak table appeared before Quetzi. The table groaned with great bottles of pulque, large baskets of fruit, a roast pig, and many other delicacies. Quetzi's eyes focused on the pulque and he grew frightened as he remembered how he was made a fool of by the god Tezcatlipoca who, disguised as a spider, had offered Quetzi his very first taste of alcohol. But his mouth watered as he remembered the feel of booze in his mouth and the wonderful burning sensation it made as it flowed down his throat and into his belly. Quetzi shook his head and closed his eyes for a moment to clear his mind of all temptation.

"No," said Quetzi, knowing that the more he resisted, the more La Diabla would push him to drink. "I am here to offer you a bargain."

"No," said La Diabla. "You must accept my hospitality and only then will I hear you out."

So they sat down, Quetzi at one end of the table and La Diabla at the other. I am still a great god, he assured himself. I can hold my liquor. I will not fail to present my bargain. And so they ate and drank in silence, each keeping sharp eyes on the other. Finally, after an hour of this, La Diabla said, "So what is the purpose of this visit?" As she said this, she could see that Quetzi was getting loose with the pulque. La Diabla smiled a noxious smile and waited for a response.

That poor son of a bitch Quetzi! He hadn't had a drink in two months and now the pulque softened his resolve and made him think corrupt thoughts as his eyes perused La Diabla's unblemished brown skin and enticing body. He shook his head again and reminded himself of his noble mission. Quetzi cleared his throat of the phlegm that pulque tends to invite to most men's throats and said, "No, I'd rather hear from you first."

La Diabla continued to smile. "Well, O magnificent Quetzalcoatl, you no doubt have heard of my plan to rid this world of the old gods. Otherwise why would you be here?"

"Go on," he said.

La Diabla leaned forward and began, "I am sickened by the puny efforts of your hermanos and hermanas to maintain a presence in this land. They are beyond irrelevant and they do nothing more than cause a low level of nausea to permeate my very essence."

"If we are so little, why do you care?" Quetzi thought he had made a good point with this question and he rocked his head back and forth to show that he was still in command.

La Diabla leaned even closer to Quetzi and the oak table creaked. She hissed, "Because as long as the Mestizos and Indians know you're still here—and they do know because of the stupid pranks you fallen gods do at night—I cannot fully rule."

Good answer, thought Quetzi. As La Diabla spoke, Quetzi allowed his eyes to drink further of her beauty. His heart beat strong within his chest and his groin flushed with the warmth of lecherous blood. What should he do? Could he forsake his fellow gods and cut a bargain to save himself and perhaps bring him a little closer to this beautiful creature? He kept still and let La Diabla continue.

"So, great Quetzalcoatl, I offer you a bargain: do not stand in my way and in exchange you may have a role under my reign."

Quetzi thought for a moment. Since the conquistadors had come and banished the Aztec gods, he had lived less than a life. If he rejected La Diabla's offer and followed through with his plan to help his brothers and sisters, maybe he could rule again. And didn't he owe it to his sister after he had defiled her long ago? But what if he failed? This powerful dark deity of Christianity could destroy him. If he aligned himself with her, maybe he could save himself and get a little power to enjoy life again! Quetzi looked into La Diabla's eyes. He could lose himself in those eyes! Screw the others! What had they ever done for him? They'd never even visited him before this whole mess started. Screw them and his sister!

"I accept your bargain!" And he drank another large goblet of pulque.

La Diabla laughed, walked over to Quetzi, and said, "Let us go to the outside world and start!"

So they left the cave, arm in arm, and went to the shore, where they stood facing east. The smogless, late-summer sky gleamed a blue that no longer exists and cool wind from the ocean blew hard and clean. La Diabla touched Quetzi's sleeve and within a breath, they were standing in the Santa Ana Canyon by the northeastern desert. She lifted her hands to her mouth and screamed a mute scream and, at that very second, Quetzi saw the true power of this god. La Diabla emitted a hot and relentless wind that began as a mere breeze but then erupted into a torrent of withering heat. La Diabla blew and blew and blew for precisely three hours and Quetzi stood there without the power to move, for he was in awe.

The too-beautiful Mexicans who were once great Aztec gods could not withstand La Diabla's wind. They withered and eventually their human forms died within those three hours. Their souls rose up and went to a place beyond the moon far from their earthly home. La Diabla was now supreme!

La Diabla kept her bargain with our friend Quetzi. She let him live different lives throughout the centuries to bring his own brand of misery to the human race. He began as a banker, then became a governor, a lawyer, a movie producer, an editor, a mass murderer, a literary agent, a plumber—and right now, as I speak, he is the owner of a major league baseball team. However, Quetzi never got very close to La Diabla. But his dating life was full and so far Quetzi has walked down the aisle at least a dozen times.

And our friend La Diabla is doing her best to strangle our world in her own way. But because of her paranoia, and despite killing all the old gods except Quetzi, she still blows the Santa Ana winds—the devil winds, as we call them today—to make certain that the former great gods of the Aztecs will never rise again.

Is there a moral to this story? No, not really. But there is an old Mexican dicho that applies: "Si se muere el perro, se acaba la rabia." If the dog dies, the rabies will be gone. But, mis amigos, I promise you this: the dog is not dead. She is alive and well in a little town called El Pueblo de Nuestra Señora la Reina de los Ángeles de la Porciúncula.

LA QUEENIE

My grandfather, Daniel "Danny" Brennan, spent the first sixteen years of his life hemmed in by what he called that "goddamn southern man's world." Gramps, even as a teenager, couldn't stomach pre-civil rights Mississippi and left home as soon as he was old enough to earn a real wage. He still likes to tell me how one Saturday morning, before his parents and younger brothers woke, he packed a patched-together cardboard suitcase with a few pieces of clothing, gathered up $16.25 from a sock he had tucked away under his mattress—money carefully saved working for two years as a soda jerk in town—and left Biloxi forever.

Mississippi. The word still emanates from Gramps's mouth with disgust. Why his father, Sean Brennan, decided to leave Ireland and settle with his new wife in Biloxi never made any sense to Gramps. After all, what was wrong with Chicago, New York, Boston, or even the West Coast for a good Irish family? But Sean Brennan was, by all accounts, a bit off. He thought he could make his fortune selling men's suits in Biloxi. He said the Irish had helped settle the place a couple of hundred years back so the Brennans should fit right in. But a couple of hundred years in a place could change a people. Those old Irish families now resembled all the other good southern clans while the newly arrived Brennans did not. The fresh-off-the-boat Irish immigrants were just one step above Jews and Blacks as far as the town was concerned. This simple fact did not help the men's suit business. Even with the establishment of Kessler Air Force Base in 1941, Sean Brennan couldn't sell enough to make a decent living. Suffice it to say that when Gramps slipped out that morning, his father had little to show for his efforts other than an impossible mortgage on a small house, a ridiculous five-year lease for a less-than-elegant storefront, four growing sons, and one despondent wife. It was probably a relief that he had one fewer mouth to feed.

So Danny Brennan, in glorious 1948, hitchhiked to sun-soaked Los Angeles to make his life among the movie stars, palm trees, and ethnically diverse population. Houses were going up like crazy to make room for the returning G.I.s. Culver City, Canoga Park, North Hollywood, everywhere. Gramps found work pretty fast in construction, helping to bring these new neighborhoods to life. Danny Brennan looked much older than he was, and at six foot one, with an easy smile, he found steady work without too much trouble. He eventually became a foreman with Boyle Construction, the youngest man on the payroll. James Boyle was an Irishman too, and he kind of saw himself in Gramps. But then it was easy to like Danny Brennan. Sure, everyone teased this big Irish boy who spoke like a southern gentleman. But he laughed at each joke and made certain he sounded more southern than before.

That charm held him in good stead. It even landed him a date with James Boyle's niece, Katherine Elizabeth Boyle, who worked as the receptionist for her uncle's business. Katie's father had been an officer in the army but he didn't make it back from the war. And her mother died of breast cancer a year later. Boyle and his wife took Katie in without a moment's hesitation. Anyway, after a half dozen dates, and with James Boyle's blessing, Danny and Katie got engaged in 1951. But then the Korean conflict intervened and Gramps enlisted with the Marines rather than be drafted. He came back in one piece two years later to a relieved, steadfast Katie. They married on February 6, 1954, in a fine Roman Catholic ceremony at St. Agnes Church on Vermont near Adams, the Reverend Joseph T. G. Ryan officiating. That church still bustles with parishioners in the new structure built in the 1960s, but most of the masses are now held in Spanish, with one in Korean. It's a few blocks from USC, where I went to law school. Gramps and Grammy now attend Corpus Christi in Pacific Palisades. A really rich parish. Anyway, Gramps did pretty well for himself at Boyle Construction. James Boyle happily made him a full partner a few years after Gramps married Grammy. And Gramps eventually took over day-to-day operations and tripled the company's size by implementing modern business theory mixed in with a lot of sweat and common sense.

About ten years ago Gramps sold Boyle & Brennan Construction for more than I even want to think about. At first I thought it was crazy to sell, but in the end it made perfect sense even to my teenage logic. You see, Gramps and Grammy could only have one child, my mother, Anne. And there was no way Mom was going to run a construction company. She had other plans, like majoring in biology and then going on to medical school. Which she did. Mom's in obstetrics at Cedars-Sinai. And Dad practiced with the district attorney's office for about fifteen years before running for an open seat on the Superior Court, which he won pretty easily four years ago when I started law school. They have nothing against the building industry. They just had other interests.

How all this relates to my dating La Queenie will make sense in a moment. Particularly with respect to Gramps. You see, I'm a true believer in telling the whole story, not just the bits and pieces that suit me. It's the lawyer in me. So be patient with my storytelling. Let me begin at the beginning. If you don't let me, you won't get the whole picture and you'll walk away from all this feeling a little uncertain and very confused. And you certainly won't understand La Queenie and what she did that rainy Monday morning four years ago.

It began on a Sunday. I was a first-year law student at USC. God, that was an exciting time. Dad just about floated above the clouds with joy at my decision to go to law school. And the fact that his alma mater accepted me, well, I don't think he could have been prouder. And Mom was pleased that I was able to maintain both my Catholicism and liberal politics, just as she had. Even when she couldn't bear sermons that dwelt too heavily on the abortion issue, Mom attained some kind of sublime peace when she attended Mass. And so did I when I started law school. But I didn't really like going to Mass at Our Savior Catholic Center on University Avenue. I had more than my fill of other students during the week and I wanted to be out with regular people. You see, my plan was to do something to help the world with my law degree. Maybe poverty law or perhaps the public defender's office. So I decided that I might as well attend

Mass at St. Agnes, which was only a few blocks away from my little apartment and on the hallowed ground where Grammy and Gramps got married.

My Spanish was not too shabby after spending the last three summers before law school in Cuernavaca and taking Spanish all through high school and college. So going to Spanish Mass at St. Agnes was pretty cool, and it reminded me of my time in Mexico. I liked to attend the 5:00 service so that I could grab dinner afterward at this little Mexican place that served the best damned carnitas I ever tasted. And this was a great Mass to attend if you enjoyed people-watching. But you'd have to choose a good place to sit to take it all in. The back of the church was best for that. When I got there the last pew was usually empty. But a few minutes after the Mass started, the stragglers would shuffle in looking kind of embarrassed and trying not to be noticed by the priest. Which means they ended up with me. Because my white face was pretty rare in that church, these folks would usually do a double-take but then they'd nod, smile, and settle in without another acknowledgment of my being different. Eventually, after a few weeks, I recognized the stragglers and they got accustomed to seeing the lone, tall "gabacho."

One Sunday evening, about ten minutes into the Mass, I saw La Queenie for the first time. She came in later, even later than the stragglers, and stepped over everyone to get to the one small empty spot next to me. She panted heavily as if she'd been running. From the second she took her place until just before Communion, La Queenie kept her eyes on the altar, not the priest. And I kept my eyes on her. She was pretty, not beautiful, but something about her attracted me. La Queenie looked to be about twenty-five or thirty years old. She stood no more than five foot one or two. Her clothes were inappropriate for church: an oversized man's dress shirt tucked tight at the waist of dark-blue Dickies. La Queenie's outfit—if you could call it that—was clean but wrinkled, as if it'd been lying in a pile most of the day. She smelled of sweat and too much perfume. A battered pair of white Chuck Taylor high-tops encased her little feet. Maybe because I'm tall like Gramps, I've always gravitated to tall women. At least five seven. But at that moment, I imagined what it would be like to get into La Queenie's bed. Her white Oxford shirt accented both the deep brown of her neck and the brilliant blackness of her hair, which curled this way and that down to her shoulders. I imagined lying on a big bed with this tiny woman on top of me, arching her back, tossing her hair away from her face and then falling forward and encasing me in that black shroud of curls.

The more I stared at her, the more she seemed to concentrate on the altar. I wanted to get her to acknowledge my presence but I didn't want to be a jerk about it. It wasn't like I hadn't dated Mexican women before. But this one was different. My opportunity eventually came with the natural rhythm of the Mass. I don't know if you're Catholic, but just before Communion is served, the priest tells us to offer each other a sign of peace. When I was with Mom and Dad, this would include a hug and a kiss on the cheek. But here at St. Agnes, with folks I didn't really know, it meant a handshake, a nod, and a mumbled "La paz está con usted." So I turned to La Queenie, held out my hand, and offered an abbreviated "Paz." And what she did surprised me.

She took in a deep breath as if she were screwing up her resolve and turned to me, head-on. "My name is Reyna Escondida," she said in softly accented English, even though I had spoken in Spanish. She held out her hand and kept her eyes on mine. "But people call me La Queenie," she added.

I reached for her hand and grasped it. La Queenie flinched but then immediately smiled and tightened her own grip. Her little hand almost disappeared in my oversized paw.

"I'm Bobby," I said. "But people don't call me anything else."

"Hello, plain, simple Bobby."

I started to laugh but remembered that we were in church. La Queenie held my hand for several seconds longer than you should with a stranger. For some reason my touch seemed to calm her. She eventually pulled her hand away and turned her gaze back to the altar. La Queenie seemed to be mouthing something, not to me, but to whatever kept her eyes locked at this spot just below the huge crucifix and to the left, by the wooden throne-like chairs where the priest and attendants would sit at several points during the Mass.

After everyone finished giving the sign of peace, it was time to receive Holy Communion. The ushers came to each end of the pews, beginning with the ones up front. They'd nod to let each row know when they could join the Communion line at the edge of the altar. When an usher finally reached our pew, I tried to let La Queenie go first but she only shook her head and sat down. I didn't think twice about it then. Receiving Communion is a personal thing and sometimes when I haven't been to confession for a few weeks, I don't feel ready for it. But now I know why she didn't go that day.

After Mass we walked out of St. Agnes without saying a word. The parishioners slowly filed out, at first quietly. And then, as families and friends joined up in little huddles and the children were freed of the holy shackles of Mass, Spanish filled the air and laughter took the place of solemn prayer. This was my favorite part of attending Mass at St. Agnes. I miss it. Anyway, I think the only two people who weren't talking were me and La Queenie. We stood looking around, not quite sure what to do next. At least I didn't know.

"Did you drive?" she finally asked.

I turned to her. "No," I answered. "I live just a few blocks away."

"Why?"

"Not everyone in L.A. is afraid of walking."

La Queenie narrowed her eyes. "No," she said, looking a bit annoyed. "Why do you live around here?"

Before I could answer, the crowd started to react in a different way. I looked up to the church's front doors and saw that the priest had parked himself where he could meet and greet his flock. He wasn't the usual priest. His name was Padre Novas and he came from El Salvador. During his sermon he'd said that he'd be visiting for a couple of months and was already enjoying Los Angeles very much. He was pretty young, probably no older than thirty-five or so. He had a full head of black bushy hair with just a touch of gray at the temples. The female parishioners fawned over him and he seemed to enjoy the attention. Even the older women chatted him up. Watching this, I didn't notice at first that La Queenie had started walking down the street.

"This direction?" she asked, without turning around.

"No," I said. "This way."

She turned and walked past me. I had to trot to catch up.

"Let me make you dinner, just plain Bobby," she said.

"I don't have much in the fridge."

But I was more concerned about what my apartment looked like. I tried to remember if I had picked up my clothes from last night and if the toilet was clean. But no matter. La Queenie had her own plans for that night.

Even though I'm engaged now and truly love Brenda, that first night I spent with La Queenie will be with me forever. And we didn't even make love. In fact, we really didn't do much other than spend time together, barely talking. I did eventually explain that I attended law school nearby, hoping that would impress her. It didn't. She wanted to know more about my family and where they came from. So I ended up talking mostly about Gramps. La Queenie listened to the whole story about him running away from home and starting in L.A. from scratch.

"I think I'd like him," she said.

"He's getting up there in years, though."

"My father used to say: Viejo el aire y todavía sopla."

I laughed.

"Do you know what it means?"

My Spanish is pretty good and I like these old Mexican sayings. "Old is the wind and it still blows," I proudly announced.

La Queenie clapped. "¡Bravo!" she cheered.

After dinner I served up some Ben & Jerry's Cherry Garcia, the only really good thing I had on hand. La Queenie loved it. Actually, that doesn't quite describe her reaction to her first taste of the ice cream. She put a little on her tongue, closed her eyes, and went to a different world. I can't explain it otherwise. She let out a little moan when she swallowed and then her eyes popped open. "This is now my favorite," La Queenie announced.

I laughed.

"When we finish," she added, "I want to lie down over there and take a short nap." She tossed her head back in the direction of my big leather couch in what I called the living room. It was my best piece of furniture by far.

"Sure," I said, with less than gentlemanly thoughts running through my head.

"And you, just plain Bobby, you can sit next to me in that chair and read a law book."

Dreams of wild passion dashed. At least I had the Ben & Jerry's.

But that was fine. Because I had a feeling—eventually proven correct—that something would happen between me and La Queenie. Anyway, after another serving of ice cream, she put our bowls in the sink and let out a yawn. "Do you have a blanket?"

She was serious about that nap. I ran to the bedroom and grabbed a blanket and a fresh pillow from the closet. I came back to the kitchen but La Queenie was already curled up on the couch. As I approached, she put out her hands to receive the pillow, which she slid under her head. She smiled. I covered her carefully with the blanket and she closed her eyes. I grabbed my civil procedure book and settled into the chair next to her.

Within a few minutes little snores emanated from La Queenie. I felt good and just a bit proud of myself, as if I had taken in a stray kitten. I read a few pages, looking over to La Queenie every so often. Before too long I grew tired and dozed off too.

I woke with a start as the front door clicked closed. In La Queenie's place on the couch was the blanket, neatly folded, with the pillow placed carefully on top of it. I looked at my watch. Almost midnight. I sighed but felt good about the evening. It had been odd, nothing like any other time I'd spent with a woman. But that was okay. Then a wave of panic came over me. La Queenie had never given me her phone number or told me where she lived.

All through my classes the next day, I worried about how I could find her again. I even went to Monday night Mass hoping to find her. Padre Novas was there again but the crowd was light, which is pretty common for weekday services. It seemed that mostly the older folks prayed that often. But I had hoped that La Queenie would be an exception. I went to Mass each night that week looking for her. I got to recognize the regulars and they started acknowledging me. Even Padre Novas nodded and smiled at me right around Wednesday when I went up for Communion. But I didn't see her at any of these masses. It wasn't until Sunday that she appeared again. And again, La Queenie came in late, again looking wrinkled but wearing a different outfit. And yet again she didn't go up for Communion but focused on an invisible spot on the altar.

This time I had made certain that my apartment was clean and that my fridge and cupboards were filled with as many dinner options as I could dream up. La Queenie seemed pleased. She settled on spaghetti with a salad. And I had overstocked the freezer with six different kinds of Ben & Jerry's. But she went straight for the Cherry Garcia. I couldn't blame her for that. And afterward, instead of La Queenie taking a nap while I studied, she kissed me and led me to my bedroom.

This became our routine. I'd only see La Queenie on Sundays, at Mass, and then off to my apartment for dinner, dessert, and bed. She always waited for me to fall asleep before she snuck out. I tried to stay awake but never managed to, and La Queenie possessed a preternatural talent for disappearing when I was dead to the world. And during those five weeks I told her more about my life and family but she didn't tell me much about hers. It's not as if I didn't ask. She just found a way to answer without giving away much and then she'd change the subject. She never divulged her phone number or address or even what she did for a living. La Queenie evaded my queries so expertly that I didn't realize until much later that I knew virtually nothing about her.

On our fifth Sunday together, after dinner but before dessert, she made an announcement. "I must meet your grandfather."

I blinked. She hadn't met my parents yet. It wasn't as if I was hiding her or anything. My parents are cool with my dating women of different backgrounds. But at the time they'd wanted me to focus on law school so I'd been hesitant about mentioning her to them. And La Queenie had never asked to meet my parents. But now she wanted to meet Gramps. No one else. Just Gramps.

"Why him?"

"Because he's like me," La Queenie said very slowly, as if she wanted to be careful about how much she revealed. "He took a chance for a new life."

"And?"

She shifted in her chair, clearly not comfortable with my probing. But I persisted. "And what else?"

"And I think he's someone I can trust," she answered.

I didn't push her any further, though in retrospect I probably should have. Anyway, we planned a nice little dinner for the three of us at my place for the next Sunday after Mass.

Gramps had to fib a little to Grammy. He knew that I wanted to keep La Queenie a secret, at least for a while longer. He kind of found it exciting and quite flattering. "But do I have to call her 'La Queenie'?" asked Gramps when we spoke on the phone the day before our planned dinner date. "I mean, Bobby boy, 'Reyna' is so much prettier, don't you think?"

He was right, of course, but La Queenie had been so insistent about what I should call her that I never broached the subject again. "Gramps, you'd have to ask her."

He thought for a moment. I could hear him take a sip from his Saturday night treat of Jim Beam on the rocks. The ice cubes tinkled just a bit. "Why does she go by 'La Queenie'?" he finally asked.

"Her real name translates to 'queen,' so I guess that's where it comes from."

He took another sip of his drink. "Makes sense," he said. And then he surprised me: "Do you mind if I join you two for Mass before dinner?"

I didn't think that Gramps went to Mass much anymore. But what the hell, I thought. Why not? "Sure, Gramps, but you won't understand a word."

"Not to worry, Bobby boy," he laughed. "I think I'll know what's happening." And then another pause. Finally, he added: "How about I pick you up and then we'll swing by Reyna's place so we could get to Mass together?"

I hesitated. I didn't want Gramps to know that I had no idea where La Queenie lived or that I didn't even have her phone number. To me this wasn't odd but Gramps, he'd smell something fishy. I thought fast. "She said she had something to do before Mass and that she'd meet me there," I said, trying to sound nonchalant.

"Oh," said Gramps.

"Why don't you come by my place and we'll walk over to Mass? It's only a couple of blocks and I want you to see the neighborhood."

"Don't forget I got married at that church."

"But a new building went up after that," I reasoned. "And the area has changed a lot. Some people say not for the better, but I like it."

That seemed to assuage him. Anyway, the next evening Gramps showed up wearing a blue blazer, gray slacks, and a crisp dress shirt, the ensemble anchored by a brilliant red tie. He looked sharp. I wore my usual Levi's and a sweater over a white T-shirt. He shook his head and teased me and my generation for how we dressed, even for Mass. After an appropriately short tour of my tiny apartment, we headed over to the church. He looked around at the neighborhood shops and restaurants, grinning. "These folks knew where to settle when they left their countries," said Gramps. "Not like my da," he added.

When we approached St. Agnes, Gramps let out a sigh. I almost could hear his thoughts: things have changed so much over the years, from the church itself to the parishioners, with their dark skin and different language. I didn't see sadness in his face, just a wistfulness that must come with age. We walked up the steps and found a place in the back pew, even though Gramps had wanted to sit up front. When Mass started and La Queenie was nowhere to be found, Gramps grew impatient. He craned his neck to the left and right, searching for her, even though he didn't know what she looked like.

"Relax, Gramps," I whispered. "She always shows up around ten minutes late."

Gramps frowned at this bit of information. He thought lateness was a sign of disrespect. Luckily, La Queenie showed up at that moment. She had dressed up for the occasion in an outfit I had never seen before: a baby-blue silk blouse and a navy skirt. Simple, but it accentuated her petite figure and made my mind wander to our times in bed. I almost regretted that Gramps was there. I looked at him. His face had broken into a wide grin, his eyes crinkled up with delight. La Queenie gave him a big hug and he hugged back. She had enchanted Gramps in seconds. After settling in, we all turned our attention to the altar. La Queenie's smile fell from her face. She leaned into me. "Where's Padre Novas?" she asked in an almost panicked voice.

Sure enough, a different priest was up there where Novas had been these last six weeks. I shrugged. "He was only visiting," I ventured. "Maybe he went back to El Salvador."

Throughout Mass, La Queenie shifted and squirmed as if she wanted to make a break for it and flee the church. When it came time for Communion, she again stayed put while Gramps and I went up. Gramps found this odd—at least that's what his expression told me. La Queenie didn't calm down until Mass finished and we went out to the cool evening air. As we started our walk to my apartment, Gramps asked what was on our menu.

"Chilaquiles, nopales salad, and Ben & Jerry's," announced La Queenie.

"I understood only that last part," laughed Gramps.

"You'll love the rest," I said. "And it's a fast meal to cook."

Gramps suddenly stopped in his tracks. "Say, Bobby boy, mind if your lady friend and I let you go ahead and we'll drop by a store to get dessert?"

"But we have ice cream."

"Can't do dairy anymore, Bobby boy." He added in a confiding tone as he tapped his midsection: "Gets me sick to the stomach, if you know what I mean."

La Queenie grabbed Gramps's arm. "Yes, Bobby, I know where we can get some great pan dulce. Go ahead and start cutting up the tortillas for the chilaquiles."

"Okay," I said. "But if Gramps can't have dairy, you'll have to skip the cheese in the chilaquiles."

Gramps waved his large hands as if he were shooing away flies. "Cheese doesn't bother me. Just ice cream and milk."

"All right," I said. "Go get the pan dulce and I'll prepare the tortillas."

"But don't rip them with your hands," she instructed. "Use a knife and make pretty triangles."

As we separated, I could hear Gramps announce to La Queenie with a chuckle: "Even I know what pan dulce is."

I strolled back to my apartment. A beautifully restored Buick Riviera coupe glided by blasting a Reggaetón song for all of us to enjoy. A couple of young cute girls looked up and waved at the occupants. The driver honked. Normally I would have enjoyed this scene, but something about the way Gramps maneuvered this time alone with La Queenie made me suspicious. Gramps was nobody's fool. And neither am I. I racked my memory. I was certain that I'd seen him enjoy mounds of ice cream at every recent family birthday party. But what could I have done? Accuse him of lying?

When I got back to the apartment, I pulled out the tortillas from the fridge and located my sharpest knife. Pretty little triangles, La Queenie had instructed. By the time I heard them walking up the creaky wooden steps that led to my front door, I'd cut a huge plateful of tortillas and had time left over to heat the oil in a skillet and set the table. The door opened and La Queenie came in first, looking radiant. Her face expressed something beyond happiness. It was relief; she'd looked as if she'd just gone to confession and unburdened her conscience. And Gramps followed closely. He sported a wide tight grin. But his eyes expressed strain, something akin to pain but not quite. La Queenie presented me with a large pink bakery box and then inspected my handiwork. "Pretty little triangles," she said as she proudly held up a specimen for Gramps to admire. "¡Excelente!" she added and then kissed my cheek as if I were a well-behaved child.

Gramps nodded. "My grandson is a smart boy," he said. "A smart boy."

Dinner went exceedingly well and my prior suspicions slowly faded away. La Queenie let Gramps call her Reyna and Gramps relaxed after a couple of cold Dos Equis. La Queenie easily persuaded him to regale us with tales about Biloxi and his first days in L.A. She was a perfect and adoring audience. After dessert Gramps called it a night, claiming that Grammy was a distrustful old lady who would surely think he was running around with a loose woman. We all laughed and tried to imagine the kind of "loose woman" Gramps would fall for. He eventually left, but not before La Queenie gave him a tight hug. Her face reached only as high as his chest—just as it did with me. Gramps, patting her dark hair, looked at me over the top of her head. I couldn't decipher his look then, but the next day I understood what his eyes were saying.

"You're lucky," said La Queenie as we lay in bed that night.

"I know," I answered as I pulled her in closer.

"No, that's not what I mean."

She untangled herself from my arms and propped herself up on one elbow so she could examine my face. The streetlight outside my bedroom window offered just enough of a glow so that we could discern each other's expressions. A curl fell over La Queenie's left eye. "I mean to have a grandfather like that," she said.

I reached up and tried to move her hair away but it simply

fell back over her eye with a slight bounce. I then coaxed her into my arms and pulled the blanket up to our necks. It was a cold night and I thought that maybe, if I held her tight enough, La Queenie would stay until morning. But my plan failed.

When the phone rang, I sat up abruptly, not remembering where I was. With each sharp ring, reality seeped in. La Queenie was gone. I glanced at my alarm clock: 7:00. My first class didn't begin until 10. I finally reached over to the nightstand and grabbed my cell.

"Bobby boy," said Gramps.

"Hi."

"Is she there?"

"No," I mumbled as I rubbed my chin's stubble.

"I figured as much."

"What?" I said. "Gramps, what do you mean?"

Silence. Then: "Bobby boy, can I buy you a cup of coffee this morning? So we can talk?"

We settled on a Coffee Bean midway between my apartment and his home. It had rained a bit the night before and the streets were slick. It looked as if it could shower again at any moment. I found Gramps already sitting at a table with two cups in front of him. He seemed ready to give me his impression of La Queenie. And I tried to brace myself for the worst. But I wasn't prepared for what he did say. "She's a pretty girl," he began as he wrapped large hands around his coffee cup. "And I think she has a good heart."

"But. . . ," I said.

"But," Gramps ventured, "but she has a couple of problems."

I took a sip of coffee and burned my upper lip. "Shit," I blurted.

"You need some cold water?"

"No, thanks," I said. "I'm ready, Gramps. Let me have it."

Gramps patted my arm. "She's disturbed, Bobby boy."

"Well, so am I," I said as I patted my lip with a napkin.

Gramps took his hand off my arm and sat back. "She's mentally ill," he said.

I didn't really understand what he'd just announced. I mean, I knew what the words meant, but I couldn't quite absorb them.

"But we had a great evening," was my inappropriate response.

"She told me a few things when we went for the sweet bread."

I focused on his eyes. The usual twinkle was nowhere to be found. He looked, well, I don't know how to describe his face. It was as if he were about to tell me that my parents were dead or something. Gramps gritted his teeth. And then he let it all out. "Reyna told me that she's pregnant," he began. "But the baby isn't yours."

I didn't expect this. La Queenie was as petite as the day I met her. Not a sign of pregnancy. And why would she tell Gramps this? Why not me? Didn't she trust me? And how does this make her "disturbed"?

"Did she tell you who the father was?" I finally ventured. And then it struck me. That priest, Padre Novas. La Queenie had seemed so shaken by his absence yesterday. I asked Gramps if my suspicions were correct.

"No," he said. "If she had said that, I think we could deal with the situation. After all, it would have been fairly normal in the whole scheme of things."

"Who then?"

Gramps looked over to the line of people waiting to order their lattes, Earl Greys, and Guatemala Antiguas. His eyes rested on a young woman who held a squirming girl in one arm while she chatted on her cell phone. The girl wore Hello Kitty pajamas and big pink slippers. She smiled at Gramps. He offered a grin and a little wave, to the girl's delight. And for a moment Gramps seemed to forget that I sat across from him waiting for an answer. Finally he turned back to me.

"So?" I asked. "I don't see how she's crazy."

"I didn't say she was crazy," he said, a bit annoyed at being misquoted. "I said 'disturbed,' which is not as coarse."

"Okay, why is she disturbed?"

"Bobby boy, Reyna told me that"—and then Gramps coughed as if he couldn't get the words out—"she said that Jesus was the father of her baby."

I blinked hard. "You mean Jesús, right?" I said. "It's a common Mexican name."

Gramps shook his head slowly.

"She couldn't really believe that," I said.

"Let me tell you everything she told me, Bobby. This isn't easy to say, but I better."

"Okay," I said as I fell back into my seat. "Shoot."

And Gramps did. He said that La Queenie had wanted to unburden herself of this secret but she'd been fearful that I wouldn't understand. She felt that someone like Gramps would be good to talk to because of his age. She wanted some reassurance. Anyway, she told Gramps that Jesus had first appeared to her two weeks before I met her at Mass. In fact, it was the first Mass that Padre Novas had said as a visiting priest. During his sermon, La Queenie learned of the atrocities that Padre Novas had witnessed in his country. She felt that he was wise and serious and brave. After Mass La Queenie introduced herself to him. She asked him to hear her confession, which he did. Afterward, as La Queenie walked back to her apartment, she heard a voice behind her. She turned. By a mailbox a few yards away stood Jesus. La Queenie told Gramps that she was a bit startled, not because Jesus stood right there on Vermont Avenue, but because she knew without question that he was, in fact, Jesus.

"He smiled at her," said Gramps. "And then said: 'Be my bride, Reyna.'"

"You don't believe this?" I said. It was a stupid question but the words came out of me before I could think.

"Of course not, Bobby boy," Gramps whispered without taking offense. He took a sip of coffee. "But she believes it without question."

"What happened next?"

"Reyna said that she had to obey because no one can deny Jesus. But she immediately went back to Padre Novas and told him what she had heard and seen. The priest offered to walk her home so they could talk in private. She said the priest believed her. After that Padre Novas would make a habit of visiting Reyna for an hour or two each Sunday before Mass. They'd pray, or so she said. And each time the priest left to get ready for Mass, Jesus would appear to Reyna—standing in her bedroom, not wearing a stitch of clothing, ready to embrace his new bride. And that's how she believes she got pregnant."

My mouth hung open and I'm certain that I looked like an

idiot. I wasn't certain what to do or what to ask. I eventually let out a weak, "What else?"

"Well," said Gramps as he cleared his throat, "after that first time she and Jesus made love, Reyna met you at Mass. That's when Jesus appeared to her during the Mass itself, standing on the altar. She said that Jesus told her that you were a good man and that she should give herself to you as freely as she had to him." Gramps leaned close. "That's pretty much it, Bobby boy."

"Oh, so I'm a gift from Jesus," I sneered.

"Now, Bobby, don't."

I felt like strangling someone. That damn priest. He had preyed on La Queenie knowing full well that he could take advantage of this beautiful but delusional woman.

"Bobby boy, listen: Reyna is a sweet girl, a kind person, but she's broken. And I don't think you or I have the ability to fix her."

He was right and I knew it. But I felt adrift, lost. I asked Gramps what I should do.

"Maybe suggest a counselor," he said. "Your mother must have some names. And then move on with your life, Bobby. You have too much to lose."

He walked me to my car and gave me a big hug. Gramps had nothing more to say; he had said all that he could. As I drove home I replayed my nights with La Queenie. Yes, she was a bit quirky, but I couldn't put my finger on one thing she'd ever said or done that would have betrayed her mental illness. Nothing.

It started to sprinkle. As I approached St. Agnes, I almost jumped when I spotted La Queenie and Padre Novas on the sidewalk just outside the church. The priest sheltered under a huge black umbrella. Several suitcases were stacked neatly by his feet. And La Queenie stood about a foot away, gesticulating wildly, yelling something. It looked as though the priest had been waiting for a taxi and La Queenie had ambushed him. Maybe she'd come to her senses and realized that Jesus had not gotten her pregnant—this handsome charismatic man of the cloth had. I don't know. As I came closer, I could see nothing but embarrassment on the priest's face. He turned away from La Queenie, searching for his taxi, I'm sure, and then caught my eye as I eased closer in the thick traffic. His eyes seem to say: Save me, please.

And I'll never forget what happened next. La Queenie turned

to see what Padre Novas was looking at and she saw me. She immediately stopped her tirade. It seemed as if everything had become clear to her at that moment. Traffic started to pick up and I moved faster along the slippery street. I didn't want to stop. I needed to get to my apartment and think. But then something happened. As I accelerated my tires hit a puddle or grease patch, I don't know what, and I began to lose control of the car. I pumped the breaks once, twice, three times, but I couldn't regain control. My car began to fishtail; I heard several honks. And at the last moment before Padre Novas fell in front of me, my eyes met La Queenie's. Her smile broadened. The priest died before the ambulance came.

At the trial I testified about the incident just as it had happened. I tried to help, though. Over the objection of the district attorney, I said that I didn't think La Queenie meant to push Padre Novas, that she was troubled because she had found out she was pregnant by him. She never took the stand. I think if she had, she could have gotten convicted of a lesser charge because everyone would've understood just how troubled she was. But the jury found that she had planned to kill the priest and if it hadn't been my car, it would have been someone else's. I doubt that. I think seeing my face is what gave La Queenie the strength to do what she did. When we locked eyes. . .I'm haunted by the thought she might have misinterpreted what I did. I'd nodded, just a bit, and she'd nodded back. You know, like we had agreed on a plan of action. I didn't mention this on the stand because I figured it wasn't relevant, not really.

It's been four years since the trial. La Queenie used to write to me a lot from prison and I wrote back a couple of times. But I stopped answering after the first year, though her letters kept on coming. Eventually, I guess, she gave up. The last letter I got was in December, a few days before Christmas. I just couldn't bring myself to maintain contact. I had to begin fresh and put the whole thing behind me.

Brenda and I plan to marry this summer. She's absolutely brilliant; no doubt she'll be a judge someday. We both graduated last year in the top 5 percent of our class. Brenda now works for the antitrust division at the U.S. Department of Justice and I landed a nice job downtown with one of California's largest firms. I figure

I can do public interest law later, a few years down the road, after I've paid off a few debts. Some of my friends say I sold out. But they don't realize that some good things are worth waiting for, right? You have to set your priorities and think long term. That's what Gramps taught me. And he's the best role model a boy could ever have.

DEVIL TALK

YSRAEL RAMÍREZ preferred to take the stairs despite the stiffness in his knees. He was still trim, straight-backed, and brown as a nut, but his high school football days had finally caught up with him ten years ago. He lifted one leg after the other up toward his neat and simplified life in the brand-new condominium, freshly painted and hermetically sealed, on Burbank Boulevard. Not as spacious as his split-level home in West Hills but he did not need all that room anymore. Cancer had taken Ruth three years ago this August. Their son Nathaniel, a lawyer with the Oregon Attorney General's Office, had flown down to Los Angeles for the unveiling of Ruth's tombstone, and then spent two full weeks helping his father find just the right place to live.

"You're going to go crazy rattling around this huge place all by yourself," Nathaniel had said, spooning tortilla soup past his thin lips as the two sat in a booth at the California Pizza Kitchen. "Absolutely loco, Pops."

So it was planned, a bit too fast for Ysrael's liking. Though he himself had been a lawyer for many years, he had grown somewhat passive in retirement. And then with his wife's passing, he seemed, at times, lost. So Nathaniel took care of everything. He even made a tidy profit for his father on the house on Valley Circle and got a good deal on the condominium two miles away. "Close to two malls, Pops," Nathaniel had said. "Topanga Plaza and the Promenade." Ysrael had offered his son a wan smile. "Me, Pops, I prefer the Promenade. They've got Macy's and a multiplex there."

Ysrael reached his floor, paused for but a moment, and breathed deeply. The hall smelled of different foods (Chinese takeout, enchiladas, pizza, some kind of fish), dinners now past. He then turned to the left and walked four doors to his unit. He pulled his key from his pocket with his left hand and touched the mezuzah with his right. Both the key and the mezuzah felt cool, solid. Ysrael brought his hand down from the mezuzah, kissed his fingertips, slid the key into the lock with a *shoonk,* and then turned it with a *cleenk*.

He settled down comfortably in his favorite recliner with a mug of decaffeinated Mocha Java (Ysrael was pleased to learn from his son that he now can buy Starbucks whole bean or ground at Ralphs), Vivaldi on the stereo, and the *Los Angeles Times* spread upon his lap. Within an hour Ysrael was dozing noisily. And he dreamed. The vibrant colors and sounds of spring swirled about him. And Ruth stood there by his side, incandescent and beautiful, whispering, "I'm waiting for you, my love." A brook gurgled happily and birds flew in and around lush oaks, singing Vivaldi's spring (the *largo e pianissimo sempre*, to be precise) with such rapture that Ysrael's heart swelled with each successive note. And what must have been a woodpecker rapped softly, rhythmically, on a branch somewhere nearby. But the rapping grew louder, more deliberate, impatient. Eventually the brook, trees, and Ruth dissolved and Ysrael's great brown eyes popped open. He was back in his den and the woodpecker's rapping moved from a disappearing tree to the front door.

"Damn!" Ysrael muttered as he pulled himself out of his chair. He walked slowly to the door as the knocking grew louder. "I'm coming, I'm coming!" But he stopped, suddenly, two feet from the door. Who could be knocking? he thought. I haven't buzzed anyone in. Must be a neighbor. Perhaps that widow Mrs. Gurley from down the hall. Probably having trouble with her dishwasher again, or so she says; in reality she has her eyes on me. ¡Dios mío! That's all I need!

Ysrael took one more step and lifted his left hand to the doorknob. The smooth brass felt warm to the touch. That's odd, he thought. He turned it with a quick, irritated flick of his wrist and opened his mouth to say something rather unpleasant to Mrs. Gurley but then froze, mouth agape, as the door swung open. Before him stood a man, head tilted to Ysrael's right, away from the mezuzah, smiling and humming to the Vivaldi that still played on the stereo. He held a beautiful brown leather briefcase.

Ysrael composed himself. "How did you get in the complex? Who buzzed you in?"

The man, who wore a finely tailored blue pinstripe suit, a gleaming white shirt, and a crimson necktie, walked past Ysrael, through the small foyer, and into the living room, where he gently lowered himself onto the middle of the long green leather sofa. He placed the briefcase on his lap, snapped it open, gestured toward Ysrael's still-warm recliner and said in a voice so soft it was nearly a whisper, "Please, sit."

Because the man easily weighed fifty pounds more than he did (the man clearly made it to the gym on a regular basis), Ysrael closed the door and went back to his recliner. As the man shuffled through his briefcase, Ysrael realized that he must be some kind of insurance salesman.

"I'm insured to the hilt," Ysrael said.

The man looked up and laughed a short, sharp laugh. "Oh, no. I'm not selling anything. I am, however, here to bargain a bit." As he whispered this last statement, he pulled out a manila folder from his briefcase, which he then closed and set down by his radiant Bostonians. He opened the folder. "Mr. Ramírez?"

Ysrael leaned back in his recliner and wondered what would come next. "Yes?"

"Mr. Jesús Ramírez?"

"No, no. I don't go by 'Jesús' anymore, I mean," Ysrael said through a cough. "I changed my name to Ysrael after I converted." He didn't know why he was answering this stranger at all, but somehow he couldn't help it.

"Converted?"

Ysrael coughed again. "Why, yes. To Judaism. Thirty-five years ago."

The man riffled through the file. "No. That can't be. It's not in here."

"I was raised Catholic, you see. But after I met my wife, Ruth, who was a Jew, I fell in love with Judaism. I studied for years. Converted after we married."

"No," the man repeated as he put the folder down on his lap. "There's nothing of this in your file."

"It's true. I do not lie." Ysrael smiled. "I changed my name after I converted because, as you can imagine, you get a lot of strange looks at Temple when you say your name is Jesús. Even if it is pronounced the Spanish way and even though Jesus Christ was a Jew himself."

The man's eyes widened in surprise. And then, ever so slowly, his eyelids lowered as he let out a little snicker. "Ah! That explains the mezuzah. I figured it was left by the prior owner."

"No. My wife bought that for me when I converted."

"Wait until they hear about this at the home office!"

"And where's the home office?" Ysrael asked, finally getting curious again.

"Hell, of course."

At that moment Ysrael knew he should have been startled or, at the very least, confused. Perhaps, he thought, after several decades as a criminal defense attorney, he was not easily shocked because he had heard millions of very strange utterances. Ysrael laughed. "Hell? That's rich."

The man returned the laugh. "Well, you see, Jes—I mean, Ysrael, you are going to die tonight, in your sleep, very peacefully, and I wanted to make a little deal with you. But because you're no longer a Christian, my hands are tied." He reached for his briefcase, snapped it open, and slid the file back in.

Oddly, Ysrael was not afraid, merely puzzled. "Why can't you make a deal with a non-Christian?"

"Well, you realize that Torah makes no direct reference to either Heaven or Hell, don't you?" He snapped his briefcase shut for emphasis, not without a little irritation.

This whole issue of the afterlife was the biggest chasm Ysrael had had to leap when he started his Judaic studies all those years ago. Heaven and Hell, for a Mexican Catholic, were as real as the nuns and priests who taught him how to be a "good" Christian. But then, reaching back to his wonderful long meetings with Rabbi Burke (as well his son's Torah worksheets from grammar school), Ysrael said, "Ah! What of Gan Ayden and Gehenna?"

The man paused, scratched his goatee, and thought for a moment. "Hhhmmm. Interesting point, Ysrael. Interesting point. But those were concepts of Talmudic times. And besides that, those were actual physical places, here on Earth. Very different from reality. My reality."

The man was, of course, correct. As a post-Talmudic Jew, Ysrael believed in the immortality of the soul. But as Maimonides wisely noted, there are neither bodies nor bodily forms in the world-to-come, only the souls of the righteous. He looked at the man and said simply, "You are right."

"I must be going," said the man as he stood up, knees cracking just a bit. "Many more trips tonight. I apologize for the inconvenience."

Ysrael stood as well, and his knees echoed the man's. "No problem, really." Ysrael suddenly laughed. "My father used to say, 'De puerta cerrada el diablo se vuelve.'"

"Languages were never my forte," said the man.

"From a closed door, the devil goes away."

The man chuckled. "Again, Mr. Ramírez, I'm sorry about all this."

"Except that business about me dying tonight, and all, it was sort of nice having a little company. But I have two questions for you, if you don't mind."

"It's the least I can do. Shoot."

"First, by your existence, does that mean Jesus Christ was indeed the Messiah?"

"No. Next question."

"Yes, well," and Ysrael looked around and coughed a bit. "Well, what was the bargain you planned to offer?"

"Oh, that. You know. The usual. I'd bring back your wife and the two of you could live for ten happy years together."

"In exchange for my soul, I suppose."

"What else would I want?"

Ysrael rubbed his hands together. "Now that would be tempting indeed!"

"But I can't offer it. I couldn't offer it to a Buddhist, a Hindu, an atheist, or any other non-Christian. I'm sorry. Rules are rules." With that, the man headed toward the door, nodded a good-night, and was gone.

Ysrael sighed and sat down in his recliner. Vivaldi still played in the background. He let out another sigh, closed his eyes, and quickly fell asleep. His mind eased into the same wonderful dream he'd been having before the man came to visit. The lush greenery, playful brook, singing birds, and his beautiful Ruth. And in his sleep, Ysrael's heart stopped. And as he slipped from this world into the next, he found himself lying in Ruth's arms as they lay in the clover.

"My love," Ruth said. "I've been waiting. What took you so long?"

Ysrael kissed Ruth's soft young cheek (for they were both in their twenties now), and noticed with delight that she smelled of fresh lemons. He said, "Oh, mi amor, I had a visitor. Please forgive me."

She pulled him closer and nuzzled his thick black hair with a laugh. "Of course, my love," she cooed. "Not another thought of it."

LOS OTROS COYOTES

Espero que la salida sea alegre,
y espero no volver nunca más.
—FRIDA KAHLO

Nadie construye muros mejor que yo, créeme

THE GUARD gently led Rogelio out of the lookout room. The boy shook his head so hard that tears flew from his eyelashes, hitting the guard's green uniform and making dark petaled blotches on the thick fabric. Rogelio was trying to shake from his mind the image of his huddled sobbing parents. But he couldn't. And though he was only in fifth grade, Rogelio was smart enough to know that he'd never be able to wipe away the memory of waving good-bye to his parents through the cloudy bulletproof Plexiglas.

The president's executive order explicitly laid out the design of the detention centers that connected to the Great Wall, and explicitly prohibited the expenditure of funds for more humane farewells. Children who belonged in the United States—because they were born in the country or were otherwise naturalized—could have no more than thirty seconds to gaze upon their soon-to-be deported parents through the Plexiglas. Because the president prohibited the installation of microphones and speakers, the good-byes would consist of silent, tearful pantomimes: mouthed expressions of love, promises to behave, vows never to forget.

Soon Rogelio and his older sister, Marisol, would pack their meager belongings and be sent to live with their tía Isabel in Los Angeles. And his parents would be with the other sobbing parents on a large black bus that would take them through one of the reinforced gates in the Great Wall and back to Mexico—regardless of which Latin American country they called home. The grieving parents would disembark in Tijuana and be left to fend for themselves.

The president had designed this process, praising himself for coming up with such a clean, fast, and beautiful way of MAKING AMERICA GREAT AGAIN! He had tweeted: "Only a Very Stable Genius could come up with this very GREAT system! And Mexico will someday PAY for my Great Wall!"

The guard led Rogelio past the other children, who waited in two snaking lines—one for boys, the other for girls, as the president had decreed—along the walkway toward the nurse's office for a quick visit before going back to the barracks to pack. Above the cries, shouts, and laughter of the other children, Rogelio could hear the recurring audio loop of the president's voice blaring over the intercoms that spotted the ceiling: "I will build a great wall—and nobody builds walls better than me, believe me—and I'll build them very inexpensively. I will build a great, great wall on our southern border, and I will make Mexico pay for that wall. Mark my words." Rogelio's teacher, Ms. Becerra, had noted in class one day that Mexico had yet to pay for the president's wall, which cost more than $21 billion to build.

As he walked with the guard, Rogelio blinked away his tears and looked out the large floor-to-ceiling windows that allowed perfect views of the Great Wall. Enormous spotlights were trained on the wall at intervals, also lighting up the cool San Diego evening. Rogelio thought that the wall was a dreadful, hideous thing even though the president had paid "good money, the best money" to one of his most supportive Twitter followers—a contractor from Alabama—to design the outlandish golden curlicues that were painted along the wall's top and bottom edges. Between the borders of gold paint, the president wanted to share with people on either side of the Great Wall his life's accomplishments as depicted in bas-relief, captioned scenes beginning with his childhood (*I was the best son!*), his education (*Only the greatest schools and top grades!*), his careers in business and television (*I had the highest ratings!*), his run for president (*Biggest victory ever!*), his swearing in (*So Presidential!*), and him signing executive orders (*Making America Great Again!*).

The president saw on Twitter that the bas-relief scenes on the Mexican side of the Great Wall had been defaced in obscene ways, but his staff convinced him that photographs of the defacement were nothing more than fake news designed to embarrass him. And this attack on his greatest accomplishment simply confirmed in the president's mind that he had been justified in imposing martial law and suspending the 2020 election four years ago. The president had seen numerous preelection polls that showed him losing the general election in a landslide, which he blamed—in an early-morning tweet—on the "Lying Liberal Media, Fake Polls, and Chinese Interference!" He had no choice but to call off the election and order the military to keep "the peace." In a rambling hour-long prime-time address to the world on October 15, 2020, the president had promised that once a full televised Senate investigation into traitorous activities could be completed, he would lift martial law and only then could free, fair elections resume. He was true to his word: most evenings during the last four years, the Senate's hearings had been broadcast on Fox, the only television network with a federal license to disseminate news, in which witness after witness divulged in exquisite detail the plots against the president and America. The hearings would take another two or three years, said the president, but they would eventually come to an end, and a full unredacted report would be released. This is what the president promised, and who but the nastiest traitor could question his sincerity?

The guard brought Rogelio to another line, this one in front of the nurse's office. Unlike the lines to say good-bye to their parents, there was only one line here, where boys and girls could mix and talk. The guard gently touched Rogelio's shoulder and said: "Wait here until it's your turn." The boy nodded, and the guard turned on his heel and went back to the lookout room to fetch the next child.

Rogelio watched a sobbing girl came out of the nurse's office, rubbing her right forearm. Another guard guided her toward the girls' barracks. Rogelio sighed. He figured the children were being forced to receive some kind of booster inoculation. Rogelio hated shots, but he liked that word: *inoculation*. He let it roll around in his mind. He'd learned from his teacher that all words had origins—roots—in other languages. French. German. Latin.

Where did "inoculation" come from? And what about the very first words? How could those words have any roots if nothing had existed before?

When Rogelio's turn finally came, a guard opened the door of the nurse's office and said, "Go in." Rogelio complied, stepping into the darkened room, lit by a lone lamp over a phlebotomy chair. The moment the guard closed the door with a loud click, the president's audio loop about the Great Wall disappeared, and the room was enveloped in the most beautiful song Rogelio had ever heard. Two women's voices, singing in a language he did not understand, seemed to come from every corner of the dark room.

The nurse stood to the left of the chair swiping at an iPad. He reminded Rogelio of his cousin Mateo who lived in Los Angeles, the only son of his tía Isabel, except the nurse had blond hair and a neatly trimmed beard. The nurse suddenly stopped swiping and looked up at the boy. "Beautiful, isn't it?" said the nurse.

The boy nodded.

"It's called 'The Flower Duet.'"

The boy nodded again, feeling calm for the first time since Homeland Security had rounded up his family in their home in Chula Vista two weeks ago.

"It's from an opera called *Lakmé* written a long time ago."

The boy listened.

"Here, this part—it's so beautiful when the two voices play off each other."

Rogelio nodded.

The nurse sighed, then looked back at the iPad. "Rogelio Acosta?" He pronounced "Rogelio" as "roe-*jell*-io."

Rogelio had heard his name mangled too often to even notice. He nodded.

"Show me your dog tag."

Rogelio pulled the dog tag out from the top of his T-shirt and showed it to the nurse. The nurse bent forward, squinted, nodded, and then typed something into the iPad. "Please sit."

The boy went to the phlebotomy chair. It was a green padded contraption that had seen far too much service. The right arm of the chair, set in the down position, was cracked, revealing white stuffing, and the dilapidated seat bore witness to the many bottoms that had nestled uncomfortably waiting to be poked. The left arm of the chair was propped in the upright position, allowing Rogelio to slide in.

"I'm getting a shot?" said the boy as he settled in. He tried to sound brave, but his voice cracked, something that was happening more often lately. He then tried to impress the nurse: "An inoculation?"

The nurse let out a muffled laugh that ended in a sloppy snort. "I guess you could call it that," the nurse said as he picked up what looked like a long fireplace lighter from a table that stood in the shadows behind him. "It'll feel like a shot." He used the other hand to grab a bit of cotton. The strong smell of alcohol hit Rogelio's nostrils.

"Put your arm down, keep still," said the nurse. Rogelio complied. The nurse quickly swabbed the boy's forearm. The boy's entire body tensed.

"Look up at the corner," said the nurse, with a nod to a spot above and to the left of Rogelio's head. "It's better not to look. It'll be over fast."

Rogelio obeyed. The music seemed to grow louder, and the women spoke to him in a mysterious language that he felt almost on the verge of understanding. The corner's darkness filled his eyes, and the music removed all thought from the boy's mind. Rogelio felt the nurse take hold of his wrist, heard a click, felt a small pinch on his forearm, and it was over.

"Good job," said the nurse. "We're done here. Just let me put a bit of cotton and tape on because it will bleed a little for the next couple of hours." The nurse worked fast. A few seconds later, Rogelio looked down at his forearm where the nurse had expertly wrapped a wad of cotton with blue stretchy tape. "Easy-peasy," said the nurse. "You can go now."

Rogelio stood. The women's voices reached an apex of beauty. He couldn't move.

The nurse smiled. "Stunning, isn't it?"

The boy nodded.

"Almost as if God is singing."

Rogelio nodded. "What are they saying?" he whispered.

The nurse shrugged. "Beats me. But does it really matter?"

Before Rogelio could answer the music ended, and a sharp

rap on the door shook the two out of their mutual reverie. As the door opened, the president's audio loop invaded the room ("Nobody builds walls better than me, believe me"), and a different guard stuck her head into the room. A teenage girl stood silently near the guard, waiting for permission to enter.

"Time to go," said the nurse.

The boy nodded and slowly walked to the door.

A mí la muerte me pela los dientes

THE LARGE BLACK BUS rocked back and forth on the I-5 freeway toward Los Angeles. An hour earlier it had made its way from the six-level parking structure at the base of the Great Wall to the freeway entrance. Rogelio rested his head on Marisol's shoulder. His sister snored softly. He felt safe with her. The forty-two children on the bus made little noise save for exhausted snores, muffled sobs, terrified whispers. The bus driver had turned off the interior lights just before backing out of the parking structure, explaining through the intercom system that it would take several hours to drive to Los Angeles and "deposit" the children at their designated new homes. She'd said that the children should enjoy the box of snacks that had been set on each seat: bottled water, a bag of pretzels, an apple, a wrapped mint. Not much, but their new families would feed them, she was sure of that. In the meantime, enjoy this free and very excellent nourishment courtesy of the president, and then try to get some shut-eye. Most of the children had quickly made their way through the snacks, then fell asleep. With the lights turned off, few could fend off the brutal fatigue that encased them in the aftermath of their farewells to their parents.

The rhythms of the freeway and the traveling shadows that shifted across the bus's interior soothed Rogelio. Before drifting into an unavoidable slumber, the boy remembered his father's favorite dicho when things got difficult: A mí la muerte me pela los dientes. When he first heard his father say this, the boy had wondered: Why would Death peel anyone's teeth? And could teeth even be peeled? But as he now capitulated to sleep, Rogelio believed he finally understood that old Mexican saying.

"MARISOL AND ROGELIO ACOSTA!"

Rogelio's eyes popped open as the bus driver called their names over the intercom. His sister was already zipping up her backpack. Rogelio figured Marisol must have been awake, reading a book with her mini-reading light. His sister loved to read—poetry, novels, short stories. That's why Marisol did so well in high school, their mother often said. Loving books will lead to success in life, she asserted. Rogelio preferred to entertain himself with video games when he couldn't be outside playing basketball or soccer. But he hoped that someday he'd like to read books as much as his sister did, and maybe then he'd get better grades.

"We're here," Marisol whispered. "At Tía Isabel's house."

Rogelio looked out the window and saw his aunt standing in her driveway. She looked so much like his mother even though Tía Isabel was eight years older than her sister, Alma. In fact, there was a time—when Alma was in her mid-twenties and Isabel in her early thirties—that many who met them thought the sisters were identical twins. Sometimes at family gatherings, whether in Chula Vista with Alma and her family or here in Los Angeles with Isabel and hers, the sisters would deliberately confuse the neighbors who had been invited over to celebrate.

Despite the 127-mile distance between Los Angeles and Chula Vista, the sisters' families remained close. In fact, Rogelio knew his tía Isabel quite well because he had interviewed her for an oral history project last year. He had learned that with the cunning and expensive assistance of a coyote, Isabel and her now late mother, Abuelita Belén, had come to the United States seven years before the infant Alma and their father could. And because of this simple accident of timing, Rogelio's aunt and grandmother had become U.S. citizens under President Reagan's 1986 Immigration Reform and Control Act. Tía Isabel did well in school, majoring in business administration at San Diego State University, then landed her first job in Los Angeles working the registration desk at the Double Tree downtown. Now Tía Isabel was the hotel revenue manager at the Courtyard Marriott near LAX. At fifty, she looked years younger, her actual age betrayed only by a streak of white that ran from the top of her forehead that she brushed back over her otherwise black hair. The women in that side of the family kept their youth, Rogelio's father, Alejandro, often said. Good skin, great hair, nice teeth. Alma would always add: And we're smart, too.

Yes, Tía Isabel was healthy, but her late husband, Tío Manny, who had suffered from type 2 diabetes for years, survived three strokes before a heart attack took him on Christmas Day 2016. Rogelio's father said that it was really the election that killed Manny, but Rogelio couldn't figure out how an election, even *that* one, could cause a heart to stop.

A few years after Manny passed away, Tía Isabel's son, Mateo, came down from Sacramento, where he had earned a master's in English literature at UC-Davis. He didn't want his mother to be alone, and he could easily find a teaching gig at a high school in Los Angeles. Mateo didn't need much to live, just enough to keep himself clothed and fed while he worked on a novel. He moved into the small house that stood in the large backyard that Abuelita Belén had enjoyed as her haven. But it had been vacant since her death, so in many ways it was a perfect solution. Mateo saved money on rent and helped his mother stave off sadness and loss. He quickly found a teaching job at Cathedral High School. "Not a big paycheck, but enough to keep body and soul together," Mateo liked to say, "while I write the Great American Novel." But his mother knew he had sacrificed the full life he had fashioned up in Sacramento to save her from the loneliness of widowhood. Mateo was her only child; though young when she had Mateo, Isabel could not conceive again. "Quality, not quantity," Mateo joked whenever his mother fell into a funk because she could not give him at least one sibling. And he'd add: "And that way I have you all to myself."

Rogelio and Marisol stepped off the bus. The night had gotten very cold. The crickets chirped loudly. Tía Isabel opened her arms wide and said, "Come here, my babies."

ROGELIO AND MARISOL had settled into a comfortable if not wholly normal routine in the month they had been living their new lives with Tía Isabel and Mateo. The house, built in 1933 in northeast Los Angeles, was just six miles from downtown in an area known as Glassell Park, near Eagle Rock, Highland Park, and Mount Washington. These communities had undergone aggressive gentrification over the last fifteen years, and Tía Isabel's modest 1,450-square-foot home was now worth well over $1 million, according to Zillow and Redfin. But Isabel would never sell. She and her late husband had toiled to scrape together the down payment when they were newly married, and the house held too many memories. And now that her niece and nephew were living with her, Isabel needed the house more than ever. She had converted the study of her wood-framed home back into the bedroom it had been when Mateo was young. Isabel furnished it with sturdy bunkbeds, two dressers, and two small desks that she bought at Ikea. She knew that she could never replace Marisol and Rogelio's parents, but at least she could make their home as comfortable as possible.

Marisol enrolled as a high school senior at the Sotomayor Learning Academies on North San Fernando Road, a short drive away. Rogelio enrolled at the same campus in the middle school program. Because he had been identified on the enrollment form as one of the relocated children, the school granted a waiver allowing him to enter the sixth grade early to be on the same campus as his sister. "Small kindnesses," his aunt had said when the waiver was approved. Each morning Mateo would drop off his cousins at school and then head to his teaching job at Cathedral High School. The children would then stay on campus doing schoolwork or attending club meetings until 6:30 p.m., when Isabel would drive to campus and gather them up for dinner. Structure. Activities. Near normalcy.

And part of that normalcy was their weekly government-sanctioned—and monitored—video call with their parents. Each Sunday night Isabel would set up her laptop at the kitchen table for Rogelio and Marisol, click onto the Homeland Security-approved weblink, type in her family password and code, and connect with her sister and brother-in-law, who sat 1,576 miles away in a small apartment in Ocotlán, Jalisco, their hometown about 150 miles southeast of Guadalajara. They were allowed fifteen minutes each week to gaze upon each other and share as many bits of news about themselves as could be managed in that short time. Since cell phone and internet connections to all Latin American countries had been blocked by Homeland Security under Executive Order 9066, they were forced to savor each of these minutes. At the end of the video calls, Rogelio's mother would always break down in tears, and his father would valiantly try to comfort her as tears fell freely from his own eyes. The one thing that kept their parents sane was knowing that the children were in safe hands and clearly thriving despite the pain of separation. And so this was the new normal: parents on a computer screen, fifteen minutes a week.

ROGELIO had his suspicions about Marisol.

At first he thought he dreamed what was happening. But one night, as the glowing alarm clock numbers read 11:02 p.m., Rogelio forced himself to stay awake while pretending to sleep—complete with fake snores—as he waited in his perch on the upper bunk. Marisol whispered: "Are you awake?" The boy did not answer. After a minute Marisol slowly got out of bed. Even in the shadows, Rogelio could see that his sister was fully dressed in a sweatshirt and jeans. She slipped on a pair of sneakers, grabbed her backpack, and gingerly opened the window. Within a few seconds she was outside standing in the flowerbed. Marisol closed the window and was gone.

Rogelio blinked in disbelief. He heard a car start up—he thought it sounded like Mateo's battered Honda Civic that was always parked out front—then a car door open and close, followed by the sound of the engine revving then slowly making its way down the street. As the last sounds of the car disappeared, fatigue overcame Rogelio, and his fake snores soon became real. His final thought was that he would confront Marisol and Mateo in the morning as they drove to school. Rogelio felt as though he had no choice but to find out the truth. He did not like being lied to.

Los caminos de la vida

"Turn it up," said Marisol, even though she could have reached over from the front passenger seat and done it herself.

But Mateo complied, pushing the volume control on his steering wheel. Marisol bobbed her head to the song. Rogelio thought it was funny how his sister had gotten into the habit of exploring their aunt's vast CD collection. So old school. Fortunately, Mateo's ancient Honda had its original CD player, so

Marisol could bring the music with her on the rides to school. Lila Downs had become Marisol's musical crush of the week. Rogelio's Spanish was not as good as his sister's, so he strained to understand the words to "Los caminos de la vida." He eventually gave up and remembered the task at hand.

"Where did you go last night?" asked Rogelio. He kept his eyes trained on the back of his sister's head, which stopped bobbing at the question. Marisol turned toward Mateo as if for guidance, but he kept his eyes on the road, mindful of the children who were walking to school and crossing streets.

"Are you two dating?"

"Oh, gross!" said Marisol.

"No, dude," said Mateo. "I wouldn't date my cousin, and I certainly don't date seventeen-year-olds. Want me to go to prison or something?"

Then Marisol said: "Look, we were going to wait to tell you." She kept her eyes on Mateo, who nodded his approval to continue.

"Tell me what?"

Marisol twisted her body so she could look at her brother. "We go to meetings," she began.

"What kind of meetings?"

"They're planning meetings," said Mateo.

"And we volunteer after the meetings," added Marisol.

"For what?" said Rogelio. He kept his body still, his voice under control. He wanted the truth.

"Meetings of Los Otros Coyotes," said Marisol, keeping her eyes on her brother. "They help reunite separated families."

"Where do you do this. . .meeting and volunteering?"

"They have an office downtown, at the Bradbury Building," said Mateo. "They pretend to be event planners. You know, special events like weddings, quinceañeras, and retirement parties."

Rogelio knew the Bradbury Building from that old movie *Blade Runner*. Marisol, a self-proclaimed sci-fi nerd, had made her little brother watch that film with her three times, though she believed the Philip K. Dick novel on which it was based was far superior. The five-story office building, best known for its astonishing skylight atrium, marble stairs, tiled walkways, and wrought-iron elevators, had been a Los Angeles landmark almost from the moment it opened in 1893. With a shiver, Rogelio remembered the creepy scene where Harrison Ford, his blaster drawn, makes his way through the darkened, dank, dilapidated atrium in search of a renegade android. *This* is where Marisol and Mateo snuck off to each night?

Marisol saw the confusion on her brother's face. "The Bradbury is filled with businesses and law offices," she said. "It's nothing like what you see in *Blade Runner*."

Rogelio appreciated his sister's explanation. Now he could move on to his next question: "Can we be reunited. . .with Mamá and Papá?"

Marisol again looked at Mateo for guidance, but her cousin kept his eyes on the road. She turned back to Rogelio. "Do you want to be?" she said.

Rogelio blinked. Tears filled his eyes. He nodded.

"Okay," said Marisol. "Okay."

Mateo pulled into the school's drop-off lane and said: "We're here. We'll talk tonight."

Rogelio nodded again. "Yes," he finally said. "Tonight."

El Señor es contigo

AFTER DINNER that night, Tía Isabel logged onto her laptop at the kitchen table to work on bills. Marisol and Mateo saw this as the perfect time to get out of the house and take Rogelio to the Bradbury Building.

"Tía," began Marisol as Rogelio handed her the last dish to dry. "Mateo said that he'd take me and Rogelio out for ice cream at Grand Central Market."

Isabel kept her eyes on her screen, nodded, and said: "Well. . ."

"It's Friday, so no school tomorrow," added Marisol.

"Okay, I guess so," said Isabel.

Marisol continued: "Do you want us to bring you anything? McConnell's has your favorite, double peanut butter chip."

"No, thank you," said her aunt without looking up, but betraying a hint of temptation. "I'm gaining too much weight. Go have fun. I need to finish the bills."

Marisol nodded at her brother. Rogelio smiled. He appreciated how his sister plotted.

MATEO DROVE HIS HONDA on Broadway through Chinatown.

The evening was warm, the streets teeming with people enjoying the weather. But dotting the street were dozens of tents and jury-rigged structures of multicolored tarps: the homes of people who could not afford apartments. The happy pedestrians made their way around these makeshift abodes without stopping.

Marisol riffled through her aunt's CD holder, found what she wanted, popped it in the player, and "La cumbia del mole" came on. She was still on her Lila Downs kick. Rogelio liked this song—and truth be told, he preferred the English version that comes later on the CD—but he wanted his sister and cousin to explain the next step.

"Tell me," he said from the backseat. "How do we get to see Mamá and Papá?"

Marisol turned down the music's volume and twisted back to face her brother. "We have to volunteer tonight anyway, so we can go early and introduce you to them."

"Them?"

"Vivaporú," said Mateo, catching Rogelio's eye in the rear-view mirror.

Rogelio blinked. "Vivaporú?"

Marisol nodded.

"That's how Mamá pronounces Vicks VapoRub," said Rogelio. "You know, because of her accent." He closed his eyes and tried to remember the feel of his mother's warm hand as she rubbed the ointment on his chest whenever he got a cold. She'd whisper, "Ave María" as she slowly applied the Vicks to her son's narrow chest. He could almost hear her voice: "Ave María llena eres de gracia, El Señor es contigo. . ." Rogelio opened his eyes, which were now moist. He said again: "Vivaporú?"

"That's the name they go by," said Mateo.

"They?" said Rogelio again. "How many people am I meeting?"

"Just one," said Marisol. "And they go by the name Vivaporú, okay?"

"Okay," said Rogelio, still feeling confused, but he didn't press the issue.

"We'll park in the structure on Spring Street and then go through the courtyard to enter the Bradbury from the rear entrance," said Mateo. "It's safer that way."

"Okay," said Rogelio. "Okay. And tell me about Los Otros Coyotes."

Mateo said, "We've told you all we should for now."

"Vivaporú will explain," added Marisol. "Be patient."

Rogelio nodded. The boy knew he had little choice but to wait.

THE THREE took the elevator down from the seventh level of the Broadway Spring Center, a large parking structure on Spring Street. "We cut across here," said Marisol as they exited.

Rogelio looked across the courtyard toward the red-bricked building his sister pointed to. Along the pathway stood a long gray wall that looked like the kind of reverse timeline that he and his classmates made for their history class. As they walked, he looked up at that first section of the wall that had the year "1900" chiseled at the top over the words: "Los Angeles mourns and reveres Grandma Mason."

"Biddy Mason lived right here, after the Civil War," said Marisol. They stopped in front of a replica of a photograph of the former slave. "She ran the city's first childcare center out of her home and founded the city's First African Methodist Episcopal Church in her home."

"Wow," said Rogelio.

They started to walk again, but slowly so that they could read the legends in the wall.

"She was born into slavery in Georgia," said Marisol. "A Mormon family owned her. But when the family moved to Southern California, she sued for her freedom because California entered the Union as a free state in 1850."

"You mean when Alta California was stolen from Mexico," added Mateo.

"What happened?" said Rogelio.

"She won," said Marisol and Mateo in unison. They laughed: "Jinx!"

As they read the entries on the timeline wall, Rogelio learned that after winning her freedom, Biddy Mason worked as a nurse and midwife, delivering hundreds of babies during her career. She also was one of the first African American women to own land in Los Angeles. Biddy Mason became a successful businesswoman who shared her wealth with charities. She spoke fluent Spanish, was much loved, and even dined on occasion at the home of Pio Pico, the last governor of Alta California. They got to the end of the reverse timeline with the year "1810" and the words: "Biddy Mason born a slave." Rogelio shivered, but he didn't know why.

"Up these stairs," said Mateo. They marched up the ten concrete steps. Mateo opened one of the large wood and glass doors, and they were in the Bradbury Building. As they walked down the hallway, Rogelio was not impressed by what he saw. Yes, the floor was beautiful, with its Italian marble and Mexican tile—which Marisol proudly pointed out as if she'd designed the building herself—but it was nothing like what he knew from *Blade Runner*. They turned, went down a few steps, and then entered the magnificent atrium area. Ah! This was it!

"Pretty fucking amazing, eh?" said Mateo. Marisol elbowed her cousin.

"What?" said Mateo. "I suspect he's used that word before."

Rogelio blushed but he liked how Mateo treated him like a peer.

"Okay, fine," said Marisol. "Now up to Los Otros Coyotes. Let's take the stairs."

Rogelio could not hide his wonder. The Bradbury was a functioning office building, and even though it was after the dinner hour, tenants—and a few tourists oohing and aahing and taking photos—wandered about. On the second floor they passed several large doors whose beveled glass windows had painted on them the names of different businesses and law firms, such as "Charoenpong, Eskandari, & Lundgren LLP," "Toma + Van Gelderen Architectural Concepts," and "Pletcher & Jones Designs." They finally arrived at a door with the name "Los Otros Coyotes: Party Planners." Under the lettering was a painting that resembled a woodcut showing three coyotes howling beneath a full moon. Marisol pushed a small button, and they waited. After a few moments, a thin young man opened the door. He smiled at Marisol. She smiled back. The young man said, "Come in."

They entered. Rogelio observed about a dozen young people at standing desks typing away on laptops, their faces aglow from the screens, almost all with earbuds, listening to their own personal soundtracks. At the back of the room a large table groaned with soft drinks, bottled waters, plates of fruit, coffee pots, paper cups and plates. To the left of the table was another door with VIVAPORÚ painted across it in bold black letters.

They walked to the door, and Marisol knocked.

"Adelante," came a voice that was the most beautiful Rogelio had ever heard.

Marisol opened the door, kissed Rogelio on his forehead, and said: "Don't be afraid." He nodded and walked into the dark room as Marisol closed the door behind her brother. Rogelio turned and set his eyes on a figure who sat in an oversized green leather chair in front of a large old wooden desk. A brass lamp at the desk's edge offered the only illumination in the room. Seven or eight books in Spanish and English sat in a stack just beneath the lamp. Rogelio could discern titles on four of the spines: *Under the Feet of Jesus, La metamorfosis, The Children of Willesden Lane,* and *La hija de la chuparrosa.* The figure looked up from a large ledger. Rogelio lifted his eyes from the book titles, noticing for the first time that, unlike in the main office, no computer or laptop adorned this room. And instead of earbuds, the person in front of the boy had a record turntable on a credenza just behind the large chair, the words "love supreme" repeating out of two large speakers. The figure reached back and lowered the music to a whisper.

"Siéntate por favor," said Vivaporú, pointing to one of two guest chairs that were stationed at angles in front of the desk.

Rogelio sat as Vivaporú stood up, looking down on the boy. Rogelio had never seen such a perfect person in his life. Vivaporú wore a luminous white three-piece suit accented with a shocking green shirt, collar spread open wide across the suit's large lapels. Vivaporú's earlobes were stretched with large golden gauges accented by a great golden chai—Rogelio thought it was a dog or some other animal—that hung on a thick chain around their long muscular neck. Vivaporú's lustrous black hair was parted neatly down the middle and hung to their shoulders. They must have been at least six feet tall, with the lean proportions of a ballet dancer. Vivaporú's hazel eyes almost never blinked, and their smooth brown skin gleamed. They pointed down at the ledger while keeping their eyes on the boy.

"Rogelio Acosta," said Vivaporú, not as a question but a statement of fact. Rogelio remembered how the nurse at the detention center had said his name before checking the boy's dog tag. But while that nurse had spat out a mangled version of his name, Vivaporú said "Rogelio Acosta" in an almost musical manner, softly pronounced in Spanish, as if the boy were a melody to be shared with an invisible audience. Vivaporú's voice reminded Rogelio of a sound he'd once heard while hiking the Mother Miguel Trailhead with his father a year before the separation at the Great Wall: a beautiful bird's song that filled the boy's mind with thoughts of his home back in Chula Vista.

"Yes," said Rogelio. "That's me."

"Your hermana tells me that you want to be with your parents again," said Vivaporú. "¿Es cierto?"

"Yes," said Rogelio. "It's true."

"They're in a safe city. Safe for children. We know this."

Rogelio listened silently.

"Show me your right forearm," said Vivaporú. The boy was confused at first, but then he realized Vivaporú wanted to look at the inoculation site. Rogelio pulled up his shirtsleeve and showed it to Vivaporú. The skin had healed, leaving a small, square, shiny scar.

"Do you know what that is?" said Vivaporú.

"My inoculation."

Vivaporú let out a gentle melodious laugh. "No," said Vivaporú. "A microchip."

Suddenly a black and white cat jumped onto the boy's lap. It purred wildly and made itself comfortable. Rogelio smiled and petted the feline.

"Su nombre es Sophie," said Vivaporú.

"I like Sophie."

"Sophie likes you."

Rogelio extricated his right arm from beneath Sophie and showed Vivaporú the scar again. "Why did they put a microchip in me?" he said.

Vivaporú leaned forward. "So that Homeland Security can track you to know that you're still in los Estados Unidos."

"What for?"

"Pues, because they need us as much as they hate us," said Vivaporú with a loud sigh. "The country desires young people to grow up and then take the jobs that need taking. ¿Entiendes?

All kinds of jobs, from janitors to engineers. The white population is aging, not—¿cómo se dice?—reproducing as fast as we are. Too many jobs, not enough people."

"I want to be with my parents."

"Por supuesto," said Vivaporú. "But I don't know if that's possible."

The boy sat up straight. "You said it was safe."

Vivaporú shook their head. "No, niño, I said your parents are in a safe city. That is a different fact."

"What do you mean?

"It is a dangerous journey back," said Vivaporú. "Children have been caught by Homeland Security before they could get back to the other side."

"And what happens to them?"

"Pues, they get sent far away, to places like Kansas and Nebraska and even South Dakota. They become—¿cómo se dice?—foster children, put with families that are not blood."

"I don't care!"

"No, it's too risky."

"I need to be with my parents!"

Vivaporú sighed, turned, walked to the turntable, and increased the volume. Vivaporú closed their eyes and swayed slowly to the rhythm of the jazz. Rogelio sat in silence for several minutes. Tears fell from his face. The track ended. Vivaporú turned off the music and turned to face the boy. "The answer should be no," they said.

The boy held his breath.

"Pues, the first step will be to remove that microchip."

Rogelio wiped the tears from his face, smiled, and sat up. "Yes?" the boy said.

"Sí."

Rogelio then grew serious, looking at his forearm. "But the government will know it's been removed," he said.

Vivaporú laughed. "¡Qué inteligente eres!" Vivaporú walked around the desk to the boy and gently lifted Sophie from Rogelio's lap. "My beautiful gato will become you."

"What?"

"We usually use rescue pets. I had been saving Sophie for a special person, and we have one here: you!"

Rogelio shifted in his seat. He was trying to follow what Vivaporú was saying.

Vivaporú returned Sophie to the boy's lap, sat down in the other guest chair, crossed their long legs, and leaned toward Rogelio. "Once we have identified a child who wants to be with their parents, we contact the parents by hacking around Homeland Security," began Vivaporú. "Your sister is already in contact with your parents because she works with us. That's what those beautiful young people are doing in the front office. ¿Entiendes? Pues, first, we remove the microchip from that child and put it into a dog or cat. That way the government thinks the chip is still on this side of the Great Wall, even though the children are transported back to their parents on the other side. It is like a reverse—¿cómo se dice?—Underground Railroad."

Rogelio nodded. His class had learned about the Underground Railroad last year when they studied the chapter on slavery. He thought of Biddy Mason, who hadn't needed to use a secret escape route because she'd successfully sued for her freedom in California. "How will I get back to Mexico?"

Vivaporú took in a deep breath and smiled. "In the belly of the beast."

"What?"

"Those big black buses that take the parents through the Great Wall and into México, like the one they put your parents on. ¿Entiendes? We have identified several sympathetic drivers and guards who have gotten even more sympathetic with a little mordida—¿cómo se dice?—bribe. And we do not charge you. We are supported by many churches, mosques, synagogues, and temples of all types."

Rogelio nodded. "And what about my sister?"

"Pues, she has decided to stay here for now. Marisol is one of our best hackers, and she has become invaluable. Ella es brillante. And she has excellent ideas for the Reconquista."

"The what?"

"No es importante," said Vivaporú. "At this moment the question is: Do you want to be reunited with your parents even though it is risky?"

"Yes," said Rogelio after a few moments of thought. "Put my microchip into Sophie, and get me into the belly of the beast."

Vivaporú clapped their hands and stood. "Your hermana will alert your parents and get you ready."

En el vientre de la bestia

After Mateo and Marisol had finished their two-hour shift at Los Otros Coyotes, they walked Rogelio to a place called Tina's Café two blocks from the Bradbury Building. They strode in silence, the evening's cool breeze beginning to make itself felt. In the back room of what was an otherwise normal coffee shop, a man removed the microchip from the boy's arm and placed it in a tube of disinfectant for eventual implantation into Sophie. The chip's slow descent through the blue liquid enthralled Rogelio. Removal of the microchip hurt the boy more than expected, but he was happy that it was no longer inside of him.

As they drove back home through Chinatown, Marisol explained the plan. She would contact their parents in the morning so they can begin their journey from Ocotlán to Tijuana. In one week, before dawn, Rogelio and small group of other children would be picked up by a school bus a few blocks from their home. It would look like any other bus taking children to school, but instead of books and folders, the children were instructed to have in their backpacks several changes of clothes, toiletries, water, snacks, and anything else needed for the trip. About a mile from the large parking structure where the black buses were parked, the children would be moved into a van of the kind used by Homeland Security, and from there they would be taken to a particular black bus whose luggage compartment—the belly of the beast—would be waiting for its young cargo. Bribes would be paid at each step. Once the bus passed the Great Wall into Tijuana, if all went well, the children's parents would be waiting to take them back to their homes. Many of the parents, who had lived in places like Guatemala, El Salvador, or Honduras, had been given asylum by the Mexican government, so their children would settle with them in their new homes in Mexico. Marisol would not tell their aunt until after Rogelio was safely with their parents. Tía Isabel would be upset, no doubt, but it was the only way.

THE BELLY OF THE BEAST WAS HOT. The black bus rocked back and forth as it made its way down three levels toward the exit gate at the base of the Great Wall. Even through the rumbling of the vehicle's engine, Rogelio could discern the audio loop of the president that was broadcast in the detention center and parking structure: "I will build a great, great wall on our southern border, and I will make Mexico pay for that wall."

Rogelio and five other children were huddled together in the dark. Two of them softly whimpered. The beaten-up luggage and duffel bags of the adults who rode above made the small space feel even more confining, like an ancient tomb. Rogelio sat in a corner, hugging his backpack. He willed himself not to cry. He had cried too much already. He was done with tears. He would soon be in Tijuana. He would soon embrace his mother and father. And after a few weeks of living in Mexico with his parents, Rogelio would contact his sister to find out more about this thing Vivaporú called the Reconquista. This was the boy's promise to himself. And he always kept his promises.

The bus suddenly jerked to a stop. Rogelio heard shouting in both Spanish and English. He held his breath, and the other children's whimpering grew louder. What was happening? Rogelio could hear cars honking and speeding by the bus. He then heard footsteps on the gravel of the freeway's shoulder. More shouting, by both men and women. Arguments, cussing—both languages mixing into one cacophonous commotion. Then silence, adults whispering, a clicking and sliding of the locking mechanism that kept the children in the belly of the beast. Suddenly light—three, maybe four flashlights aimed at the children. And then Rogelio—blinded by the flashlights—heard a woman scream: "Oh, my God!"

THE CHICANO IN YOU

THE FIRST TIME Javier Zambrano experienced it, he was four years old. JFK had been assassinated the week before, and the country was still in the throes of mourning, Roman Catholics like Javier's family suffering this violent loss more than others.

Javier stood still, silently watching a stray calico cat carefully make a path through the succulents that lined the fence in his abuelita's backyard. The Los Angeles sky was clear save for a few fainthearted clouds, the midday temperature already hitting eighty degrees even with the sun sitting low in the sky, the same sun that warmed the boy's back through his favorite faded green T-shirt. The calico, suddenly sensing Javier's presence, stopped its progress, its left forepaw frozen above a level patch of grass, and set its eyes on the boy. Javier smiled, wondering what it would be like to creep through his abuelita's plants with such perfect control, one paw at a time.

And then it happened.

Javier blinked, the low-hanging sun, now in his line of sight, making the long shadow of a figure jut toward him. Who was that? A boy, like him. Wearing the same faded green T-shirt he wore. Javier blinked again, realizing that he was much closer to the ground than before. He looked down and saw one white and orange paw firmly on the ground, the other lifted before him, frozen in mid-step. Javier looked up and recognized the boy as himself. A wet foam of fear covered him, and he closed his eyes as tightly as he could. When Javier opened them a few moments later, his line of sight had returned to where it had been, sun at his back, and he was watching the calico.

Over the years Javier gradually learned to exert some control over his ability, but that control was far from perfect. First, he learned that he could not enter a person—or animal—he knew too well. Too much connection seemed to block his ability, although he certainly had tried—especially when his father beat him. Second, Javier could use his ability no more than once a year, and even then only if everything fell into place perfectly. Third, while in another person or animal, he retained some measure of control while enjoying the particular skill, knowledge, and experience of his host. And perhaps most important, Javier discovered that he could remain in another being for months at a time while the real Javier went about his life as he would normally.

As the decades passed, Javier grew more cautious with the targets he chose, honing his ability as if in preparation for a great goal, a history-altering finale. For he'd learned while in college that he could use his ability not only on people he met or saw from afar, but also on those he encountered solely through television, radio, magazines. Another lesson Javier learned: never could he aim his ability at a target with intent to cause harm, gain a selfish advantage over others, or fulfill carnal desires. That's not to say he didn't try; Javier was no more perfect than you or I. But once he knew the restrictions of his ability, he aimed to stay within those constraints, feeling a bit chastened and quite embarrassed by his failings as a person.

So, over the decades Javier went to college, married and divorced quickly before the age of twenty-five, then twenty years later married Celia Norte, who had sole custody of two teenage boys from a previous marriage. Javier worked several jobs until settling on a comfortable career with the city's building permit department which, combined with Celia's salary as a paralegal for a large law firm, allowed them to purchase a lovely 1923 Craftsman house northeast of downtown that kept their commute within the realm of reasonable as the boys attended Loyola High School.

But he kept his ability a secret from his beloved Celia—and everyone else, for that matter. Throughout the years, before and after he had married, Javier had experienced many remarkable things: flying through the Los Angeles skies on feathered wings and in the cockpit of a Cessna Skycatcher; lecturing two class sessions of a course titled "The Oceanic Imaginaries: Postcolonial

Literatures" to graduate students at UCLA—despite majoring in economics while in college; conducting Mahler's Adagio Symphony No. 10 at Walt Disney Concert Hall; fabricating thin sheet metal products that eventually became rain gutters, outdoor signs, and ducts for heating and air-conditioning; delivering three babies in one day.

His wife never suspected that he possessed this special ability—of course, how could she?—but Celia was particularly impressed by Javier's rather eclectic and precise knowledge of airplanes, music, literature, sheet metal, and medicine, to name a few of the many interesting subjects Javier could opine on. She had married a savant, a kindhearted, sometimes distracted savant.

And Javier grew accustomed to his ability, figuring it would be something he would utilize until his death. But one night he realized his ability had a purpose beyond self-improvement and experiential diversity.

Javier and Celia lay in bed as talking heads on television gesticulated in an almost disoriented manner. When the stunned commentators called Pennsylvania, Celia could watch no longer; she had fallen asleep weeping, her face partially buried in her pillow. Javier still stared at the screen. Celia had predicted that this could happen—she could see the momentum—but until this moment Javier had optimistically believed that America would never, ever reward such a man with its highest prize. After all, this was a man who had based his candidacy on a promise to build a great wall to keep Mexicans—criminals and rapists, to use his words—out of the United States. People like Javier's long-dead abuelita, one of the kindest souls he had ever known. No! Not in Javier's lifetime. Never, ever.

And when the networks called Wisconsin—giving that man enough Electoral College votes to become the forty-fifth president—Javier knew the identity of his next target. This would be the greatest test of his special ability. It would require control, will power, a resigned acceptance that he would be away from his family for four or even eight years. But Javier had to do it. He had no choice. It would be Javier's one heroic chance to make America great again.

PERMISSIONS AND SOURCE ACKNOWLEDGMENTS

THE STORIES in this book appeared in earlier form in the following publications:

"How to Date a Flying Mexican": First published in *Exquisite Corpse* (2008). From *The Book of Want: A Novel* (The University of Arizona Press, Tucson, AZ, 2011). ©2008 by Daniel A. Olivas. Reprinted by permission of The University of Arizona Press.

"After the Revolution": First published in *Margin* (2005). From *Anywhere but L.A.: Stories* (Bilingual Press/Editorial Bilingüe, Arizona State University, Tempe, AZ, 2009). ©2009 by Bilingual Press/Editorial Bilingüe. Reprinted by permission of Bilingual Press/Editorial Bilingüe.

"Elizondo Returns Home": First published in *Fourth & Sycamore* (2015). From *The King of Lighting Fixtures: Stories* (The University of Arizona Press, Tucson, AZ, 2017). ©2015 by Daniel A. Olivas. Reprinted by permission of The University of Arizona Press.

"Good Things Happen at Tina's Café": First published *in LA Fiction Anthology: Southland Stories by Southland Writers* (Red Hen Press, 2016). From *The King of Lighting Fixtures: Stories* (The University of Arizona Press, Tucson, AZ, 2017). ©2016 by Daniel A. Olivas. Reprinted by permission of The University of Arizona Press.

"Don de la Cruz and the Devil of Malibu": First published in *Exquisite Corpse* (2000). From *Devil Talk: Stories* (Bilingual Press/Editorial Bilingüe, Arizona State University, Tempe, AZ, 2004). ©2004 by Bilingual Press/Editorial Bilingüe. Reprinted by permission of Bilingual Press/Editorial Bilingüe.

"Señor Sánchez": First published in *Nemeton: A Fables Anthology* (Silver Lake Publishing, 2000). From *Devil Talk: Stories* (Bilingual Press/Editorial Bilingüe, Arizona State University, Tempe, AZ, 2004). ©2004 by Bilingual Press/Editorial Bilingüe. Reprinted by permission of Bilingual Press/Editorial Bilingüe.

"Driving to Ventura": First published in *Outsider Ink* (2001). From *Assumption and Other Stories* (Bilingual Press/Editorial Bilingüe, Arizona State University, Tempe, AZ, 2003). ©2003 by Bilingual Press/Editorial Bilingüe. Reprinted by permission of Bilingual Press/Editorial Bilingüe.

"Franz Kafka in Fresno": First published in *LatinoLA* (2009). From *Anywhere but L.A.: Stories* (Bilingual Press/Editorial Bilingüe, Arizona

State University, Tempe, AZ, 2009). © 2009 by Bilingual Press/Editorial Bilingüe. Reprinted by permission of Bilingual Press/Editorial Bilingüe.

"The Fabricator": From *Anywhere but L.A.: Stories* (Bilingual Press/Editorial Bilingüe, Arizona State University, Tempe, AZ, 2009). © 2009 by Bilingual Press/Editorial Bilingüe. Reprinted by permission of Bilingual Press/Editorial Bilingüe.

"Eurt": First published in *The Paumanok Review* (2000). From *Devil Talk: Stories* (Bilingual Press/Editorial Bilingüe, Arizona State University, Tempe, AZ, 2004). © 2004 by Bilingual Press/Editorial Bilingüe. Reprinted by permission of Bilingual Press/Editorial Bilingüe.

"The Fox": First published in *Octavo* (1999). From *Devil Talk: Stories* (Bilingual Press/Editorial Bilingüe, Arizona State University, Tempe, AZ, 2004). © 2004 by Bilingual Press/Editorial Bilingüe. Reprinted by permission of Bilingual Press/Editorial Bilingüe.

"Belén": First published in *New Madrid* (2008). From *The Book of Want: A Novel* (The University of Arizona Press, Tucson, AZ, 2011). © 2008 by Daniel A. Olivas. Reprinted by permission of The University of Arizona Press.

"The Horned Toad": First published in *Fables* (1999). From *Devil Talk: Stories* (Bilingual Press/Editorial Bilingüe, Arizona State University, Tempe, AZ, 2004). © 2004 by Bilingual Press/Editorial Bilingüe. Reprinted by permission of Bilingual Press/Editorial Bilingüe.

"Chock-Chock": First published in *Del Sol Review* (2005). From *Anywhere but L.A.: Stories* (Bilingual Press/Editorial Bilingüe, Arizona State University, Tempe, AZ, 2009). © 2009 by Bilingual Press/Editorial Bilingüe. Reprinted by permission of Bilingual Press/Editorial Bilingüe.

"The Plumed Serpent of Los Angeles": First published in *Southern Cross Review* (1999). From *Devil Talk: Stories* (Bilingual Press/Editorial Bilingüe, Arizona State University, Tempe, AZ, 2004). © 2004 by Bilingual Press/Editorial Bilingüe. Reprinted by permission of Bilingual Press/Editorial Bilingüe.

"La Queenie": From *Anywhere but L.A.: Stories* (Bilingual Press/Editorial Bilingüe, Arizona State University, Tempe, AZ, 2009). © 2009 by Bilingual Press/Editorial Bilingüe. Reprinted by permission of Bilingual Press/Editorial Bilingüe.

"Devil Talk": First published in *Facets Magazine* (2001). From *Devil Talk: Stories* (Bilingual Press/Editorial Bilingüe, Arizona State University, Tempe, AZ, 2004). © 2004 by Bilingual Press/Editorial Bilingüe. Reprinted by permission of Bilingual Press/Editorial Bilingüe.

"Los Otros Coyotes": First published in *Both Sides: An Anthology of Border Noir* (Agora Books, 2020). © 2020 by Daniel A. Olivas. Reprinted by permission of the author.

"The Chicano in You": First published in *Roanoke Review* (2020). © 2020 by Daniel A. Olivas. Reprinted by permission of the author.

ABOUT THE AUTHOR

DANIEL A. OLIVAS, the grandson of Mexican immigrants, was born and raised near downtown Los Angeles. He is an award-winning author of ten books of fiction, nonfiction, plays, and poetry, including *The King of Lighting Fixtures: Stories*, *Crossing the Border: Collected Poems*, and *Things We Do Not Talk About: Exploring Latino/a Literature Through Essays and Interviews*. His work has been widely anthologized, and he has written on culture and literature for the *New York Times*, the *Los Angeles Review of Books*, *BOMB*, *Jewish Journal*, *High Country News*, and *The Guardian*. Olivas is also a playwright whose work has been produced in readings and for the stage by Playwrights' Arena, Circle X Theatre Company, and The Road Theatre Company. He writes regularly for *La Bloga*, a site dedicated to Latinx literature and the arts. Olivas received his bachelor's degree in English literature from Stanford University and his law degree from UCLA.